BERLIN BLUES

Sven Regener is the lead singer and songwriter of the band Elements of Crime. *Berlin Blues* is his first novel.

Sven Regener

BERLIN BLUES

TRANSLATED FROM THE GERMAN BY
John Brownjohn

VINTAGE BOOKS
London

Published by Vintage 2004

18

Copyright © Sven Regener 2003
English translation © John Brownjohn 2003

The publication of this work was supported by
a grant from the Goethe-Institut Inter Nationes

First published in Great Britain in 2003 by
Secker & Warburg

Vintage
Random House, 20 Vauxhall Bridge Road,
London SW1V 2SA

www.vintage-books.co.uk

Addresses for companies within The Random House Group
Limited can be found at: www.randomhouse.co.uk/offices.htm

The Random House Group Limited Reg. No. 954009

A CIP catalogue record for this book
is available from the British Library

ISBN 9780099449232

Penguin Random House is committed to a sustainable future for
our business, our readers and our planet. This book is made from
Forest Stewardship Council® certified paper.

Printed and bound in Great Britain by Clays Ltd, Elcograf S.p.A.

BERLIN BLUES

1 THE DOG

THE CLOUDLESS NIGHT sky was already displaying a pale glimmer in the distance, over East Berlin, by the time Frank Lehmann, whom they'd recently taken to calling 'Herr Lehmann' because word had got around that he would soon be thirty, walked home across Lausitzer Platz. He was feeling tired and wrung out after his stint at the *Einfall*, a bar in Wiener Strasse. Some lousy night that was, Herr Lehmann reflected as he entered Lausitzer Platz from the west. Working with Erwin is no fun, he thought. Erwin's an idiot – all bar owners are idiots, he thought as he passed the big church that dominated the whole square. I shouldn't have drunk all those shorts. Erwin or no Erwin, I shouldn't have drunk them, he told himself as his absent gaze became entangled in the wire mesh fence enclosing the playground. His legs were leaden with work and hard liquor, so he wasn't walking fast. Those shorts were a mistake. I ask you, tequila and Fernet Branca . . . I'll pay for it in the morning, he told himself. Work and booze don't mix – anything stronger than beer is a mistake, and someone like Erwin, of all people, shouldn't talk his staff into drinking shorts. He thinks he's being big-hearted, encouraging his staff to drink shorts, but he only does it as an excuse to get smashed himself. On the other hand, thought Herr Lehmann, it isn't fair to put the blame on Erwin. The truth is, nobody's ever to blame for drinking shorts but yours truly.

Human beings have a will of their own, he thought as he neared the other side of Lausitzer Platz. We can't fail to know what we're doing or not doing, and the fact that Erwin's an idiot and talks you into drinking shorts doesn't mean he's to blame – far from it. At the same time, he thought contentedly of the bottle of Scotch he'd swiped and stowed away in the big inside pocket of his overcoat, which was really far too warm for September. Although he himself had no use for whisky, not having touched spirits on principle for ages, Erwin needed teaching a lesson now and then, and he could always make a present of the bottle to his best friend Karl.

And then he saw the dog. Herr Lehmann, as they called him nowadays, although the people that did so weren't much younger than himself (in fact some of them were even older, for instance Erwin and his best friend Karl), was no expert on dogs, but he couldn't, with the best will in the world, conceive that anyone had bred such an animal deliberately. It had a big head with huge, slobbery chops and two flabby ears that hung down on either side like a pair of wilted lettuce leaves. Its rump was fat and its back so broad you could have parked a bottle of whisky on it, but its legs, which were disproportionately thin, protruded from its body like snapped-off pencils. Herr Lehmann, who didn't think it overly amusing to be addressed as such, had never seen such a hideous animal. He shrank back and froze. He didn't trust dogs, and this one was growling at him.

No false moves, thought Herr Lehmann, who did not, on the other hand, see any point in getting worked up over a stupid nickname. Look it steadily in the eye, that intimidates the brutes, he thought, and he focused his gaze on the two black, blank holes in his adversary's skull. The dog, whose jowls were rhythmically rising and falling in time to its growls, returned his gaze. They were about three paces apart. The dog didn't move; nor did Herr Lehmann. Don't look away, he commanded himself. Don't show you're scared, just walk past, he thought, and edged aside. The dog growled even louder – a vicious, nerve-jangling sound. Don't show you're scared, the brute will sense your fear and take advantage of it, thought Herr Lehmann. Another little sideways step. Don't take your eyes off him. Another little step, and another, and then straight ahead. But the dog edged sideways too, so they were face to face again.

It won't let me past, thought Herr Lehmann, who wasn't planning to celebrate his forthcoming birthday in style because of his conviction that it was just a birthday like any other, and he'd never liked celebrating his birthdays anyway. This is absurd, he thought. It shouldn't be happening – I haven't done it any harm, after all. He looked at the big yellow teeth and quailed at the notion of the dog's huge jaws sinking them in one of his legs, in his arm, in his throat – indeed, he even feared for his balls. Who knows what sort of dog it is? he reflected. Perhaps it's been trained for a specific purpose – perhaps it's a canine killer, a crotch-biter, or the kind that goes for the jugular. Then you'll bleed to death in the middle of Lausitzer Platz. There's no one around, the square's deserted. Who *would* be around so early on a Sunday morning? All the bars are shut – the *Einfall* is always the last to close apart from the *Abfall*, but that doesn't count. The only people around at this hour are demented Berliners with trained killer dogs – perverts who jerk off in the bushes while they watch their vicious dogs play lethal games with people.

'Who does this dog belong to?' he called across the deserted square. '*Who owns this fucking dog?*' There was no response. The dog merely growled even louder and cocked its head so its eyes took on a red glow. It's only the retinas, Herr Lehmann told himself reassuringly – the retinas, that's all – the brute turned its head, and now the light is falling on its eyes so the retinas reflect it in my direction, it's the retinas that are red, carotin, vitamin A, stuff like that – it's common knowledge they're good for the eyes. He had a dim recollection of this from his school-days. I always did well in biology, thought Herr Lehmann, but that was a long time ago, and biology won't do me much good now. I've got to get out of here, he thought, and he was filled with an unprecedented longing for his home, the one-and-a-half-room flat in Eisenbahnstrasse where his books and his empty bed awaited him less than a hundred yards from the spot where his life was currently under threat from a dog he'd never seen before.

If it won't let me past, thought Herr Lehmann, whom everyone had regularly addressed as Frank until that childish trick of calling him Herr Lehmann caught on, I'll simply have to turn back. And he visualised the route he would have to take in order to give this rabid beast in Lausitzer Platz a wide berth: Waldemarstrasse, Pücklerstrasse, Wrangelstrasse, and then into Eisenbahnstrasse from the far side. Child's play. Retreating can sometimes make more sense than attacking, he thought; strategically speaking, a shrewd tactical withdrawal can result in victory. But he didn't dare turn round. Don't turn round whatever you do, he told himself – keep looking the beast in the eye. He took a few cautious little steps back, and the dog, still growling, advanced a few little steps. Don't rush things, thought Herr Lehmann, who had been looking forward to the footbath to which he'd lately been treating himself after work, although he doubted if he'd manage one in his present state. Just don't rush things, he told himself, and resisted the temptation simply to turn and run. That would be fatal, he thought; the dog can run faster than me – it would pounce on me from behind. I'd be defenceless, so that's out. He took a few more steps back, whereupon the dog, which was now augmenting its growls with an occasional bark, veered off sideways and slunk past him with its head down, with the result that Herr Lehmann, rather than lose sight of it, had to turn on the spot until they were confronting each other precisely the other way round. That's okay with me, thought Herr Lehmann; I wanted to go in that direction anyway. He took another few steps back, at which point the whole procedure repeated itself in reverse: the dog slunk past, Herr Lehmann turned as it did so, and they wound up back where they'd started. I'd better try talking to the animal, he thought.

'Listen,' he began in a low and, he hoped, soothing voice. The dog sat down on its haunches. That's a good start, thought Herr Lehmann. 'I sympathise,' he said. 'You don't have an easy life either.' He rummaged in the pockets of his overcoat for something to give the animal. Sometimes bribery's the only answer, he thought. It doesn't have to be something to eat, maybe it simply wants to play – the owners of dogs like this always claim they only want to play – so maybe I've got something on me it can play with. But all he found was his bunch of keys and the bottle of Scotch, because he wasn't – he regretted this for the first time – one of those people who cram their pockets with all kinds of forgotten oddments and tote them around for years on end. The dog was growing a trifle restive, so he stopped rummaging. 'Just sit there nice and quietly,' he told it. 'I was only looking to see if I had something for you. I'm sure you'll get something sometime from your master, or maybe even your mistress – "master", "mistress", good God, what ludicrous expressions! Who on earth thinks them up?'

The dog didn't seem to care either way. It folded its spindly forelegs, and its obese body flopped down on the asphalt.

'That's right, lie down for a bit,' said Herr Lehmann, for whom lying down had been a favourite occupation in recent years. He went on talking without a break as he gradually edged aside. 'I'm the last person not to let a sleeping dog lie,' he burbled on. 'Sleep, boy, go to sleep, I know what it's like to be pooped, I know the feeling, I'm pooped myself, but you, you poor bastard, are a whole lot more pooped than me . . .' He continued to sidle crabwise by slow degrees. 'It tires a dog out, running around menacing people, heaven knows what possesses a dog to act that way, I'm almost a whole yard to the left of you, and now I'm going to take a tiny little step forward, and another, and another . . .' The dog watched this for a while, then jumped up with a vigour and alacrity Herr Lehmann would never have thought possible in view of its spindly, feeble-looking legs, and growled and barked so belligerently that his fear turned to utter fury.

'*Fuck this!*' he yelled across the deserted square at the top of his voice. '*Someone take this blasted dog away! Someone take the godforsaken brute away, damn it all! And you, shut up!*' he bellowed at the dog, which actually fell silent.

Herr Lehmann calmed down. I must pull myself together, he told himself − I must keep my nerve. 'You see?' he said apologetically. 'You made me lose my temper.'

The dog sat down again. Herr Lehmann, whose work-weary feet were aching, felt as if his legs were filled with lead and every bone in his body had been smashed. He squatted down so as to take the weight off his legs, however briefly, but it didn't do much good − in fact it was even more uncomfortable in the long run. It doesn't matter now, he thought − I may as well sit down properly − so he subsided on to his bottom and came to rest in a kind of lotus position. If anyone sees me, it flashed through his mind, they're bound to think I'm a hopeless down-and-out. The asphalt beneath his buttocks felt cold, and he was shivering. This is the coldest time of day, he reflected, and adjusted his position so that he was sitting on the skirt of his overcoat. It's cold as charity at this hour, he thought, even though it's still so warm during the day. How light it is already – it must be nearly morning. It occurred to him only now how many birds were visible everywhere. They sat perched in the trees, in the bushes, on the tall fence around Bolzplatz, and on the nearby semicircle of benches regularly occupied during the day by a few alkies or old folk or both. The birds weren't flying around, Herr Lehmann was surprised to note; they were simply sitting there making a din – and what a din, he thought. There's a lot of wildlife in this city, he reflected as he saw two dark shapes – rabbits, probably – flit across the expanse of grass near the church.

'Why don't *you* chase rabbits?' he asked the dog, which had stretched right out on the asphalt with its head between its forepaws. He remembered the bottle of Scotch he'd acquired by rather reprehensible means. Extracting it from his overcoat, he unscrewed the cap and took a hefty swig to ward off the cold.

'That doesn't matter either,' he told the dog. 'You're probably too dumb or too slow to catch rabbits, with those funny legs of yours.'

The whisky tasted as foul to him as spirits in general – Herr Lehmann drew no subtle distinctions in that respect – but it did generate some internal warmth and dispelled the headache that was already giving him a foretaste of the hangover to come.

More and more often of late, Herr Lehmann had caught himself looking back on his childhood with a touch of melancholy, and without inwardly resisting the impulse as he used to in the past. 'Yes,' he told the dog, 'you look a bit like those animals I used to make out of conkers as a boy, the ones with matches stuck in them for legs and so on. If I simply ran off, who knows if you'd manage to catch me, with those legs of yours?'

He took another swig. The dog did nothing. 'Not that I'm a very fast mover myself,' he added, just for something to say. 'What's your name, I wonder?'

He put the bottle down beside him, drew up his knees, and clasped them to his chest. The dog blinked at him placidly.

'Maybe we ought to find out what your name is,' said Herr Lehmann, who thought this a good idea. All I have to do, he thought, is find out what he's called, then he'll simmer down. He's familiar with his name – he's got a collar, after all, so he must have an owner and a name. All I have to do is say his name and he'll feel at home – feel I'm in authority. 'Bello?' he hazarded. 'Hasso?' No reaction.

Then he heard footsteps behind him. He turned to see a woman approaching, a fat, voluminously attired woman wearing a headscarf. Ah, he thought, perhaps she could take over from me. But although he knew he must look rather bizarre, sitting on the ground with a bottle of whisky beside him, he didn't get up. He was far too tired, and besides, he didn't want to provoke the dog. Craning his neck, he peered at the woman, who – doubtless because she'd caught sight of him and the dog – quickened her step and steered well clear of him.

'Excuse me,' he began, when she drew level, but she didn't look at him as he spoke, just stared straight ahead and put on more speed. The dog averted its gaze with an impassive air. 'No, wait,' Herr Lehmann called desperately, 'I've got a problem here. The thing is . . .' Fat as she was, the woman broke into a run and disappeared before he could finish his sentence. The dog growled contentedly.

'Stupid cow,' said Herr Lehmann, and readdressed himself to the dog. 'Wolfi?' That name proved just as unproductive. 'Putzi? Rudi? Fifi – no, you don't look like a Fifi. Hulk? Rambo? How do those dogs' names go, damn it? Schnappi?' A long-dead great-aunt of his had owned a dog by the name of Schnappi, a long-haired miniature dachshund that had ended up beneath the wheels of a delivery van. Still a child at the time, he'd loathed it from the bottom of his heart. 'Hansi? Boxi? Lassie?' The dog showed no interest.

Herr Lehmann was tiring of this game. It's all balls, he thought – I'm drunk, after all. He took another swig of Scotch and shuddered.

'There's something I should tell you,' he said. 'I always hated dogs, even as a boy, and that's a long time ago. Dogs don't belong in towns – I've always been scared of them. Hey! Hello there, police!' he called feebly as he saw a patrol car cruising the square. He raised a hand and waved, but no one noticed. The car drove on.

'Think yourself lucky,' he told the dog sternly. 'They'd have shot you in double-quick time. You still think you've got the edge on me, but you can forget it. Strategically, you're at a disadvantage. Humans are superior to animals. If you were a wolf and I was some country bumpkin plodding through the forest, you might have a chance, but this is the city. People will come and rescue me, and they'll lock you up. Besides, unlike animals, humans are capable of using tools. Tools, you brute, so put that in your pipe! That's the crucial difference between us, tools – that's how it all began. Take this bottle, for instance!' He raised the bottle, and the dog growled. 'I could hit you over the head with it, then you'd look stupid! This is twelve-year-old whisky – Scotch whisky. Costs forty marks or more, and Erwin charges six marks a shot, imagine!' Drinking shorts always makes one talk too much, thought Herr Lehmann, and talking crap to dogs takes the cake.

Just for something to do, he poured himself a screwcapful of Scotch and was putting it to his lips when he noticed the animal's air of interest. Experimentally, he waved the screwcap to and fro. The dog followed it with its eyes, panting excitedly with its jaws open and its tongue lolling out.

'Aha!' said Herr Lehmann. 'I get it. Okay, watch this!'

Leaning forward, he tossed the screwcap so that it landed between the dog's forepaws and formed a tiny puddle of whisky there. The dog sniffed it, adjusted the position of its malformed body, and proceeded to lap it up.

'Here, have some more,' said Herr Lehmann, and he flooded the asphalt, which, as luck would have it, sloped in the dog's direction. 'Looks like you're used to it,' he said, when he saw how avidly the dog was lapping up the rivulet of spirits flowing towards it. 'You probably belong to some alky,' he said, and took another big swallow himself. 'Fair's fair,' he added. The dog glanced at him briefly, glassy-eyed, and went on lapping.

'It'll knock you out in no time, that stuff, take it from me. Boo!' Herr Lehmann brandished the bottle at the dog, but it didn't react, just lapped away until there was nothing left, then endeavoured to get to its feet.

'Not so easy now, huh?' Herr Lehmann took a final swig, squirted some of it over the dog just for kicks, and then got back on his own unsteady legs. The dog made a feeble attempt to bare its teeth when he very gently tickled it under the chin with the toe of his shoe. The gurgle it emitted was doubtless meant to be a growl.

'Out of my way, you brute!' Herr Lehmann cried imperiously, and thrust the animal aside with his foot as best he could. It snapped at the foot but missed. He pushed it over.

'Come on, then! Go for me if that's what you want, you lump of lard!' The dog struggled to its feet, turned sideways on, and leant against his legs.

'Get off me!' said Herr Lehmann. Now that the hideous creature was so trustfully nestling against him for support, however, he felt a trifle sorry for it. He stepped back a little, and the dog slid slowly down his legs until its ponderous bulk was lying on his feet. He lost his balance, flailed the air with his arms, and fell to the ground athwart the dog's body. It was all he could do to avoid smashing the bottle.

'What's going on here?'

Herr Lehmann looked up and saw two policemen looming over him. He hadn't heard them coming.

'I had to keep this dog at bay,' he said. 'There's never one around when you need one. One of your lot, I mean, not a dog. Problem's solved. Everything's under control, gentlemen, honestly.'

'He's drunk as a skunk,' said one of the policemen, who was about Herr Lehmann's age.

'Come on, get up,' said the other, who was a bit older.

'Easier said than done,' said Herr Lehmann. 'It's this confounded dog, see for yourself.' Laboriously, hampered by the dog squirming beneath him and the bottle still in his hand, he propped himself on his knees and elbows. The younger policeman relieved him of the bottle and hauled him to his feet – unnecessarily roughly, it seemed to Herr Lehmann.

'Is this your dog?' the other man demanded sternly.

'No, goddammit!' Herr Lehmann stood facing them, swaying a little. He tried to grab the bottle, but they wouldn't let him have it. 'It menaced me, the brute. Wouldn't let me go home.'

The policemen looked at the dog, which now made a far from menacing impression. It simply lay there panting, staring into space with its tongue hanging out. The younger man squatted down and stroked its head. The dog tried to stand up, but it was past doing so.

'It's pissed,' said the crouching policeman.

'That's cruelty to animals,' said his colleague. 'Cruelty to animals is a criminal offence. You could be charged.'

'With cruelty to animals.'

They're repeating themselves, thought Herr Lehmann. People always do that – they keep saying the same things over and over.

'You've been pouring booze down its throat, the poor thing. That's cruelty to animals, that is. You ought to be ashamed of yourself. A poor, defenceless creature like this!'

'Defenceless? Pah!' Herr Lehmann said indignantly. 'It was *self*-defence, I had no choice.' He was far too tired to go into details. 'Self-defence, it was. No choice, period,' he said. 'Quite straightforward, case closed.'

The policemen didn't believe him. They asked to see his ID and made a note of his particulars.

'Right, Herr Lehmann,' said the older of the two as he returned his papers. 'You'll be hearing from us. And now, get off home. We'll take the dog with us. You'll never see it again. Cruelty to animals, this is. I'm a dog owner myself. A disgrace, that's what it is.'

'Hopefully,' said Herr Lehmann.

'Hopefully what?'

'Hopefully I'll never see it again.'

'Push off quick, before I forget myself!'

Herr Lehmann departed with weary tread. At the mouth of Eisenbahnstrasse he looked back and saw the two patrolmen lugging the corpulent animal over to their vehicle.

'Poor creature,' he heard one of them say. Just then the dog awoke from its torpor and bit him. Herr Lehmann walked on quickly. He refrained from laughing until he rounded the corner.

2 MOTHER

'FRANK, IS THAT you? You sound so odd. It went on ringing for such a long time before you picked up, I thought you weren't there at all. I was just about to hang up.'

Herr Lehmann loved his parents. He was grateful to them for many reasons, one of them being the fact that they lived a long way from West Berlin, in Bremen, which was two national frontiers and several hundred kilometres away. Another of the reasons why he cherished them so much was that it would never for a moment have occurred to them to address him as Herr Lehmann. The only problem was, they liked to get up early and call him at the crack of dawn.

'Mother!' said Herr Lehmann.

'I was just about to hang up.'

Why didn't you? he thought. I myself, thought Herr Lehmann, who thoroughly prided himself on his consideration for other people, would have done just that. To be more precise, I wouldn't have let the phone ring thirty times. Here we go again, he thought. Five times is okay, especially as most people own answering machines which cut in – for a very good reason – after four or five rings. He regretted that he still hadn't acquired such a gadget, but he shrank from the prospect of traipsing out to some suburban warehouse to pick one up cheap.

13

'Frank, are you still there?'

Herr Lehmann sighed.

'But mother,' he said, 'mother, it's only . . .' It was long since Herr Lehmann had needed a clock that worked, because he'd developed an excellent sense of time and could always, at a pinch, fall back on the speaking clock. He debated for a moment. 'It can't be ten o'clock yet, and you know I work nights!'

'It's a quarter past ten. Nobody's still asleep at that hour – I'm surprised you were still asleep. *I've* been up since seven.'

Her tone was so triumphant that Herr Lehmann, who considered himself a thoroughly equable person whose temperament had settled over the years like the sediment in some fine old vintage burgundy, felt sufficiently provoked to deliver a sharp riposte.

'Why?' he demanded.

'I was just about to hang up, but then I thought, no, he can't have gone out already, seeing as how he always works so late.'

'Exactly, mother, exactly,' said Herr Lehmann, firmly resolved not to let her get away with what was, in his experience, a typically maternal attempt to sidestep. 'But that wasn't the question, mother.'

'Question? What question?' she retorted irritably.

'*Why*, mother? That's what I asked you. *Why* have you been up since seven?'

'What nonsense! I always get up then.'

'Yes, but why?' Herr Lehmann persisted.

'What do you mean, why?'

'Mother!' Herr Lehmann had gained the upper hand. She's listening to me, he thought happily. She's reacting instead of acting – she's on the defensive now. Don't let her off the hook, follow up your advantage, bring the subject to a satisfactory conclusion, settle it once and for all, get things straight, et cetera . . . Unfortunately, he'd rather lost the thread.

'What do I mean?' he asked, annoyed with himself. 'Why? That's obvious . . . I mean . . . Surely I can ask why, it's a perfectly reasonable question . . .'

'You're talking rubbish, Frank,' she said sternly. 'And speak a bit more clearly, I can hardly understand you.'

'Come off it!' snapped Herr Lehmann, who was now feeling decidedly ill-tempered and totally aware of his wretched situation. It's humiliating, he thought, for someone who's nearly thirty years old – someone who's had only three and a half hours' sleep preceded by a brush with a canine killer and two dumb policemen, someone with a throbbing head and a dry mouth – to be insulted by a member of his family, let alone by his own mother, the one person in the world who's supposed to be wholly in sympathy with every act committed by the fruit of her womb. Celebrated examples flashed through his mind: mothers of serial killers who declared that they loved their sons above all else and blamed themselves for everything – who rose at dawn every morning and went to the prison to bring their depraved offspring home-cooked meals and/or supplies of heroin. That brought him back to the point at issue.

'Now listen, mother,' he said, resuming his counterattack. 'My question was this: Why—'

'You're very indistinct. Have you got something in your mouth?'

'*Yes*,' Herr Lehmann said spitefully, '*a tongue!*' If you want plain speaking, mother, he thought, you can have it. '*Is that better?*'

'No need to shout, I'm not deaf. All I ask is that you speak a little more clearly or at least refrain from eating while we're talking. It really isn't good manners.'

'Don't change the subject, mother.' Herr Lehmann spoke with exaggerated clarity, which wasn't easy in view of his dehydrated condition. Dehydration is a major cause of hangovers, he told himself, but so is lack of electrolytes. 'Why do you get up at seven, that was the question. You're a housewife, and besides, today is Sunday. You don't have anything to do all day, or at least, nothing you couldn't do later than seven o'clock, so why, if I may make so bold – why, in the name of all that's holy – do you get up at seven purely in order to terrorise me with a phone call whose main purpose is to inform me that you've been awake for three hours? Why, mother, why?'

'Well . . .' The voice on the line sounded rather nettled and very far from defeated. 'Why not?'

That, thought Herr Lehmann, is remarkable. She's tough, you've got to hand it to her. It must be one of the traits I inherited from her, thought Herr Lehmann, who had always felt that tenacity – instilled by long experience of life without a regular income – was one of his most salient characteristics.

'Why not? *Why not?* Because it's not good manners.' Herr Lehmann went for broke. He noticed with relief that his wonted eloquence was returning, courtesy of adrenalin and self-discipline. 'If you yourself say it's bad manners to speak with one's mouth full, mother, even when a person hasn't asked to be called but has been wrested from his slumbers by the phone ringing umpteen times and robbed of his well-deserved sleep – a sleep earned by the sweat of his brow, I might add – if you call *that* bad manners, how in God's name can you assume that it's acceptable to wake someone who slaves the whole goddamned night for a hard-earned crust, if I may put it that way? How can you think it's good manners to let the phone ring umpteen times, when it must be obvious that the person is either out or fast asleep? Not to mention the fact that, if you simply say "Why not?" when asked why you get up at seven, the same thing naturally applies in reverse. If you're surprised that I should still be asleep at ten and ask me why, I myself could just as easily answer

"Why not?" — *if* that's an answer at all, and not a wholly impermissible way of dodging the issue!'

There, thought Herr Lehmann, it had to be said sometime. On the other hand, now that he had woken up a bit and been able to let off steam at some considerable length, he felt rather sorry to have given his mother such a dressing-down. He wasn't sure if it had really been necessary. It really wasn't right to speak to one's mother like that, he thought. After all, he loved his mother. He owed her the gift of life, that was undeniable, and it certainly wasn't her fault for not being too bright. She's just an ordinary woman, thought Herr Lehmann, although the expression 'ordinary woman' had an unpleasant ring. It's not a good expression, 'ordinary woman', he thought — it smacks of middle-class snobbery.

'Ernst, won't you speak to him? He sounds so odd.'

'What is it now, mother?'

A defensive murmur issued from the depths of his parents' distant living room.

'*I'm* the one that always has to call him,' Herr Lehmann heard his mother saying, 'but it was *your* idea . . .'

'What now, mother? What's wrong? Would you sooner have a quiet word with the old man and call me back later?' Herr Lehmann played another trump card. 'Think of your phone bill.'

But his mother wasn't listening. Herr Lehmann, who was only wearing his underpants, having always gone to bed in his underpants ever since a former girlfriend had told him it was unhygienic to sleep in the buff, and that constantly boiling his dirty sheets — a chore he'd never asked her to perform — was environmentally polluting in the extreme, now made the most of the time his mother was engaged in fighting a battle that had probably been in progress for thirty years. Straining both telephone cables to their fullest extent, the straight but forever entangled one and the one that was spiral by nature, he made his way into the kitchen, where he drank several glasses of tap water and put a kettle on for coffee.

'Hello? Hello?' he called into the mouthpiece while lighting the gas stove with difficulty. 'I'm still here,' he added as he deposited two spoonfuls of coffee in a mug, although he was actually enjoying this breather in spite of the awkward angle at which he was compelled to hold his head in order to remain on the ball.

'*You* always say we should call him, but *I* always have to do it.'

Murmur, murmur. '. . . didn't.'

'That's the limit! Who was it that . . .'

'How can I help it if . . .'

'I never said . . . I only said someone should let him know . . .'

'What do you mean, someone? Who's going to tell him, if not me?'

'Tell me what?' Herr Lehmann interjected into the ether. He couldn't stand coffee machines. He believed, in any case, that filters were one of the greatest mistakes in the history of coffee-making, and that coffee with boiling water poured straight on to it was far healthier, if only because the suspended particles retained by a filter helped to spread the effect of the caffeine over a longer period, thereby precluding any form of adverse effect on the circulation. He poured himself a mug of what he now, since the demise of his old coffee machine, euphemistically referred to as 'cowboy coffee'.

'*Tell me what?*' he yelled into the mouthpiece, less in anger than in a straightforward desire to cut this nonsense short. '*Hello, hello mother, hello mother, hello mother, hello mother . . .*'

At that moment someone hammered on the wall. Although he had long ceased to care what the neighbours thought of him because he regarded them all as antisocial idiots, especially when they indulged their predilection for flash-frying and smoked out the stairwell, and sometimes even his apartment, with cheap fat, Herr Lehmann was nonetheless annoyed by this. It's that stupid bitch with the dreadlocks, he thought, conscious of the misunderstandings that might arise if that woman, of all people, overheard him calling loudly and incessantly for his mother.

'What do you want, Frank?' demanded the selfsame mother.

'*You* called *me*, mother, or had you forgotten? I've been standing around here, listening to you quarrelling.'

'We aren't quarrelling, what makes you think we're quarrelling, a quarrel is something quite—'

'Think of your phone bill,' Herr Lehmann warned a second time. 'And now, please tell me what you want. Please, mother,' he demeaned himself by adding, 'what was it you wanted?'

'Well, can't a mother call her son occasionally for no special—'

'Yes, mother,' he broke in soothingly, 'yes, of course.'

'I really don't have to explain my reasons for calling my own—'

'No, mother, it's all right,' said Herr Lehmann, at pains to defuse a situation which could, he knew, escalate to an infinite extent. Anything was possible, even tears.

'We're coming to Berlin!'

Herr Lehmann wasn't prepared for that. It was a hard blow – so hard that it reduced him to silence. They're coming to Berlin, they're coming to Berlin, he told himself, quite unable to conceive of such an eventuality.

'Frank? Are you still there?'

'Yes, mother. Why are you coming to Berlin?'

'But Frank, we've always wanted to.'

'That's news to me, mother,' Herr Lehmann said testily. 'I've never, in all the years I've been living here, detected any sign of your wanting to come to Berlin.'

'But of course, we've often talked about it.'

'No, mother,' said Herr Lehmann, 'you never did. What you always said was, you *didn't* want to come to Berlin because you felt uneasy about the GDR and travelling through the Eastern Bloc, et cetera, and you didn't want to be humiliated by the frontier guards and all that crap.'

'But Frank, honestly, things aren't anywhere near as bad these days. Don't make such a fuss.'

'Me, make a fuss? What do you mean, don't make a fuss?'

'That's all water under the bridge. Things aren't half as bad these days, what with the treaties and so on.'

'That's what *I* always told you, but *you* said—'

'Now don't go making such a fuss about a few policemen. We haven't committed any crime, so we've nothing to fear.'

'I'm not making a fuss.'

'It didn't sound like that just now.'

This is pointless, Herr Lehmann thought resignedly. There's nothing to be done.

'When are you coming?' he asked, to change the subject.

'That's the fantastic thing,' said his mother. 'It's all inclusive: coach fare, hotel, theatre tickets, everything.'

'Yes, but when are you coming?'

'It's on at a theatre in the Kurfürstendamm, Ilya Richter's supposed to be in it. It's called, it's called . . . Ernst, what's the name of the thing they're doing? . . . At the theatre, of course! . . . Of course, with Ilya Richter . . . What? . . . No, surely not . . . Are you positive?'

'*Mother!*'

'Harald Juhnke, it's with Harald Juhnke, your father says,' said Herr Lehmann's mother.

'But when, mother? *When* are you coming, for God's sake?'

'Oh, not for a while yet – not till the end of October. When exactly is it, Ernst?'

'The end of October?' Herr Lehmann blurted out the words more fiercely than he intended. 'The end of October? Good God, that's not for another six weeks or more . . .' He wasn't quite sure of today's date, but it was somewhere around the beginning of September, that much was certain. 'You're coming at the end of October, and you call me about it at *this* stage?' Still, he thought, it's a mistake to make a fuss. It's only fair to warn someone well in advance, these things need arranging.

'But aren't you glad? How could you take such a tone when . . .' – her voice began to quaver at this point, and he realised that the floodgates were about to open – '. . . when your own parents are coming to visit you after all the years you've been living there, and I was so looking forward to seeing . . .' The tears were now in full spate, Herr Lehmann could tell from her voice – not that they quenched it. She can simultaneously weep buckets and go on talking quite normally, he thought, working himself up into a lather of resentment – go on talking on and on and on. '. . . so looking forward to seeing what sort of life you lead,' his mother pursued, 'and the restaurant where you work, and what your friends are like, and anyway, it's high time we—'

'What are you planning to do,' Herr Lehmann said before he could stop himself, 'visit me or check up on me?'

Actually, he felt tempted to give way and assure her of what she must realise in any case, namely, that he hadn't said anything to suggest that he wasn't glad too, and that, on the contrary, she ought to be pleased that her own son was sorry their visit was still such a long way off. But he didn't want to do that. That would have signified total defeat, and he had to put a stop, once and for all, to total defeats at his mother's hands. It mustn't end like this, he thought, or the whole day will be ruined. Recently, he recalled, he and his best friend Karl had watched a TV programme on manic depressives, and one of the interviewees had said, 'Mornings are the worst time – that's when the day begins.' Well, that was just the way he felt now, and that was why he had to venture a final onslaught.

'Check up on you? *Check up* on you? What do you take us for?' came the shrill response from Bremen. The tears had stopped. They come and go like a tropical rainstorm, thought Herr Lehmann.

'Why don't you come a bit later on?' He realised, thanks to this sudden flash of inspiration, that he was back in the game.

'Later on?' his mother said suspiciously. 'What do you mean?'

'Think about it . . .'

'But Frank, what is it now?'

'You mean you'd forgotten my birthday?' Herr Lehmann hated doing this, but what the hell, he thought, all's fair in love and war.

'Of course I hadn't forgotten your birthday,' said the voice in his ear, 'but that's not till November.'

'So?' Herr Lehmann said triumphantly.

'Why bring that up? It's still a long way off.'

'Not much longer than the thing you called me about.'

'What thing?'

'Well, your trip to Berlin.'

'Oh, *that*. That's quite different, that's at the end of October.'

'End of October, beginning of November, where's the big difference? You'd forgotten my birthday,' Herr Lehmann said gleefully. 'You booked a trip to Berlin and forgot I'd be thirty a few days later.'

'Nonsense, how could I have forgotten it?'

'That's what I'm wondering,' said Herr Lehmann, brightening. I've won, he told himself.

'A mother doesn't forget something like that. Thirty . . . My God, thirty already. Of course I hadn't forgotten. Thirty, and it seems only yesterday I was holding you in my arms . . .'

'Yes, yes,' Herr Lehmann said soothingly.

'Such a delicate little thing, you were. We were so worried about you. You were always ill.'

'Yes, yes, okay!'

'You cried so much, too, quite unlike your brother. Forget your birthday? What nonsense! No mother would ever forget her child's birthday.' Herr Lehmann heard his mother calling over her shoulder. 'Ernst, could we travel a week later?'

'No, no, it's all right,' called Herr Lehmann, who found this a thoroughly unappealing idea, but the thread was already broken. He listened awhile to another heated exchange at the other end of the line, but this time, worse luck, he couldn't catch a word of it because his mother had remembered to put her hand over the mouthpiece. Meanwhile, he sat at the diminutive table in his diminutive kitchen – in a rather lopsided, unhealthy posture, so the phone would reach – and sampled his cowboy coffee. The only trouble with cowboy coffee, he thought, was the impossibility of ensuring that all the grounds really settled, because basically that's what they did. He remembered an old saying of his East Prussian grandmother's: tea must draw, coffee must settle. That, he thought, was why filter papers, as such, were completely pointless. Even so, a few grounds always remained floating on the surface. Strange, that, thought Herr Lehmann, and he wondered what was so different about those particular grounds that they behaved so utterly unlike their fellows.

'No,' his mother reported back, 'we can't, I'm afraid. What a shame.'

'Why can't you?' Herr Lehmann demanded remorselessly, and rubbed salt into the wound by adding, 'After all, I'll only turn thirty once in my life.'

'I know, I know.' He could literally hear his mother writhing with remorse at the other end of the line. 'But it's the Meierlings' silver wedding – they're counting on us, we can't back out now. Still, you will *be* in Berlin at the end of October, won't you? You never leave there in any case.'

'Hm, that depends . . .' Herr Lehmann said with relish.

'But we're coming specially for your sake.'

'I find that hard to believe, mother.'

'Frank!' She sounded almost imploring now. 'If we come to Berlin after all these years . . . I'm sorry about your birthday. If I'd known it was so important to you . . .'

'It's not as important as all that . . .'

'I'm really sorry we can't make it any later.'

'Oh, sure.'

'We weren't to know it meant so much to you.'

'Well, worse things happen at sea.'

'You weren't there for *my* birthday in February, nor was your brother, so maybe you shouldn't make such a song and dance about it. Your birthday, I mean.'

'Hm . . .'

'If your father and I come to Berlin for once, surely you can be there for us?'

'Of course, naturally.'

'It's a weekend. The twenty-eighth and twenty-ninth of October, it is.'

'I'll write it down, mother, so I don't forget. I'll make a note of it right away.'

'Surely we must see each other if your father and I come to Berlin for once?'

'Of course, mother.'

'No, really!'

Herr Lehmann sighed. Fair enough, he thought. Fair enough, mother, let's call it a draw.

3 BREAKFAST

HE SHOULD HAVE known it was a stupid idea to look in at the
Markthalle at this hour on a Sunday – he realised that as soon
as he entered the place soon after his mother's phone call. Why
on earth did I come, he asked himself. What on earth possessed
me to go in, he wondered as he stood, near the door but already
inside, and absorbed the whole sad truth at a glance: that there
was absolutely no point in patronising the *Markthalle* on a Sunday
– in fact one reason why he hated Sundays so much was that
on Sundays the logical transition from his digs to the nearby
Markthalle was invariably spoiled for him by the positively inhu-
man bunch of breakfasters who always, as if to order, made it
their Sunday rendezvous.

I can't stand this place, not even for ten seconds, Herr Lehmann
said to himself as he lingered near the door for no good reason,
surveying the left-hand room and its occupants. The breakfast
trade is ruining everything the way it ruins everything every
Sunday, he thought. For completeness' sake he looked in the
other direction, at the right-hand room, which led to the toilets.
It held only a few tables, but these were as predictably chock-
a-block with breakfasters as Herr Lehmann's observations had
taught him that every bar in the city was chock-a-block with
breakfasters on a Sunday. Breakfasters are the ultimate enemy,

he thought absently as a scrawny waitress – he didn't know her, oddly enough – squeezed past him bearing an enormous tray, and it's always breakfast time on Sunday, at least till 5 p.m., even in the *Markthalle*, although it claims to be a restaurant as well as a bar – which doesn't make it any better, he thought.

A bar that also serves breakfast shouldn't call itself a restaurant, Herr Lehmann reflected as he continued to stand aimlessly near the entrance, feeling rather foolish. It's unworthy of a chef – insofar as these so-called restaurants employ a genuine chef at all – to spend his time arranging slices of cheese and sausage on plates. It's bad for the counter staff, too, he thought, to be so preoccupied with breakfasters that they fail to notice a friend and colleague standing forlornly near the entrance. It ought to be the duty and moral obligation of all restaurant owners or managers – even if they're called Erwin and feel they have to rake in every last mark, and even if the restaurants are bars as well (not that that's anything against them in itself, he conceded, because drinking is a universal occupation and makes sense, in a bar) – to keep their establishments free from breakfasters, because breakfasters are the most intolerable people on earth, Herr Lehmann thought as he continued to stand near the entrance like a spare prick at a wedding, refusing to budge an inch because he didn't want to give the breakfasters, who occupied the whole place, the satisfaction of driving him, of all people, out of the *Markthalle*. It's no wonder, he thought, that a person's own friends fail to notice him and help him find a table to himself and a bit of peace and quiet, if they have to cope with the kind of scumbag breakfasters that are roaming around loose in this place.

A term like 'orange juice' is legally protected, so only orange juice a hundred per cent extracted from oranges can be called 'orange juice', thought Herr Lehmann, whose legs were gradually growing heavier as he continued to stand forlornly near the entrance, whereas the other stuff, depending on its fruit content, has to be called 'orange nectar' or 'orange-flavoured fruit juice'. Why doesn't the same apply to the term 'restaurant', which is far worthier of legal protection than the term 'orange juice'? The term 'restaurant' should be protected against breakfasters most of all, he thought, but not the term 'orange juice' – there'd be no point. Such were the ever more meaningless thoughts that circulated in Herr Lehmann's unwontedly hung-over head as he continued to survey the big, mercifully muzak-free premises in which no one, but no one, was making any attempt to clear the table that would have been his only salvation – apart, of course, from instant flight, which would now have struck him as the best course of action had it not betokened surrender and left him at a loose end thereafter.

His desperation was such that it almost impelled him to sit down any old where, as he occasionally did on weekdays, though never, of course, at a table where someone was breakfasting. In Herr Lehmann's experience, breakfasting was an altogether absurd activity that took up a lot of space. Despite this, it occurred to him yet again, as he defiantly clung to his post near the entrance, that breakfasting seemed to be the breakfasters' whole *raison d'être*. They came to life as they reverently slid their little plates to and fro, dissected slices of sausage, decapitated boiled eggs, folded up garnishings of lettuce leaves that were never intended to be eaten and thrust them into their mouths, trimmed the rind off cheese, and broke open bread rolls in slow motion. They not only consumed this muck, which was bad enough in itself; above all, they indulged in a collective ritual whose sole purpose, Herr Lehmann now felt convinced, was to deny him access to the *Markthalle*.

They're insane, he thought savagely as he lingered near the

door like someone awaiting a miracle, harassed by the intolerable comings and goings of people who, as if sexually frustrated, brushed against him in passing even though he considerately left so much space between himself and the nearest obstacle that even the most uncoordinated imbecile would have had room to get past without occasioning any physical contact. Breakfast . . . The very word is loathsome when you come to think of it, he reflected. Break-fast . . . Violate your fast . . . It must have been invented by some religious killjoy, he thought while repeatedly compelled to change position to avoid the breakfasters who kept getting up and jostling him on their way from somewhere to somewhere else, to the loo and back or whatever, but who never quit the premises, which would have been the only acceptable course of action on their part. Breakfast . . . It seemed to imply that hunger was admirable, and that assuaging it was a form of gluttony. More loathsome even than 'breakfast', however, was the word 'breakfaster', he thought, inwardly reluctant to calm down, as he continued to stand there waiting for someone to notice him and feeling more and more embarrassed. Breakfasters are human too, he conceded, but why do they have to indulge in their awful, shameless hobby in public? They're like nudists or clubbers. It never occurs to them how awful they look and sound when they wave their greasy hands in the air and say things like 'May I have another boiled egg?' or 'Where's that other coffee I ordered?'

I really ought to go, this is pointless, he thought as he continued to stand near the entrance, having now lost all desire to go on surveying the scene. You can't rely on anything or anyone any more, not even colleagues and old friends, he thought. He had already turned to go, temporarily obliged to delay his final departure from the *Markthalle* because he'd been elbowed aside by some people who were also leaving but hadn't left a table

completely vacant, he noted with regret, when he heard someone call his name.

'Frank!'

He knew, of course, that he was the Frank in question, and
he also knew, of course, who had hailed him – after all, he'd
waited for the call long enough – but he felt tempted to ignore
it and leave regardless. It would serve Karl right, he thought,
although – it occurred to him a moment later – that's unfair,
Karl can't help it. The breakfasters are to blame, he told himself,
although he'd naturally spotted Karl right away and been
surprised that his best friend was working there this morning.
It didn't surprise him to see Heidi, who nearly always worked
in the mornings because she liked doing breakfast shifts and was
rather peculiar in other respects as well. It was different with
his best friend Karl. Although Karl worked at the *Markthalle*, he
never worked anything but the late shift, just as Herr Lehmann
did at the *Einfall*. They'd always been unanimous that working
breakfast shifts was the daftest thing imaginable. 'We aren't waiters or coffee-frothers,' his best friend Karl always said when the
subject of breakfast shifts cropped up, which it seldom did because
the subject of breakfast shifts wasn't an issue where they were
concerned, since they never worked them. So it was no wonder
that Herr Lehmann had spotted his best friend Karl at once,
because Karl stuck out like a sore thumb, not being a person
who'd ever had any connection with all this breakfast shit, and
because he looked out of place here at this hour. What was
more, being the tall, broad, muscular ox of a man he was, Karl
could hardly escape notice, least of all when he was standing
behind a counter.

So Herr Lehmann turned round when his best friend finally
noticed him and called his name. Karl, who had both hands in
the washing-up water, grinned at him, then removed his hands

30

from the sink and beckoned him over with two big, dripping beer glasses. Without devoting too much thought to why Karl should be washing up such big beer glasses at this time of day – it seemed quite natural to him, in his present condition, that a lot of apple-juice spritzers should be imbibed here on a Sunday morning – he went over to him.

'What are *you* doing here?' demanded his best friend Karl. 'This isn't your time of day.'

'I was going to ask you the same thing,' said Herr Lehmann, 'and have a bite to eat.'

'Okay, grab yourself a seat somewhere,' said his best friend Karl. 'I'll bring you the menu right away.'

'I don't know, this place stinks.'

His best friend Karl laughed. Karl's always so good-tempered, thought Herr Lehmann – that's the strange thing about Karl, his eternal good nature. 'It's enough to drive you up the wall, this place,' he burst out. 'I mean, Jesus, look at this shower of shit!' Somehow, he felt sorry for putting it that way and for being so grouchy. It sounds so negative, he thought. I shouldn't say such things to Karl, not now. I ought to be more positive – better-tempered, somehow.

'Balls,' said Karl, 'there's still plenty of room if you share a table.'

'It's lousy, sharing a table.'

Karl sighed. 'What about that big one over there? There's only one chair taken.'

'I don't feel like it now,' said Herr Lehmann, who found his own intransigence thoroughly distasteful. Still more distasteful, however, was the idea of sharing a table with a stranger, even a non-breakfasting stranger, and possibly of being spoken to, if only along the lines of 'Would you mind passing the ashtray?' The day had got off to a bad start with his mother's phone call, and the previous day had ended just as badly, come to that. He didn't want much, only some peace and quiet and a little space to himself.

His best friend Karl sighed. 'Okay, take that one for two over there.' He pointed to a small table with two chairs near the swing door to the kitchen. 'That one really *is* free.'

'No, no, it's not on,' said Herr Lehmann. 'That's for staff, I really couldn't—'

'Frank!' his best friend Karl said firmly. 'Cut the cackle and sit down.'

'I couldn't,' said Herr Lehmann, who really prided himself on his principles. 'What would the others say? It's just not on.'

'Heidi!' his best friend Karl called to the woman who was currently excavating the orange-juice press with a knife. 'Any objection if Herr Lehmann parks himself at the little table?'

'Don't bother me now,' she called back without looking up.

'See?' said Karl. 'Nobody gives a damn.'

Herr Lehmann disliked any form of preferential treatment, although, to be honest, he *had* rather counted on getting the little staff table. 'But tell me,' he said quickly, to change the subject, 'what are *you* doing here?' And why are you in such a good mood? he felt like adding but refrained because he would have had to admit that he himself was feeling rather sour, and that would put him even more in the wrong than he was already, occupying a table reserved for staff.

'I'm helping out,' said Karl. 'Came straight here from the *Orbit* – haven't even been to bed. Erwin caught me on the phone at nine, just as I was going home. I don't know how he manages it every time.'

Herr Lehmann scanned his best friend's face, which wasn't so easy because Karl had gone back to rinsing glasses with great alacrity. He couldn't detect any signs of fatigue, which was strange, if only because Karl was as old as himself. I ought to be a tough nut like him, thought Herr Lehmann. Karl would never let himself be thrown off his stride by a dog and a phone call from his mother, that's why nobody calls him Herr Schmidt, Herr Lehmann reflected, feeling even more wretched than before.

'I'll sit down, then,' he said. Karl just nodded, and Herr Lehmann dragged his weary bones over to the little table that was really reserved for staff.

'That table isn't free, it's only for staff,' said the unfamiliar scrawny girl he'd noticed earlier.

'That's what I said,' Herr Lehmann mumbled. He turned puce and stood up again.

'It's okay,' said Heidi, who was just passing. 'Herr Lehmann's allowed.'

'Herr Lehmann?' said the scrawny girl, in what Herr Lehmann considered an inappropriately sarcastic tone of voice. '*Herr* Lehmann, eh? Do you work here too?'

'I work for Erwin, but I really don't . . .' said Herr Lehmann. He was feeling thoroughly awkward now, especially as he was attracting universal attention. People at the neighbouring tables had raised their heads and were positively gawping at him, and he had an urge to say something to them he knew he'd regret later, which was why he didn't say it. Today isn't the day to get abusive, he told himself. I should never have got up and gone to the phone. That and drinking shorts, those were my big mistakes.

'Just sit down,' said Heidi, and she took him by the shoulders and forced him back on to his chair. 'I'll take care of this myself,' she added, turning to the scrawny girl. Herr Lehmann, who found the whole situation vaguely reminiscent of the casualty department of the district hospital, which he had once visited when suffering from acute inflammation of the scrotum, felt very grateful to Heidi.

'How are things, Herr Lehmann? Like something to drink?'

'Don't know. First off, maybe a big glass of tap water.'

'You look done in, Herr Lehmann.'

'Nice of you to say so, Heidi. It makes me feel even worse.'

'You've got a hangover, Herr Lehmann. You're unbearable when you've got a hangover. I'll send Karl to you.'

'Don't forget the water.'

Not long afterwards, his best friend Karl came over with a beer glass full of tap water.

'That looks disgusting,' said Herr Lehmann. 'Was the glass really clean?'

'Okay,' said his best friend Karl. 'What would you prefer?'

'Don't know. Peach juice?'

'We don't have any, Frank. For some reason it's the only juice we don't have, you know that.'

'Yes, well, in that case I'm out of ideas . . .'

'Come on, Frank, here's the menu. How about some coffee?'

'No, I already had a bucketful at home. Something refreshing, preferably. Some cherryade, maybe?'

'Sure that's what you want?'

'Not really.'

'I'll bring you a beer.'

'Not draught beer, though – anything but that.'

'Check.'

Karl brought him a Beck's, sat down facing him, and sighed. Herr Lehmann took a first, cautious swallow. Looking at his best friend as he did so, he saw him rub his eyes. Karl's suddenly looking tired after all, he thought. It can't be good in the long run, skipping several nights' sleep on the trot. Age takes its toll, he thought, and took a second pull at his beer. He was hungry, he realised.

'I don't need the menu,' he said, relaxing.

'What'll you have, then?'

'Roast pork,' said Herr Lehmann, who never had anything else at the *Markthalle*.

'It's eleven o'clock, Frank. Can't you order some kind of breakfast like everyone else?'

'Breakfast?' said Herr Lehmann, who was feeling much better. 'Breakfast is crap.'

'I know, but have the Bunkhouse Brunch,' said his best friend Karl, and the exhaustion in his voice was such that Herr Lehmann felt sorry for being so awkward. 'That's fried eggs on ham with French fries. It's okay.'

'No thanks.'

'I could murder you sometimes, Frank, especially when you've got a hangover. The place is jam-packed, the new waitress hasn't got a clue, and there's another new girl in the kitchen. What sort of earful do you think she'll give me if I go asking her for roast pork at this hour?'

'You're scared of some girl in the kitchen?'

'You don't know her. She's a trained chef – been to college and all that.'

'So what?'

'One can't just mess her about.'

'What do you mean, mess her about? What does roast pork have to do with messing someone about?'

'Don't be silly, Frank.' Karl rose with a weary grin. 'All right, it's no skin off my nose. I'll send her out to you. You can ask her yourself.'

Herr Lehmann, who now wished he'd had the ham and eggs even though it was breakfast muck and at his age you couldn't be too careful about cholesterol, watched with concern as his best friend Karl tottered into the kitchen. I must take a bit more care of him, he thought. Karl overdoes it sometimes. Maybe I should have a word with him and tell him he ought to get more sleep, but he'd be bound to think I was overstepping the mark.

Karl reappeared. 'She'll be out right away, so be nice to her,' he said, patting Herr Lehmann on the back. 'Like another beer? Although, from the look of you, old son, I reckon you'd be wiser to get some sleep. You're looking kind of done in, if you don't mind me saying so.'

Before Herr Lehmann could think of a suitable retort, his best friend Karl was back behind the counter washing glasses.

He briefly succumbed to fatigue. Karl shouldn't have said he looked done in, let alone Heidi. You just don't say such things, he thought. If someone tells you a thing like that, you promptly feel bad, whether or not it's true. Now that his fury at his mother and dogs and breakfasters and the lousiness of the world in general had abated, he was feeling terribly tired again, especially as that first beer had taken the edge off the headache which had been his main reason for sallying forth. The scrawny girl, the one who had tried to evict him, wordlessly brought him another beer.

Just as he was broaching this second bottle, *she* suddenly appeared. Tall, statuesque and beautiful, she flopped down on the other chair and eyed him appraisingly. The neck of the bottle was still in his mouth when she addressed him.

'Isn't it a bit early for that?'

He lowered the bottle.

'Early for what?'

'Both. Beer and roast pork.'

'Not in my book.' Herr Lehmann could tell that this was going to be a hard-fought battle requiring total concentration, which was why he tore his eyes away from her substantial bosom and set about marshalling his arguments.

'I gathered that,' she said drily.

'What it's too early or too late for,' said Herr Lehmann, proceeding to evolve an impromptu theory, 'is purely a matter of social convention. To put it another way,' he went on, changing direction so as not to stray on to the wrong sociological track, 'if it's okay for these imbeciles to breakfast till five in the afternoon, it must also be okay to order roast pork at eleven in the morning.'

The beautiful girl was unimpressed. 'I'd prefer to put it the other way round,' she said. Herr Lehmann now noticed that she was wearing genuine working gear of the kind he'd only ever seen on a TV chef: baggy pants with little blue and white checks and a long white smock buttoned up in a peculiar way and absolutely spotless, unlike the dirty swab dangling from the thin chain encircling her curvaceous hips, but that, since she was sitting down, was visible only to someone who looked closely, which Herr Lehmann briefly did. 'If the world is teeming with assholes who breakfast till five in the afternoon,' she said, 'why should we need any desperate characters who order roast pork at eleven in the morning?'

Herr Lehmann, who'd never heard a woman talk that way before, was enchanted. His desire for roast pork had deserted him, in fact, but he naturally didn't feel like dropping the subject, not when she spoke to him like that.

'What's so difficult about producing some roast pork?' he asked. 'It's left over from last night anyway. All you do is cut off a couple of slices, pour some cold gravy over them, and stick them in the microwave. I wasn't born yesterday, I know the form.'

'Oh, so you know the form, do you?' she said, unmoved, and inserted a cigarette between her lips. 'Shove the ashtray across, would you?'

Herr Lehmann shoved it across.

'You bet I know the form,' he said.

'What if I tell you there isn't any roast pork left over from yesterday? What then?'

Herr Lehmann would sooner have steered the conversation in a different direction. Why, he thought, can't I ask her how old she is, what her name is, and what she's doing when she's through for the day?

'Then I'd say it may be only a quarter past eleven, but the normal lunchtime shit comes on at half past twelve, and then you'll be needing some roast pork anyway.'

'And if I told you that I wasn't born yesterday either, and that the roast pork's already in the oven, but that it'll take another hour, and that all you can have till then is a shitty breakfast like these other bleary-eyed bastards' – she waved her cigarette in the air as though bestowing a benediction on the entire establishment and everyone therein, and she also raised her voice so that everyone could hear, or so it seemed to Herr Lehmann – 'these roll-munchers with their shitty sausage and their shitty cheese and all the rest of the muck that goes down their throats . . . If I told you that's the most you can have, but that if you're set on roast pork, and that if you asked again, really nicely, at half past twelve, which, as you appear to know, is when lunch comes on, you might get some really good roast pork, if not the best roast pork of a lifetime, except that by then you'd probably be too pissed to notice . . . If I told you that, what would you say then, you . . .' – she leant forward and blew some cigarette smoke at him – '. . . you smart-ass?'

Herr Lehmann had to decide, in the ensuing seconds, how to proceed. Should he give in? Should he admit that she was right? Should he order a Bunkhouse Brunch? Should he simply change the subject and ask whether her kitchen attire included a chef's hat worn over the dark hair she'd gathered into a ponytail? On the other hand, should he really let her call him a smart-ass and get away with it?

'For a start,' he said, 'I'd say that this place opens at ten on Sundays, and that the kitchen staff, of whom I presume you're one, are bound to get here at half past nine, and that, if you start roasting a joint of pork at half past nine, it ought to be well enough done by eleven for you to cut me off a slice. Forget about the crackling, I'd have it without, but some French fries would be fine, and you've got those anyway, because they're included in the Bunkhouse Brunch. So I'd say that the roast pork was already done enough for you to cut me off a slice, just the very outside, and never mind if the crackling isn't crisp yet, crackling's overrated anyway, in my opinion, and you could throw in a few French fries, and there's never any shortage of gravy, so there you have it, QED, no problem. That's what I'd say . . .' – Herr Lehmann leant forward in his turn – '. . . being a smart-ass!'

There followed a brief pause during which she continued to smoke and eye him with serene indifference. Herr Lehmann suddenly wished he smoked too. Above all, he wished he didn't talk such bullshit. It's all balls, he thought. She must hate me – at least, he thought, I'd hate me if I were a chef and someone gave me a load of bullshit.

'I see,' she said at length. 'So the crackling doesn't matter.'

'No, the crackling's unimportant.'

'To you or in general?'

'Whichever.'

'Any more of your kind around here?'

'No.'

'Well,' she said, stubbing out her cigarette and getting up, 'that's all right, then.'

'Okay,' said Herr Lehmann, who didn't want her to go yet,

'I'll wait a bit longer. It'll soon be half past twelve in any case.'

'I could always haul a half-cooked joint of pork out of the oven and mutilate it for you, seeing we're such good friends.'

'No, no, don't bother, it's not that important.'

'It's all the same to me. I can always do it in the future.'

'No, really, don't put yourself out, I'll have another beer while waiting. Maybe I'll read the paper. Or have a coffee.'

She lingered a moment. Their eyes met, and Herr Lehmann got the impression that she didn't really hate him, which was a big relief. Then she smiled.

'Don't drink so much,' she said, tapping him lightly on the shoulder with her finger as she brushed past. 'The day's still young.'

'True,' he said. He wanted to add something, he didn't know what, but she'd already disappeared into the kitchen.

Herr Lehmann sighed and drained his bottle of beer. Then he ordered himself a coffee. The day was still young, and he'd fallen in love.

4 LUNCH

HERR LEHMANN GOT his roast pork shortly before noon, when his best friend Karl served it up 'with best regards from the beautiful chef'. Not long afterwards the beautiful chef herself sat down at his table and watched him eating.

'Okay if I smoke?' she asked.

'Yes, of course.'

'I shouldn't really.'

'It doesn't bother me.'

'Well, how's the pork?'

'Great, really fantastic.'

'That's all right, then.'

'Yes, it's fabulous. The best I've ever had here.'

'No need to be smarmy.'

'I'm not. I never am.'

'That's all right, then.'

'Good. How long have you worked here?'

'This is my second shift.'

'Did Erwin take you on?'

'The guy that owns this place? The one with long, straggly hair?'

'That's right. Getting a bit thin on top, I'd say.' Erwin always makes a good topic of conversation, thought Herr Lehmann.

You can't go far wrong, talking about Erwin.

'Yes, he engaged me. Funny customer.'

'Funny how?'

'I don't know, just funny, somehow.'

'Well,' Herr Lehmann conceded, 'he does have his points. At least he keeps everything on the boil.'

'How about Karl? Known him long?'

'We're old friends, kind of. Used to share digs when I first arrived in Berlin. You aren't from here either, are you?'

'What makes you say that?'

'Well, you sound more like you come from my part of the world.'

'What do you mean, "sound like"?'

'Just that.'

'What *is* your part of the world?'

'Bremen and thereabouts.'

'I come from Achim. If you know it.'

'Achim . . . That's out Verden way, isn't it? Near the Grundbergsee, right?'

'Not really.'

'We stayed at the camping site there – I mean, my parents and my brother and so on. When I was a boy.'

'At the camping site? Beside the Grundbergsee?'

'Yes.'

'A wonderful childhood you had, I must say. I mean, fancy camping beside the Grundbergsee! Very glamorous, really classy.'

'Very funny. I suppose it sounds a real hoot to a country bumpkin like you.'

'Watch it!'

'At least it made a nice change for us, playing with cowpats, not like you in Achim.'

'What would *you* know about Achim? You don't even know where it is.'

'Still, I did learn to swim in the Grundbergsee.'

'That's saying something, of course.'

'Definitely.'

'So you learnt to swim in the Grundbergsee. Big deal.'

'A person has to learn somewhere.'

'Sure, of course, great.'

'And fresh water's harder to swim in than sea water. It's not as buoyant.'

'That's logical. Very observant of you.'

'It was cold as a witch's tit, too.'

'Which made it even harder.'

'Absolutely.'

'That's all right, then.'

'And how does someone who lives in Achim get to be a cook?'

'A chef.'

'Okay, okay: how does someone who lives in Achim get to be a chef?'

'I trained in Bremen. At the Ibis Hotel.'

'The Ibis?'

'Yes, damn it all, the Ibis. Have I got a speech defect or something?'

'No, but it isn't exactly the height of glamour, learning to cook at the Ibis.'

'You must be the kind of guy that knows a bit about everything. Roast pork, the Grundbergsee, Achim, learning to swim, fresh water and sea water, hotels, catering – you're a universal genius, right? Speak out, don't be shy.'

'I didn't start all that bullshit about glamour. Anyway, anyone who rubbishes the Grundbergsee should bear this in mind: the

Ibis is practically the Grundbergsee of the hotel trade.'

'What am I expected to do now, defend the damned hotel? Besides, I didn't rubbish the Grundbergsee. You can't rubbish a lake; it exists, period. I don't know the Grundbergsee at all, if you really want to know.'

'Aha!'

'Anyway, what do *you* do, when you aren't bugging people?'

'I work for Erwin too, but not here. At the *Einfall* in Wiener Strasse. Maybe you know it.'

'No. I don't.'

'How long have you been in Berlin?'

'What's it to you?'

'Just asking.'

'If you really want to know, I've been here a month.'

'A month?'

'Anything wrong with that?'

'No, no, I wasn't suggesting there was. I've been in Berlin since 1980 — that's nine years already.'

'So? What am I supposed to do, applaud?'

'I didn't mean it like that.'

'Quite a guy, you must be, living here for nine years already. Some folk are really proud of how long they've lived in Berlin — I've noticed. I mean, it's a magnificent achievement, living in Berlin. Only two million people do it, after all. Fantastic.'

'That wasn't what I meant at all.'

'Oh no, he didn't mean it like that. "I've lived here since 1980," ' she mimicked. 'Do you get a medal for it, or something? Types like you only come here to get out of doing their national service.'

'Hey, hey, I said I didn't mean it like that.' Why are all the women I fall in love with so touchy, thought Herr Lehmann.

'So how *did* you mean it?'

'Well, just . . . I mean, I was trying to . . . Anyway, it's a long time since I lived in Bremen, otherwise we might have . . .'

'What?'

'Nothing.'

'That's all right, then.'

'Sure.'

'Exactly.'

'Besides, I didn't come here to get out of national service.'

'I see. Great.'

'I wasn't that smart.'

'I wouldn't have thought you were.'

'That's all right, then.'

'Exactly.'

'Sure.'

'And what do you do at the – what was it called again?'

'The *Einfall.*'

'Ah yes, the *Einfall*. Great name for a bar.'

'I didn't dream it up.'

'So what do you do there?'

'Serve behind the counter, of course.'

'You think that's worthwhile, do you?'

'How do you mean, worthwhile?'

'Well, do you think it's a worthwhile job, standing behind a counter pouring drinks? It isn't a fulfilling way of life, surely?'

'Just a minute,' said Herr Lehmann. 'What do you mean, fulfilling? "Fulfilment" is a totally idiotic expression. What are you trying to say? Is life a glass or a bottle or a bucket – a container to be filled with something, a container you *have* to fill, in fact, because for some reason the whole world seems to agree that fulfilment is an absolute must. Is that what life is – just a container for something else? A barrel, maybe, or a sick-bag?'

She stared at him bemusedly.

'Well, is that all it is?' Herr Lehmann added.

'I don't know. It's just a figure of speech.'

That's enough, Herr Lehmann told himself, I mustn't go on about it. I'm bullying her, he thought, and that's bad. 'Fulfilment is a rotten metaphor,' he went on despite himself. 'That's an established fact, but even if people use it, what do they mean by it? Can anyone tell me? Could I go over to one of the people at that table and say, "Excuse me, but can you quote me one or two examples of fulfilment?" No, nothing doing, but everyone thinks it exists – nobody gives it a second thought. Talk about fulfilment and you reduce life to a means to an end, a container to be filled with something, instead of realising that it's worth something in itself, and that if you're constantly preoccupied with filling it you may not grasp that at all.' Herr Lehmann had the bit between his teeth. 'Okay, let's stick with the metaphor of life as a container that has to be filled with something, not that anyone can tell me exactly what that something ought to be, and so, if we want to stick with the metaphor, we can only look at it the other way round: then life becomes a container that's full when we're given it – full of time. There's a hole in the bottom, and the time leaks out. If we must talk about a container at all, that's the way it works, and the stupid thing is, time can't be topped up.'

'But I never said anything about a container.'

'That's equally beside the point,' said Herr Lehmann. I'm not being romantic, he thought, romantic is something else. 'You started on about fulfilment, and anyone who raises a subject ought to think it through. A word like that needs careful thought. So what does the fact that someone works in a bar have to do with fulfilment? Fulfilment is utter bullshit. We're alive and happy to be so, that's quite enough.' Any minute now she'll get up and go, he thought, and then I'll have fouled things up for good.

But the beautiful chef was looking more surprised than annoyed. 'Jesus,' she said, 'fancy getting so worked up over one little word. It doesn't matter if I call it "fulfilment" or something else, you know what I mean.'

'No, I don't. I refuse to know what people mean when they try to rubbish my life without thinking what they're saying.'

'It isn't a decent job, at any rate. You can't just work in a bar.'

'Ah!' Herr Lehmann stuck a forefinger in the air and promptly retracted it. Wagging my finger at her on top of everything else, he thought – I'm going from bad to worse. 'Now we're getting to the heart of the matter,' he said. 'So I can't *just* work in a bar, huh? What's so bad about it? Why can't I *just* work in a bar?'

'Because it's far too boring.'

'Not to me it isn't.'

'Don't you do anything else?'

'Why do people keep asking me if I do something else?' I'm not talking to her at all, Herr Lehmann reflected sadly. I'm really talking to the rest of the world, and she's getting it in the neck. 'Most of the people I know say: Yes, I work in a bar, but I'm really an artist, I really play in a band, I'm really a student, et cetera. They mean they won't be working in a bar for evermore, and that someday the tide will turn, like with Karl and his sculptures and so on. I'm not decrying Karl and his stuff, but honestly, isn't it a bit sad when people persist in regarding what they do as a stopgap and not the real thing?'

'What sort of sculptures does he do?'

'Never mind, that's not the point. The point is: why are some jobs considered worthwhile and others not? If I were to tell people I'm really an artist, they'd all say: Ah, I see, now I get it. But what's so bad about simply standing behind a counter – and enjoying it, what's more? The whole city's full of bars, and for why? There are more bars here than churches or art galleries or concert halls or clubs or discos or whatever. People like bars – they enjoy going to them. It's a good, useful job, working in a bar. People get just as much fun out of going into a bar as they do out of going to an exhibition or a concert, so why does everyone want to be an artist or something, whereas nobody wants to be someone who only works in a bar? Would you ask an artist why he doesn't do something else? Like work in a bar, for instance? Actually,' Herr Lehmann conceded with a smile, happy to have hit on a way of softening his approach a little, 'there are plenty of artists who end up opening bars. From that point of view I'm doubly right: I'm saving myself an artistic detour.'

'I wasn't thinking of art at all. Where does art come into it? All I said was—'

'People go into bars and get drunk,' Herr Lehmann cut in. That's bad, he thought, I shouldn't interrupt her like that. 'Some more so, some less, but they all enjoy it. What would life in this city be like if there weren't any bars or cafés or whatever they like to call themselves? What's so bad about a job that consists in serving people with something they like? Fulfilment, pah! Bar staff may be the only ones who make people feel really fulfilled.'

'Oh, come on, make up your mind. That's two definitions of fulfilment you've given me. One involves getting tanked up, which means pouring it in up top, and the other assumes there's a leak down below, as you explained at great length.'

'A time leak, sure. But look at it this way: when you've had a drink, time goes slower.'

She thought for a moment. 'No, faster. You yourself get slower, so you don't take in all that's happening. Therefore, the time goes faster.'

'No, slower. When you've had a drink and things around you

seem to speed up, that's because the time passes more slowly from your own point of view. You yourself have more time – or take more time. When someone's had a lot to drink and goes to the loo, he takes maybe twice as long as he does when he's sober. In other words, he takes more time, and he can only do that because he's *got* more time.'

'Come off it, that's the exact opposite of the truth. When you're drunk you experience far less in the same time. On your way to the loo, for instance, you manage only three steps in a certain time instead of six. But that means the time has gone faster. Let's assume you normally take six steps in three seconds, whereas you need six seconds when drunk. That means the time has gone twice as fast while you're doing the same thing.'

She's good, Herr Lehmann thought admiringly. What's more, she could even be right.

'Hang on,' he said, 'that only applies if you regard time as a finite quantity, but it doesn't work like that. In my opinion, the process resembles an hourglass. Sober sand runs out faster than drunk sand; that's why drunk sand makes the time go slower.'

'*Drunk* sand?'

'Well, I'm speaking metaphorically.'

'But that's a really dumb metaphor. I mean, how can someone get worked up over a word like "fulfilment" and then start talking about drunk sand. It's plain daft.'

'No it isn't.'

'Yes it is. Besides, if we're talking about how time passes for the individual, at what speed and so on, it's quite beside the point to bring in a phrase like "taking one's time", which is something completely different. If one person takes three seconds for six steps and another takes six, time goes faster for the latter because six seconds have gone by before he's managed to do what the former does in three.'

'Wrong, wrong, wrong. That's utter bilge. The seconds aren't finite quantities, they conform to external circumstances. Six steps take three seconds either way: three sober seconds if you're sober and three drunk seconds if you're drunk. That's why my drunk sand metaphor wasn't wrong. On the contrary, three drunk seconds go by while the drunk is taking six steps, whereas six seconds go by for the sober citizen, who may be standing beside the cigarette machine while the drunk is going through his paces. Ergo, time passes slower for the drunk. If you compare those two times, the sober and the drunk, then time definitely goes slower for the drunk.'

She smiled, seemingly tickled by the situation. I appeal to her, Herr Lehmann told himself – she likes this sort of thing, and that's good. He was very much in love.

'That's illogical,' she said. 'The faster someone is, the slower the time passes. It's like mayflies. One day is a mayfly's lifetime, that's why they're so hard to catch. To you, your hand seems to be moving fast, but a mayfly sees it coming in slow motion and has plenty of time to fly away. That's because it spots things quicker.'

'A mayfly's speed of perception is greater, so time goes more slowly for it, is that what you mean?'

'Yes, of course. And sober people are quicker on the uptake than drunks. They take more in, so they have more time to spare, so time goes more slowly for them.'

Herr Lehmann was fascinated. Perhaps she's right, he thought, but perhaps not. He decided to take the emergency exit. 'And why,' he asked, 'do mayflies only live for a day?'

'Very funny. Are you implying that drunks live longer?'

'It's a possibility.'

'I think you're nuts.'

'Could be.'

'It doesn't matter, though.'

'No, somehow it doesn't.'

'That's all right, then.'

'Yes.'

'Listen, you pair of lovebirds,' said Karl, who had come up to the table unnoticed by either of them, 'I can see you've really hit it off, the two of you, but I think mademoiselle had better get back to the kitchen. I mean, I hate to say it, but—'

'Okay, okay.'

'What do *you* think, Karl? Does time go faster or slower when you're drunk?'

'Is that the sort of thing you've been talking about? You're two of a kind.'

'Don't hedge. It's important.'

Karl thought for a moment. 'I reckon it goes faster. But it evens itself out the next morning.'

'There you are,' the beautiful chef said with a smile.

'But only drunks discuss such things,' said Karl, 'and only in a bar at night.'

'You're wrong. Time goes slower when you drink and speeds up again the next morning.'

'Honestly, Frank, Katrin's got to get back to the kitchen.'

'I won't say any more, it doesn't matter anyway. That's to say—'

'Forget it, I'm off to the kitchen now. Later, maybe. I'm going swimming afterwards. At the Prinzenbad. You could come too.'

'Herr Lehmann swimming? That's a sight I'd like to see,' said Karl.

'I can swim perfectly well.'

'Sure he can. He learnt in the Grundbergsee.'

'I think I'm missing something here,' said Karl.

'Incidentally,' said Katrin, getting up, 'the Grundbergsee is

nowhere near Achim. It's somewhere near Oyten on the autobahn to Hamburg. Achim's on the autobahn to Hanover.'

'When are you going swimming?'

'When I'm through here, but only after I've been home. I
should be there around six.'

'It's ages since I've been to the Prinzenbad. Is it still open?'

'It's open till mid-September,' said Karl, and to Katrin: 'Herr
Lehmann in the Prinzenbad – I'd like to see that once before
I die.'

'Think it over,' she said, and disappeared into the kitchen.

Herr Lehmann gazed after her, almost dislocating his neck in
the process.

'Hm,' said his best friend. 'Oyten, Achim, Grundbergsee, autobahn – it all sounds romantic in the extreme.'

Herr Lehmann said nothing. He was trying to think.

'Hey, Frank, what's going on?' Karl persisted, cuffing him on
the shoulder. 'What are you thinking about, how to do the
breast-stroke?'

'Nothing,' said Herr Lehmann, trying to picture a communal existence with Katrin, the beautiful chef, who had now
acquired a name.

'Like another beer?'

'No,' Herr Lehmann said absently, 'I think I'll go back to bed.'

'Bed never hurts,' said his best friend Karl.

5 COFFEE AND CAKE

SHIT, THOUGHT HERR Lehmann, I must wake up. And he did. He always had wild dreams when he slept in the afternoon, and he usually found them quite enjoyable. They were better than television, he often thought, especially as he didn't have a TV since his little black-and-white set had packed up, and he'd always found afternoon television depressing. But this dream had been too much of a good thing. His entire body was bathed in sweat when he woke up, and not only because of the sultry heat that lay over the whole city. It was around five o'clock in the afternoon, he estimated, but in his dream it had been night-time – a night of the dark variety – and he'd run along Manteuffelstrasse until he reached a high-rise that had threatened to collapse unless the dogs turned up soon. He'd waited for them on the balcony, not being able to go downstairs because the delivery men from the brewery had blocked the whole stairwell. It must be the drink, he thought, rubbing his bare, perspiring chest. He was just thinking of taking a shower in the cubicle in the kitchen when it occurred to him that there was absolutely no need because he had to go to the Prinzenbad in any case, to meet Katrin, the beautiful chef, as his best friend Karl had called her.

He'd assembled the requisite gear before retiring to bed: a pair of swimming trunks, which had taken a lot of finding; a towel that was tolerably clean or at least dark-coloured; and the padlock he'd acquired during his last (and first and only) visit to the Prinzenbad, which was years ago, in return for a deposit of twenty marks and a rental fee of fifty pfennigs, payable on admission. Still dazed with sleep and his dream, he stuffed it all into a plastic bag, pulled on a T-shirt, and went down into the street. En route for the subway he kept to the shady side and passed all the bums without being accosted, even once, which told him something about the impression his present appearance made on those around him. He actually felt rather sick while waiting on the platform, and was toying with the idea of going home when the train pulled in and took the decision out of his hands.

This is just the sort of day *not* to be going to the Prinzenbad under any circumstances, Herr Lehmann thought morosely as the No. 1 lurched along in the direction of Prinzenstrasse in its usual slow and dreary fashion. They'll be queuing up for tickets in droves in the full glare of the sun, he thought, and the lousy season ticket holders will elbow their way to the front. Except that I'm not being fair, the season ticket holders won't be elbowing their way to the front because they don't have to queue up at the cash desk, which is only logical and fair, thought Herr Lehmann, who had had the same thought on his first (and last and only) visit to the Prinzenbad – a visit that hadn't been his own idea, he now recalled, but stemmed from his then girlfriend, who'd reckoned that he needed a bit of exercise, and that swimming was very healthy in general. Swimming is the healthiest kind of exercise there is, she'd declared, being a season ticket holder like his best friend Karl, and she'd swum a thousand metres before Herr Lehmann had even reached the cash desk. Her name was Birgit, and she'd 'gone with' him, or however one chose to describe it, for about two weeks. At least, that was what Herr Lehmann had thought, whereas she had announced, when the two weeks were up, that they'd never really 'gone with' each other, and that she'd really still been 'going with' her former boyfriend all the time. 'Going with' – that was what she used to call it, Herr Lehmann remembered, and a pretty questionable turn of phrase it was, when you came down to it. Anyway she'd still been 'going with' the former boyfriend, of whom she'd volunteered the information, only a week earlier, that it was 'all over' between them and that she was now 'going with' Herr Lehmann. Not that he'd set much store by that assurance, he recalled as he alighted from the subway at Prinzenstrasse station, still thinking of the said Birgit, because, to be strictly honest, all he'd ever wanted from her was her body.

All the same, he thought as he emerged from the subway station into the dazzling sunlight, crossed Skalitzer Strasse and plodded the last fifty metres to the Prinzenbad, she'd had an exceptionally beautiful body, and perhaps, he reflected as he went up to the cash desk and said 'Just today' and replied 'Certainly not' when asked if he was a student and had then been given a ticket of which he was promptly relieved by a man wearing white shorts and flip-flops and nothing else – perhaps swimming really is healthy. Although on the other hand, he thought as he entered the pool area, if swimming's so healthy, why do all the people I can see here make such a relatively unhealthy impression? It occurred to him only now that there hadn't been a queue at the cash desk after all, but he simultaneously grasped the reason: there'd been no one left to queue up outside because everyone was already inside.

And by 'everyone' Herr Lehmann meant everyone. He lingered near the entrance for a while, deafened by the unbelievable hubbub around him, and tried to get his bearings. Utterly bewildered by the general commotion, he at once became aware that he didn't really belong here. People were running around on all sides, half-naked people of all ages and either sex stomped through the footbath or stood in it, puffing and blowing under a cold shower. Pensioners shuffled past, Turkish youths yelled and guffawed as they belted each other with wet towels, little children hugged empty plastic bottles or stumbled along unwrapping ices on sticks, and the changing areas left and right of Herr Lehmann disgorged or swallowed up interminable streams of jostling figures. Further away could be seen the snack bar or kiosk area, where vast crowds were queuing up for something or already consuming it seated at tables. There were people everywhere, running or strolling, calling or waving to each other, and from the pool itself, which was partly obscured by orna-mental shrubs, came shouts and splashing sounds and an unin-telligible loudspeaker announcement. In the distance beyond, Herr Lehmann knew, lay a vast expanse of densely populated turf over which hung a faint odour of chlorine alloyed with a whiff of French fries.

Anxious to start off on the right foot, Herr Lehmann made for the changing area on his right, which was familiar to him because he had changed there once before, on his last (and first and only) visit. The men's area was identified by a large icon and the symbolic colour blue, and this was a good thing, because his chief fear was of incurring accusations of voyeurism and sex mania by inadvertently entering the women's changing area — a vision which assailed him like a sort of waking nightmare and made him shudder. So he took care to tag along after some other men, who were also bound for the men's changing area, and had an agreeable sense of having cleared the most difficult hurdle. Herr Lehmann had been of the opinion, even in the 'seventies, that the liberating effect of exhibiting one's nakedness in public was grossly overrated, so he retired to one of the cubicles to change into his trunks. These 'swimshorts', as they had been termed by the department store where he'd bought them as a favour to Birgit, were a frightful garment in a garish, vertigo-inducing pattern, and he'd bought them only because the other styles on sale were even worse. Such had been the prevailing fashion, Herr Lehmann reflected as he donned his awful swimming trunks, which, now that he was approaching his thirtieth birthday, were rather tight at the rear. Draping the towel over his shoulder, he took the padlock in one hand and his bundled-up clothes and shoes in the other, left the cubicle, found an empty locker with some difficulty, threw everything except the towel inside, secured the door with the padlock, and strode out into the open.

Herr Lehmann really did experience a kind of liberation as he padded through the throng and felt the warmth of the flagstones suffuse his bare feet. Somehow, he was glad after all that the place was so crowded. He welcomed the hurly-burly because it enabled him to feel unobserved. None of these people could care less what he did. It didn't matter to them that his trunks were too tight and that his skin, apart from his forearms and his face, was as white as a fish's belly. Nobody here gives a damn, thought Herr Lehmann. Nobody looks twice at anyone or anything, he thought, his one worry being what Katrin, the beautiful chef from the *Markthalle*, would think when she saw him thus attired. The other question was, how would he find her? He looked around for a clock, which, when he located it, told him it was only half past five, so he could assume she hadn't turned up yet. Good, he thought, that means I can get in a bit of practice first. It'll cool me off, and besides, he told himself rather meekly as he splashed through the footbath to the pool, it's healthy. Once there, he stood dreamily watching the swimmers in the milky water while the public address system announced that Stefan, aged three, was looking for his mummy and that smoking was prohibited throughout the pool area. Vast numbers of people were sitting or lying on towels, not only behind him and all round the pool but on a kind of stone ziggurat in the background. More people still were in the pool itself, and all were trying to lend their activities an air of purpose. Some, who were or at least looked like genuine athletes in goggles and bathing caps, were ploughing through the water so autistically that Herr Lehmann noticed at once that they had absolute right of way. A few of the other swimmers managed to maintain a skilful zigzag course, but the overwhelming majority, most of them breast-strokers, struggled along somehow, forever taking fright, taking evasive action, stopping short, plunging sideways, submerging, doggy-paddling on the spot, and doing their utmost not to get in the way. Conditions were aggravated by the tearaways, children and Turkish youths at either end of the pool, who kept jumping in, climbing out and jumping in again. Indefatigably yelling, shoving, and creating total chaos, they were the true masters of the situation. All the other occupants of the pool had sooner or later to traverse their sphere of activity, and all, Herr Lehmann felt sure, were afraid of being sunk by some ass-bombing tearaway. Ass-bombing . . . He was pleased to have remembered the term, which he hadn't heard or thought of for years. It reminded him of his early boyhood, like everything here, and he decided to preface his own swim with just such a leap into the water.

When he reached the deep end and prepared to make an ass-bombing entry, however, he suddenly changed his mind. It's undignified, he thought as the public address system announced that a male infant with no clothes on was looking for his mummy, and that children wearing swimming aids had no business in the main pool. I'll soon be thirty, he thought. Turning thirty didn't mean standing on your dignity or insisting on being called Herr Lehmann, but ass-bombing was out. Besides, he thought, it was all too easy to land on top of people and turn them into irremediable paraplegics. Furthermore, testing the water with his toes had convinced him that it was bracingly cold despite the heatwave, and he was one of those who, as a boy, had learnt the basic rules of swimming, which prescribed that one should cool off slowly in hot weather, moistening one's arms and legs before entering the water, and that heavy meals and alcoholic beverages should be avoided – but that was the last thing he wanted to think of. For one reason or another, therefore, he opted for the most sensible method of entry and climbed down one of the ladders normally used by old age pensioners. The water wasn't as cold as he'd thought, provided you lowered yourself into it by degrees, and the only time he faltered was when it reached his genitals. Immersed at last, he quickly put a few yards between himself and the ass-bombing youngsters. I ought to swim a length or two, he told himself. At a crawl, preferably, they say it's better for your back than doing the breast-stroke, though the backstroke is even better – which makes sense, considering its name, he thought as he ploughed along. Then he swallowed some water, collided with two or three other swimmers, got kicked, and decided to cut his losses. He swam back to the ladder and climbed out again. You have to know your limitations and act accordingly, he thought as he dried himself off. He consulted a clock, saw that it was already twenty to six, slicked his wet hair back, and went in search of the beautiful chef.

To begin with he returned to his point of departure, the entrance to the changing cubicles, where he stood for some time in the hope of seeing her arrive. Then, when a place on a bench commanding a good view of the entrance became free, he sat down – only to feel silly after a few minutes. For one thing, people kept sitting down beside him or even jostling him aside, simply in order to dry their feet and put on their socks and shoes; for another, it dawned on him as time went by how silly he would look if Katrin – a name he murmured softly to himself for experimental purposes – came in and caught sight of him sitting on the bench like a little boy lost. If that happens, Herr Lehmann thought grimly, I may as well hang a placard round my neck saying 'You're the only reason why I'm waiting here like a dickhead'. So he stood up and strolled around a bit to make his reunion with the beautiful chef seem like a casual, chance encounter. 'Hi, you here too? How nice . . .' That's how it's got to be, he thought: a meeting between two self-assured, unattached users of the same public amenity – a couple whose acquaintanceship is recent and whose mutual expectations are still indeterminate.

Besides, Herr Lehmann reflected while plodding back through the footbath just as the loudspeaker announced that little Marco, aged about two, was looking for his mummy and that jumping in off the side of the pool was prohibited, it's quite possible that she's already here. He strolled along the edge of the pool, scanning the innumerable horizontal bodies and wondering what she would be wearing, a bikini or a swimsuit. He secretly bet on a swimsuit, because he thought swimsuits considerably more attractive and surmised that her rather opulent figure would look far better in a swimsuit than a bikini, which he had always regarded as a fashion aberration. She may well have hurried here after work, he thought. It's unusually hot and sultry for a September day, so she may have got a move on and arrived here while I was in the pool, he thought, scanning the ziggurat and its recumbent occupants as unobtrusively as possible. A lot of the women were sunbathing topless, which rather inhibited him from scanning them too closely. He knew how easy it would be for someone looking for someone among a host of bare-breasted women to incur a charge of voyeurism, and besides, as time went by he spotted more and more familiar faces from the *Einfall*. His customers and bar-room acquaintances were present in force and starting to recognise him. They raised a hand in greeting and even waved to him, a circumstance which Herr Lehmann found extremely embarrassing because he didn't really want them to see him in such an undignified get-up.

So he walked on past the three-metre board, access to which was barred, left the main pool by a roundabout route and entered the area devoted to the non-swimmers' and multipurpose pools, although he assumed that Katrin, the beautiful chef, was not the type of person to disport herself in the non-swimmers' or multi-purpose pools. Not being entirely certain about the latter, however, he went to take a look at it. It's possible, he thought, that she may prefer the multipurpose pool, although he knew little about it other than the fact that it existed and bore a bureaucratic-sounding name. The multipurpose pool was over to the left and slightly raised, so you couldn't look into it unless you went right up to it, which was what Herr Lehmann now did, threading his way between the extended families sprawled on the intervening flagstones. There was no room to lie down on the edge of the multipurpose pool itself because it was enclosed by a low wall – and who, thought Herr Lehmann, likes to park his ass on a slab of hot concrete? The only occupants of the multipurpose pool, rowdy youngsters and decrepit oldies, were giving one another a hard time. Roped off at the far end was the non-swimmers' area, which Herr Lehmann felt he could ignore, and beyond that lay the big expanse of grass for sunbathers, but he doubted if she was there because it would be out of character.

She isn't the kind of girl who wilts after a couple of quick dips and flops down on the grass, he thought as he headed for the café and skirted the big, asymmetrical non-swimmers' pool, simultaneously running a final check on the swimmers in the main pool on his right. He splashed through another footbath and found himself outside the café, where the queues had already grown shorter, then veered off to the right in order to check the entrance once more and, at the same time, fetch some money from his trousers in the locker, because the café seemed to him to be the only place in the complex where he wouldn't feel like a fish out of water.

That's the answer, Herr Lehmann thought as he entered the changing area: I'll get dressed and park myself outside with a cup of coffee, then I can keep an eye on the entrance without looking like a weirdo. I'll simply tell her, if I see her, that I've already had a swim and am having an after-dip coffee. That's brilliant, he thought, and it isn't even a lie. So he got dressed, took another look at the entrance, where there was still no sign of her, and then joined one of the queues outside the café.

The only problem, he thought as he stood there surrounded by fidgety children who kept shoving and skipping around while placing their orders – mostly for sweets on which they found it hard to decide, pointing first to this and then to that, fumbling with the coins clutched in their moist fists, doing endless sums in their heads, and letting their little friends go ahead of them – the only problem, thought Herr Lehmann, is how I can link up with her. For instance, if she comes in now and makes for the main pool, I'm in trouble – she'll have a swim and go straight home, that's why I'll have to get a seat outside as soon as possible, one I can watch the entrance from.

It's lucky the café is on slightly higher ground, he told himself reassuringly as the queue progressed at a snail's pace, making him very nervous. On the other hand, I can't yell at these children to get a move on, that would be antisocial somehow, he thought – it wouldn't go down well. He marvelled at the angelic patience of the woman behind the counter, who, notwithstanding the exiguous turnover generated by wine-gum snakes, wine-gum devils, wine-gum crocodiles and the like, complied in a positively exemplary manner with her miniature customers' wishes and, more especially, with their frequent changes of mind. She's genuinely fond of the little buggers, thought Herr Lehmann, and he loved the woman for it. That's what we all should be like, he told himself – that's the way to be when you're serving behind a counter: everyone who comes along is equal and has equal rights. A person could really take a leaf or two out of that woman's book, he reflected. All the same, he felt edgy and couldn't wait to buy a coffee and bear it off to his observation post.

'Hello there, you're next.'

'What about him?' said Herr Lehmann, pointing to a little boy in front of him.

'He's still making up his mind,' the woman said with a smile. 'What's it to be?'

'A coffee, please.'

'Got an empty mug?'

'Is that essential?'

'No,' said the woman, 'but it'll be an extra two marks' deposit, so don't go complaining about the price.'

'Sure,' said Herr Lehmann. He was hungry, he realised.

The woman brought the coffee. 'Is that all?'

'No, I'll have a, I'll have a . . .' Herr Lehmann feverishly scanned the glass case on his right, but there wasn't much in it, just a few plastic bowls containing something that resembled rice pudding and some pieces of breaded meat which doubtless had to be

63

deep-fried, and that would take too long. 'I'll have a . . .'

'There's a few slices of gâteau left, but that's all – the rolls have run out,' the woman said patiently, and Herr Lehmann felt rather ashamed because he himself was now holding everyone up.

'Yes, fine, I'll have one,' he said, to clinch matters.

'Hey, Herr Lehmann!'

He turned round. Jürgen, an old acquaintance, had materialised behind him.

'Can you get me four beers?'

'And four beers,' Herr Lehmann told the woman automatically.

'Schultheiss or Kindl?'

Good question, thought Herr Lehmann. 'Schultheiss or Kindl?' he asked Jürgen.

'Whichever,' said Jürgen.

'Schultheiss,' said Herr Lehmann, sensing that the people behind him in the queue were growing restive.

'And some matches,' Jürgen sang out.

'And some matches,' said the woman, producing some. 'Will that be all?'

'Yes, yes,' Herr Lehmann said sheepishly, and paid.

'It's all the same, this piss,' said Jürgen, coming up alongside to help with the carrying. 'What are you doing here? We saw you earlier on,' he added.

'Who's we?' asked Herr Lehmann.

'Me and the others,' was Jürgen's meaningless reply.

'Very illuminating,' Herr Lehmann said sarcastically, but Jürgen didn't notice.

They emerged together. Once outside, Jürgen called, 'Hey, you guys, look who's here: Herr Lehmann!''

'Hi, Herr Lehmann. We were admiring you earlier on.'

'What have you done with those snazzy trunks? I'd like to have examined them at leisure.'

The others were Marko, Klaus and Michael, who were already seated at a table waiting for their beer. Herr Lehmann knew them all fairly well, having worked with Marko and Jürgen at the *Hase*, a bar Erwin had since disposed of. Erwin had fired the pair of them because of his belief that they displayed 'an excessive affinity to free beer' – his actual words, because Erwin was a former student of German language and literature and sometimes spoke that way. Marko and Klaus now worked at Jürgen's bar, the *Abfall*, which was right next door to the *Einfall*, where Herr Lehmann worked. Jürgen had called it the '*Abfall*' just to annoy Erwin – they weren't in serious competition. The *Abfall* didn't get really busy until the *Einfall* closed, which was why it always stayed open until nine in the morning at least. The other member of the party, Michael, universally known as Micha, was always around whenever Jürgen, Marko and Klaus turned up somewhere. Nobody knew how he really earned a living, but he was a journalist of some kind. Herr Lehmann sat down at their table.

'Get a load of Herr Lehmann with his coffee and cake!'

'Looks good. Nice and nourishing.'

They raised their glasses and toasted him. Herr Lehmann didn't resent their banter. They didn't mean it nastily, and he liked them. Normally he'd have been pleased to run into them here, although, if the truth be told, their paths crossed almost daily.

'No afternoon's complete without coffee and cake, I always say.'

'Least of all on a Sunday.'

The only trouble was, Herr Lehmann didn't have a good view of the entrance from where they were sitting. He naturally had no choice but to join them, however. It would have been unthinkable to sit alone at another, more conveniently situated table. What explanation could he have given them?

'Look at Herr Lehmann, always athletic, always in peak condition.'

'You're a bunch of idiots,' Herr Lehmann said indulgently, sipping his coffee. This delighted the others, who laughed contentedly.

'What's that fantastic object on your plate?' asked Marko, bending over it. 'It looks like the Kantian *Ding an sich*.'

'What's the Kantian *Ding an sich*?'

'I've forgotten. Something to do with perception.'

'Gâteau. The woman said it was gâteau.'

'I'd be careful of it, very careful.'

'What are you guys doing here, anyway?' Herr Lehmann demanded.

'We're always here Sundays,' said Jürgen. 'Marko's even got a season ticket.'

'You come to drink, or what?'

They laughed. 'Not on your life,' said Klaus, raising two puny arms. 'We swim with grim determination. Which reminds me: we were watching you earlier on. A superb display you put on. Hey, why do you keep leaning back like that? Is something going on over there we don't know about?'

'I thought I saw someone,' Herr Lehmann replied innocently.

'Herr Lehmann is always seeing things we don't. That's why he got out of the pool so quickly, because he saw something.'

'Real hardcore training, that was, Herr Lehmann.'

'Can't you give this Herr Lehmann shit a rest? It isn't funny any more. The pool was getting on my nerves, if you want to know.'

'Yes, Sundays are always tough. Sundays sort out the wheat from the chaff.'

'It's your own fault if you always come on Sundays,' said

Marko, fiddling with the swimming goggles he wore on top of his head.

'There speaks a true sports fan,' said Klaus. 'I'm going to get myself another beer. Who else wants one? You, Frank?'

'No, I'm working tonight.'

'So are we all.'

'Oh, all right.'

'Can I have your mug?' Herr Lehmann was asked by a fat little boy.

'It's still got something in it,' he said.

'I thought you were going to have a beer,' said the boy.

'What are you, a private eye or something? Anyway, there's two marks' deposit on it.'

'I know,' said the boy, 'that's why I asked.'

'Look, there's Karl,' said Jürgen.

Herr Lehmann looked in the direction Jürgen indicated, and sure enough, there was his best friend Karl with Katrin, the beautiful chef. She was wearing a black swimsuit and looked gorgeous.

'Who's the fat bird with him?' asked Marko.

'Now can I have your mug?' the little boy persisted.

'Get lost,' said Herr Lehmann. Karl and the beautiful chef were passing the café on their way to the sunbathing area. Neither of them saw him. Katrin, straight-backed and very graceful, was walking along with a white towel draped over her arm. Herr Lehmann wondered how any girl could walk so gracefully in her bare feet. Everyone else just waddled, Karl included, but she positively floated along.

'Hi there!' he called. 'Hi there, Karl!' he added, hoping that Katrin, too, would look over at him.

'Asshole,' said the little boy.

'Which Karl?' asked Michael, who wasn't wearing his glasses.

Klaus returned with some beers. '*That* Karl?' he asked.

'Yes, *that* Karl,' said Jürgen.

'Oh, *that* Karl,' said Michael.

'Hey, Karl, over here!' Klaus yelled. That did the trick. They both looked across. Herr Lehmann waved to them. Katrin, the beautiful chef, waved back. She and Karl exchanged a few words, then finally came over.

'Hi,' said Katrin, 'so you turned up after all.' She was now standing beside Herr Lehmann, looking down at him. A mercy I'm not wearing those trunks, he thought.

'Nice to see the old gang again,' Karl said to the table at large, then thumped Herr Lehmann on the back. 'Well, had a good swim?'

'He's the Mark Spitz of Kreuzberg,' Marko said drily. 'We saw him. Awesome, it was.'

'And now you're sitting around drinking beer,' said Katrin, seemingly to them all, but Herr Lehmann felt she was addressing him alone.

'No,' he said, 'I'm only having coffee.' He pointed to his mug and the unopened bottle of beer beside it.

'What?' said Klaus. 'I thought you wanted one.'

'No, I'm working tonight. Won't you join us?' he said to Katrin. She pulled up a chair and sat down, as did his best friend Karl.

'What's that?' Karl asked, indicating Herr Lehmann's slice of gâteau. 'Gâteau, huh? Not bad.'

'Be my guest,' said Herr Lehmann, still looking at Katrin, who seemed to return his gaze in a curious way. 'I've got to work later on.'

'When?'

'Eight.'

'Oh,' she said, then turned to the others. 'Anyone know when this place shuts?'

'I think swimming stops at half past seven,' Marko said, 'and everyone has to be out by eight.'

'In that case,' said Karl, 'we'd better have a quick dip.'

'And you're working tonight?' Katrin said to Herr Lehmann. 'Where, exactly?'

He explained where.

'I may look in on you. Nice place?'

'Hard to say, I can't judge.'

'All right,' she said, getting to her feet. 'I'm going to have a swim. So long, everyone.' And she walked off.

'Who was that?' Marko asked Karl. 'Where did you pick her up?'

'She cooks at our place. Well, you guys, I'm also going for a swim.' Karl stood up. 'They say it's healthy.'

'To look at you,' Marko said, eyeing Karl's massive frame, 'you're more the long-distance type.'

'Speed is secondary,' said Karl, cocking a forefinger. 'What matters is, who displaces the most water.'

They watched him as he walked off in the beautiful chef's wake, and Herr Lehmann wondered yet again how Karl managed to look so chirpy after a night without sleep. Maybe it's swimming that does it, he reflected – maybe he's more athletic than I've always thought. He's got a season ticket, after all.

'What's with Karl and that bird?' Marko asked Herr Lehmann.

'She works at the *Markthalle*, that's all.'

Klaus indicated Herr Lehmann's beer. 'Is that going begging?' he asked.

'No, give it here,' said Herr Lehmann.

'Now can I have the mug?' asked the little boy, who had suddenly reappeared.

'Yes, take it.'

'But there's still some coffee in it,' said the little boy.

'I thought you didn't want any beer,' said Klaus. 'I thought you had to work.'

'Drink it yourself,' Herr Lehmann told the little boy, and to Klaus: 'I don't care, give it here.'

'Asshole,' said the little boy, and went off with the mug.

'I don't care,' Herr Lehmann repeated. 'This isn't my day. I had a sleep earlier on, and it's made me all muzzy. Maybe I should simply have gone on sleeping,' he added pensively.

'It's a funny thing, sleeping in the afternoon,' said Michael. 'It always gives you such funny dreams.'

'Yes,' said Herr Lehmann, 'very funny.'

6 SUPPER

AFTER ALL THE day's excitements, Herr Lehmann welcomed the chance to go back to work that evening. He was always glad to go to work. There was something reassuring, something refreshingly familiar about entering the *Einfall*'s cool, shadowy interior and inhaling the wonted smell of cigarette smoke, beer and cleaning fluid. The afternoon shift had been handled by two gays: Sylvio, who had somehow made his way over from East Germany two years ago, and Stefan, his ex-boyfriend. They were both in high spirits when Herr Lehmann took over the till from them.

'Some charming people here today, Herr Lehmann, really charming.'

'My name's Frank, you easterner,' Herr Lehmann said good-naturedly.

'Did you hear that, Stefan? Herr Lehmann called me an "easterner".'

'Now don't go bugging Herr Lehmann, he's got enough on his plate. He'll be working with Erwin again tonight.'

'What do you mean, with Erwin?'

'Verena won't be coming. She's feeling off-colour, poor thing.'

'Aren't there any stand-ins?'

'Looks like Erwin's got staff problems,' said Sylvio. 'First he can't give me any extra shifts, and now he's in the poo. He said to tell you he'll be here at nine. I'm off now.'

'Me too,' said Stefan.

'Have fun with Erwin.' Chuckling blithely, they left Herr Lehmann alone behind the counter.

Trade was slack. The only customer inside the bar room itself was a man sitting at the counter drinking wheat beer. Herr Lehmann knew him vaguely because he often sat there. His name was Volker or something similar, and he never drank anything but wheat beer. The handful of people sitting at the tables outside scarcely stirred, and there was little traffic in the street. The air was so sultry and oppressive that the few pedestrians oozed along like water snails. It's going to be a bad night, Herr Lehmann told himself.

The next hour crawled by just as uneventfully. Herr Lehmann drank one cup of tea after another and ate some sandwiches left over from the previous day. He preferred them when they'd gone a bit soft, as they did after a long day at the *Einfall*. They were made by Verena, who earned a little money on the side by making the sandwiches for nearly all of Erwin's bars, and she always made the *Einfall's* sandwiches with extra mayonnaise for Herr Lehmann's benefit. Now and then someone came in from outside and fetched himself a drink; the man at the counter, whose name was probably Volker, asked for another Kristall wheat beer without lemon; and a small boy wanted some change for the cigarette machine. Herr Lehmann enjoyed this time of the evening, which gave him an opportunity to think. He daydreamed awhile about Katrin, the chef from the *Markthalle*, and made another attempt to picture living with her, but he didn't get far. It was hard to picture life with a woman who went to the Prinzenbad on Sundays and barely noticed him when she did. She probably thinks I'm dumb, he thought as he watched the street, and who knows what other flaws she has? Better *not* to know, he told himself. He took a swab and proceeded to clean up a bit behind the counter.

Erwin, his boss, turned up at nine, and with him a sense of hectic unease.

'Boy-oh-boy-oh-boy,' he said, and made himself a mint tea with milk, a habit which irritated Herr Lehmann more than anything else, and Erwin had plenty of irritating characteristics. 'Boy-oh-boy-oh-boy,' he repeated with a sigh. Erwin was a Swabian to the marrow and, at the same time, a devoted resident of the Kreuzberg district. He'd been there for ages, and had built up a little empire of bars over the years. Recently he'd even been experimenting with bars in Schöneberg, but Schöneberg was another kettle of fish. 'It's not so easy over there,' he'd once told Herr Lehmann. 'They expect value for money.' And that, to Herr Lehmann, said all there was to say about Erwin. The word was, a small inheritance had enabled him to acquire his first bar fifteen years ago, while he was still at university. That had been the *Einfall*, Herr Lehmann's present place of work. Then, little by little, with the aid of a carefully selected team of fellow students, he'd cornered the local bar trade. Although Erwin was widely rumoured to be a millionaire, his lifestyle was that of a man on social security. At the moment he was looking very much the worse for wear. He stood there, greasy-haired and unshaven, sipping his mint tea with milk, kneading the bags under his eyes, and saying 'Boy-oh-boy-oh-boy'.

'What's the matter, Erwin?' Herr Lehmann said coaxingly.

'Don't ask,' said Erwin.

'What are you doing here, anyway? Is Verena sick or something?'

'They're all nuts. She's got a migraine, can't stand the weather, wondered if I'd like to have sex with her. As if!'

'Hm,' said Herr Lehmann, who had once had sex with Verena. 'Could be. A lot of people get migraines in this kind of weather.'

'What about me? Who ever thinks of asking if *I've* got a migraine?' Erwin paused for a moment, turned up the music and simultaneously lowered his voice. 'I tell you this,' he said conspiratorially, 'people do too many drugs these days.'

'Not Verena, though.'

'You don't have a clue,' said Erwin. 'You wouldn't notice someone snorting if his face was plastered with the stuff. You go to a party and you think, ooh, what a good mood everyone's in. It's really touching of you.'

'Come on, Erwin, now you're talking bullshit.'

'What's this music, anyway? Did you put it on?'

'No idea,' said Herr Lehmann, who hadn't taken any notice of the music until now. It was boom-boom stuff without any singing, not the rock music usually played at the *Einfall*. Music meant nothing to him. In his opinion, its sole function in a bar was to enable people to shout at each other in peace. 'I'm no expert. Sylvio and Stefan must have put it on.'

'Gays are always up to the minute, believe me. That's Acid House, Herr Lehmann.'

'Frank.'

'It's the latest thing, old son, and it's all about drugs. A friend of mine was at a party in Schöneberg recently. Two or three days on the trot, and they lie there screwing in their own shit.'

'Honestly, Erwin,' said Herr Lehmann, 'this is really silly. What are you getting at?'

'Frank!' Erwin wagged a forefinger at him.

'Just a minute,' said Herr Lehmann, who had no wish to hear more. The place was gradually filling up outside. The tables were already full, so a lot of people came inside while others stood in the street, beer in hand, or sat down in the bus shelter. Herr Lehmann had to serve several people waiting patiently at the counter. The *Einfall*'s patrons were a well-behaved bunch. Erwin nodded darkly and did absolutely nothing to help.

'They've got to clear out of that bus shelter!' he shouted suddenly, jumping up off the bar stool he'd been sitting on. 'I'll only have more aggro with the licensing authority.'

'Perhaps they want to take a bus,' Herr Lehmann hazarded as he opened bottles and worked the till.

'Tell that to Berlin Transport,' Erwin shouted. 'They've already lodged a complaint, according to the licensing authority. Have you any idea how quickly those people can close a place down?'

'Jesus, Erwin, take it easy,' said Herr Lehmann. 'You get far too worked up. You probably work too hard,' he added, trying to change the subject. But Erwin wasn't having any.

'They're launching raids again. They closed the *Loch* in Schöneberg because of drugs.'

'Schöneberg's Schöneberg,' Herr Lehmann said soothingly. 'Here in Kreuzberg the most people do is smoke grass.'

'What about Speed?' Erwin shouted over the boom-boom music, which Herr Lehmann was gradually turning up. 'What about all the Speed they do in Kreuzberg, not to mention the coke? What do you think they'd find on these people in here right now, if they raided the place?'

The bar was filling up with customers demanding drinks. Even Erwin had noticed this and was working too. It didn't, to Herr Lehmann's regret, prevent him from continuing to talk bullshit, albeit in fragmentary form.

'Then there are all the junkies . . . And this new stuff, Ecstasy . . . And all these designer drugs . . .'

Herr Lehmann had ceased to listen. In his opinion, Erwin's only problem was that he read *Der Spiegel* every Monday and took what it said far too seriously. Outside, everything indicated that a storm was brewing. The customers were in an odd mood – kind of feverish, thought Herr Lehmann. From the nearby fire station came the wail of sirens and flashes of reflected blue light. A sudden gust of wind sent dust and rubbish whirling along the street and buffeted the awning.

Erwin was still drivelling on about drugs and predicting the imminent closure of all his bars. 'Erwin,' Herr Lehmann cut in, 'I'm just going to wind the awning in.'

'Sure, sure,' said Erwin, who had just poured himself a slug of his special brandy, as he called it, 'good idea. You're a treasure, Herr Lehmann!'

Herr Lehmann fetched the long crank handle from the kitchen and went outside. The first drops of rain fell just as he was winding in the awning to good-natured protests from the customers he was depriving of overhead protection. Then the rain came down in sheets and everyone dashed inside except Herr Lehmann himself, who continued to wind in the awning, and the people crowding into the bus shelter, who loudly cheered him on. He was wet through by the time he finished and came back into the bar. Erwin was very concerned.

'Boy-oh-boy, you can't go on working like that, you're soaked to the skin. I'll fetch you a T-shirt from upstairs.' Since separating from his wife and child, Erwin practically lived above the *Einfall*, which was why it was the only bar he still worked at himself. The special brandy had evidently done him good, because he was looking a lot more relaxed. 'Have one of these for a start,' he said, waving the bottle of brandy with his name on it.

Herr Lehmann declined the brandy with thanks but was happy to accept the T-shirt. In his view, catching cold for the sake of Erwin's awning would have been above and beyond the call of duty. The bar, which reeked of sweat and damp clothes, was now thronged with people squeezing past and around each other. The refugees from the rain were in a good mood. Mellowed by their communal experience, they drank like fish. That was all right with Herr Lehmann, who enjoyed serving behind the counter when the place was full. He liked the bustle and the necessity for fast work. It's better than twiddling your thumbs, he told himself as the people on the other side of the counter milled around, many of them calling out to him, others merely looking at him with mute entreaty, others elbowing their way to the fore, and others – the ones in the second row – waving money at him. They all tried to attract his attention, and he was adept at distinguishing between those who were really next and those who had pushed in front. Every movement he made was deft and economical. With a speed unrivalled by any other barman in town, he opened bottles of beer, mixed spritzers, poured shorts with a generosity dependent on how well he knew and liked the customer in question, added up bills, worked the till, greeted friends and acquaintances, stood one or another of them a drink, and felt good.

Erwin, who returned after a while, was also feeling good, to judge by his rosy cheeks. Grinning, he thrust a crumpled T-shirt into Herr Lehmann's hand.

'Go to the kitchen and get changed,' he said magnanimously. 'I can handle things out here.'

Herr Lehmann felt unconvinced of that, but it didn't really matter. This was Erwin's joint, after all. In the kitchen he saw a twenty-mark note lying on the floor beside the big bucket reserved for broken glass – Erwin's well-known and oft-derided method of testing the honesty of his staff. Herr Lehmann pocketed the note and stripped off his wet T-shirt. The one donated by Erwin was inscribed 'Stuttgart Football Club:

German Champions 1983/84'. Erwin's always full of surprises, thought Herr Lehmann.

He returned to see Erwin engaged in pouring himself another drink while chaos reigned on the other side of the counter. 'Really suits you,' called Erwin, and gave the thumbs-up, a gesture Herr Lehmann found embarrassing.

'Hey, Erwin,' he said, 'I just found twenty marks in the kitchen. Is it possible they belong to me? I've a feeling I mislaid twenty marks in there recently.'

'Twenty marks?' Erwin said innocently. He produced his wallet and thumbed through the contents. 'Wait a minute . . . No, I must have left them in there. They aren't here any longer.'

'You left them beside the bucket?'

'Yes — no, they must have fallen on the floor.'

'What were you doing in the kitchen with a twenty-mark note, Erwin, snorting coke?'

'Like hell I was. It's my money, honestly.'

'You really think so, Erwin? It could be Sylvio's and Stefan's. They were working here earlier.'

'No, no.' Erwin was becoming genuinely agitated. 'It's mine, I'm absolutely positive.'

'Maybe we should put it on one side until I've asked them.'

'I'll see to that,' said Erwin, snatching the note. 'Leave it to me.'

Herr Lehmann lost interest in this tomfoolery and devoted himself to the customers. Raging outside was a violent storm complete with thunder and lightning and all the trimmings. Everyone was in high spirits. Fascinated, they looked out of the windows while the boom-boom music, which Herr Lehmann had put on autoreverse, came pounding out of the speakers with monotonous regularity. Nobody came and nobody went, and the feeling that there was no alternative but to stay where they were and drink themselves silly had a disinhibiting effect on all present.

When Herr Lehmann returned from the cellar with some more crates of beer, Erwin had quit the counter and was playing a drinking game with a couple of acquaintances, so he resigned himself to working on his own for the rest of the night. In the next two hours it rained as if the Almighty planned to wash Kreuzberg clean for evermore. Nothing much happened apart from that, except that the bar's occupants, Erwin first and foremost, got resolutely drunk. At one stage everyone cheered when a convoy of fire engines roared past, making a hellish din, and the wheat beer drinker who was still sitting at the counter, and whose name was probably Volker, tried to engage Herr Lehmann in a conversation about the rain. 'When it makes bubbles,' he said, ' – bubbles in the puddles, I mean – the rain'll stop soon. It'll stop soon, the rain will.'

Herr Lehmann didn't argue the point, he merely nodded and rewarded the man for this intriguing notion with a Kristall wheat beer *sans* lemon. Whenever pressure of work permitted, he looked out at the rain. Summer was over, from the look of it. Well, he didn't mind. He liked the summer – it was the nicest time of year in Berlin, and he'd never understood why people went on holiday then, of all times. On the other hand, there was something so demanding about the summer. In summer Herr Lehmann was constantly assailed by the feeling that he ought to be taking advantage of the fine weather and doing things with his friends, like barbecues and excursions and lakeside bathing parties – activities of which he wasn't particularly fond and which stood equally low in his friends' scale of values, but whose theoretical possibility made him feel he was missing out on something, failing to make the most of the fine weather, and frittering his time away. The rest of the year was simpler. When everything was wet and grey outside – or, better still, cold and off-white – he could happily while away the day in bed with a book, waiting for the return of darkness and his time to go to work. Actually, he reflected as he looked out at the rain, it's silly to think like that – it's the same as that crap about fulfilment. If you think you've got to make something of the summer, you've already lost. Better simply to enjoy it without getting a bad conscience. Well, it's over now, he thought rather sadly as a swaying, brightly lit double-decker bus pulled up at the stop. Only one person got out, but Herr Lehmann recognised her figure and walk at once. She wasn't wearing a raincoat, just jeans and a T-shirt. Her first move was to take refuge in the bus shelter.

He made his way to the bar-room door, which was open, and called.

'Katrin!'

She didn't react, even though he waved extravagantly. Perhaps it wasn't her after all. 'Hello! Hi there!' he called as loud as he could.

It really was her. She came running over and joined him in the entrance.

'Hell,' she said, 'now I've got wet feet.'

'Like a drink? I work here,' he said. 'I must go back inside,' he added, because it was making him nervous, standing so close he could smell her wet hair.

'I was on my way home, actually,' she said. 'Besides, my hair's all wet. And my feet.'

'Yes,' said Herr Lehmann. 'We must do something about that. Definitely.'

She smiled and touched him lightly on the arm. 'You're an oddball,' she said cryptically. 'So this is where you work?' They were still standing in the entrance, and she peered into the *Einfall* as she spoke.

'Yes, this is the *Einfall*.'

'I didn't know. I've often walked past here — I live just round the corner. There's no name up outside.'

'Really?' said Herr Lehmann, who had never noticed this in all the years he'd worked there.

'Well,' she said hesitantly, 'I think I'll go home first. I live just round the corner,' she repeated.

'Oh yes, well,' said Herr Lehmann.

'I'd sooner get changed first.'

'Yes, absolutely,' said Herr Lehmann.

'Maybe I'll look in after that. What time is it, anyway?'

'I don't know,' said Herr Lehmann. 'Eleven, half past, no idea.'

'So late already?'

'Yes,' said Herr Lehmann. 'Sure, but we're open till two at least, usually three or four.'

'Maybe, but that'd be too late for me.'

'Yes, of course, fair enough,' said Herr Lehmann. They were still standing in the entrance. Now and then someone pushed between them, and it was an effort to maintain eye contact. 'But it's only eleven or half past . . .'

'I must change first, though. My hair's wet, too.' She was now contemplating his T-shirt.

'Well . . .' Herr Lehmann summoned up all his courage. 'Well, I think it would be nice if you looked in again.'

'You mean it?' she said archly, smiling at him.

'Yes, of course,' said Herr Lehmann. 'Then I could buy you a drink. The T-shirt isn't mine,' he explained, because she was still staring at it. 'Erwin lent it to me. I got soaked myself, earlier on.'

'Yes, it came down so suddenly,' she said, and Herr Lehmann hoped she was blathering on like this because she didn't want them to part. 'I've just been visiting a girlfriend in Charlottenburg.'

'It's a long way, Charlottenburg,' he said.

'Yes, it was a real trek.'

'Well,' said Herr Lehmann, 'we can't stay here. Besides, I think I'd better do a bit of work.'

'Ah, there's Erwin,' she said, and waved to the person in question, who was now standing behind the counter and hanging on to it for support. Erwin just goggled at them and didn't respond.

'What's the matter with him?' she asked.

'It's a long story,' said Herr Lehmann. 'Won't you come inside after all?'

'No, I'm going now. See you later, maybe.'

'Yes,' said Herr Lehmann, 'see you later, maybe.'

Nothing much happened in the next hour. The rain eventually stopped and the bar quickly emptied. Erwin went upstairs briefly to freshen up, as he put it, and was back on form thereafter. He tried to talk Herr Lehmann into drinking shorts, but Herr Lehmann was adamant and stuck to tea. The previous night had been a warning that spirits didn't agree with him. He wasn't even sure that the dog really existed, but if so, it must still be somewhere out there. Or in a home for strays. In any case, staying sober was always the best policy. At one o'clock he abandoned hope of her coming and treated himself to a beer. The place was pretty empty, and it would soon be closing time.

Then, all at once, it was action stations. The boom-boom or Acid House music, as Erwin had called it, was still playing no less loudly, which was why Herr Lehmann failed to hear anything from behind the counter until matters were well advanced. Erwin was arguing with a customer in the far corner. Herr Lehmann went over to them to be on the safe side, because you never knew with Erwin. He was short and not particularly strong, but he'd recently been capable, when drunk, of creating mayhem.

'Put that spliff out, man, or get out of here.'

'Eh? This is a perfectly ordinary cigarette.'

'Don't give me that, you asshole. No spliffs in here. If you want to smoke that thing, out!'

'I bought this beer from you, pal. Nobody's going to chuck me out.'

'You think I want them to close me down?'

It was a ludicrous but patently entertaining situation. The last five or six customers were watching this verbal sparring match with relish. Herr Lehmann decided to mediate.

'Listen, Erwin, let him drink up and then he'll go.'

'What's *your* problem, you bum?' demanded the stranger. 'A couple of wankers, that's what you are!'

Herr Lehmann had an uneasy feeling about the man. The *Einfall*'s customers were a peaceable bunch on the whole, but now and then someone like this turned up. Herr Lehmann had never seen him before, but he sensed that he was a nutter. He wasn't exceptionally tall or well built, but he was charged up somehow, which made him unpredictable – a nutter, in fact, and not one of the innocuous kind. What Herr Lehmann found particularly worrying was the way he kept jiggling his foot, pointlessly but with great rapidity. He was belligerent, he wanted some aggro, and an oaf like Erwin was just his meat. Herr Lehmann hated this kind of shit.

'Leave him be, Erwin,' he persisted. 'There's no point, it'll soon be closing time in any case.'

'I own this place, and I want this clown out of here!'

'Maybe you'd better go,' Herr Lehmann told the spliff-smoker. 'You heard what he said.'

'I'm not going to let this dwarf piss on me,' the man growled. Herr Lehmann felt really worried now. The electricity was flowing.

Erwin was less concerned. He took the man by the scruff of his neck and tried to drag him to the door. 'You're leaving!' he just had time to say before it happened: the spliff-smoker punched him smack in the face. Erwin staggered backwards holding his nose. Herr Lehmann, whose heart was in his mouth, and who was no less charged up by now than the nutter, had to do something, and fast. He grabbed him firmly by the ear and twisted it as far as it would go. The man gave a yell and doubled up, but Herr Lehmann maintained the pressure until he was down on his knees. Then he escorted him to the door. This took some time because his yelping captive had to shuffle along in a crouching position. Meanwhile, Herr Lehmann was furiously debating how to extricate himself from this mess unscathed.

The problem didn't really present itself until they were outside. Herr Lehmann came to a halt midway between the entrance and the bus shelter, twisted the man's ear even harder, and bent down to address him.

'Listen,' he panted, 'listen carefully.'

The man whimpered.

'Listen!' Herr Lehmann bellowed. 'Are you listening?'

'Yes, yes! Let go of me, you sonofabitch!'

'Now pay attention,' said Herr Lehmann. 'We can go on standing here like this indefinitely. Alternatively, I can twist your ear off. Alternatively, you can give me your word you'll piss off at once if I let you go.'

It's ridiculous asking a nutter to give me his word, he thought, but what else can I do? If I were a bouncer I'd beat him to a pulp or kick him senseless or something, but I'm not a bouncer, I'm not up to it.

'Yes, yes,' said the nutter.

'Now listen.' Herr Lehmann endeavoured to lend his words some weight. 'If I let go of you, and you make the slightest attempt to do anything except push off, I'll give you such a thrashing, I'll punch you so hard in the kisser, that . . .' – he wondered feverishly how to bring his sentence to a convincing conclusion – 'I'll give you such a thrashing,' he repeated, 'that, that . . .' – I read the wrong books, he thought – '. . . that you won't know if it's Christmas or Ramadan.' Well, he thought, let's hope it works. '*Got that, you asshole?*'

'Yes, yes! Please let go.'

Herr Lehmann let go – against his better judgement, but he had to do so sometime. The man jumped up and promptly lunged at him. Herr Lehmann fended him off.

'I'm going to knock your block off, you wanker!'

'Piss off. Get lost, man, just get lost.'

The man went for him again. Jesus, he thought, how stupid this must look. Then a fist connected with his face, and suddenly he was flat on his back in a big puddle with his adversary flailing away on top of him. Herr Lehmann, who didn't find this unduly painful, defended himself as well as his position allowed. He directed his main effort towards grabbing the man's ear again, the only thing that occurred to him on the spur of the moment, but it never came to that. All at once it was over. Someone hauled the man off him. Sitting up, he saw his best friend Karl, a big, bulky figure, holding his ex-opponent with one hand and slapping him hard in the face with the other.

'Never . . . never . . . never . . . do . . . that . . . again,' said Karl, accompanying each word with a slap. Then he hurled the man against the bus shelter and knocked him flat on his face with a kick up the backside. 'You hit Herr Lehmann,' he shouted. 'That carries the maximum sentence. Twice over,' he added, hauling him to his feet and hurling him against the bus shelter a second time. Herr Lehmann, for whom everything was going much too fast and rather too far as well, wanted to intervene, but he wasn't feeling too good and continued to sit there for the time being. 'Now you're going to say sorry.' His best friend Karl towed the nutter over to him. 'Say sorry!' Herr Lehmann scrambled to his feet. His clothes were soaked from the puddle he'd been lying in, and Erwin's T-shirt was torn. 'Are you deaf?' Karl shook the man like a sodden jacket and clouted him on the head. 'It's all right,' said Herr Lehmann, 'let him push off.' Karl put his face very close to the other man's. 'Get this, you little shit,' he said. 'You can count yourself lucky I stepped in. If Herr Lehmann had really gone to work on you, you'd be mincemeat by this time. And now, you scumbag, get lost!' He shoved the man away from him. The man took a few unsteady steps, then turned and gave them a one-finger salute. 'I'll get you sooner or later,' he said furiously, and walked off.

'He's been seeing too many movies,' said Karl. 'Let's have a look at you.' He turned Herr Lehmann to face the nearest street light and brushed him down a bit. 'Going in for a rather different type of customer at the *Einfall* these days, aren't you?'

'Oh, balls,' said Herr Lehmann. 'Forget it. And stop messing me about.'

'Someone has to,' said his best friend Karl, plucking a wet leaf out of his hair. 'Let's go inside, there's no point in hanging around out here.'

So they went inside. Erwin was standing behind the counter with his head tilted back and some ice cubes clamped to the bridge of his nose. All the customers had gone except the wheat-beer drinker probably called Volker, who was gazing equably into his glass.

'This place is dead as a dodo,' said Karl. He went behind the counter and helped himself to a beer. 'Want one too, Frank?'

'Sure.'

'What went on here, anyway?'

'Nothing much,' Herr Lehmann said dejectedly. 'The man was a nutter, that's all. This isn't my lucky day, I tell you.'

'You should get out of those wet things,' said Karl. 'Looks like closing time anyway. Better get off home quick or you'll catch your death. Hey, Erwin, say something.'

'I can't, not now,' Erwin said in a muffled voice. 'It was all my fault. That fucking bastard!'

'Let's have a look,' said Karl, removing the ice cubes. 'You'll live. But Herr Lehmann here, he got rolled in the mire for your sake – put the forces of evil to flight with his bare fists and so on. He deserves one of your special brandies.'

'I don't want to go home,' said Herr Lehmann. The very thought of going home to bed on his own appalled him. 'What are you doing here, anyway?' he asked. 'Don't you ever need any sleep?'

'Superman Karl is never out of a job. Besides, I've got something to celebrate, that's why I came looking for you jokers, but you were in the middle of a party already. Hey, Erwin, the least you can do is find Herr Lehmann another T-shirt.'

'He's already wearing one of mine.'

'Really? I wouldn't brag about it,' said Karl. 'We were going to discuss something, Erwin, so let's go upstairs a minute. Frank, I'm just going upstairs with Erwin, but I'll be right down with a clean T-shirt. You finish up in here, and when I come back we'll go next door and have a post-traumatic drink at the *Abfall*. We've got something to celebrate, okay?'

Anything was okay with Herr Lehmann as long as he didn't have to go home yet.

'You start clearing up,' said Karl. 'I'll be back right away. And lock the door.'

Herr Lehmann locked the door, collected all the bottles and glasses, rinsed them, and stood the chairs on the tables. Then he proceeded to swab the counter, watched by the wheat-beer drinker whose name was probably Volker.

'That was great, that trick with the ear.'

'Oh well,' said Herr Lehmann, half flattered, half sheepish.

'But did you see it?'

'What?'

'The rain.'

'What about it?'

'The way it made bubbles. And then: bingo! All over!'

Herr Lehmann couldn't help laughing, he didn't know why. He simply couldn't stop – he laughed and laughed until it hurt. At some stage the man whose name was probably Volker joined in, becoming just as hysterical as Herr Lehmann. Their laughter eventually subsided. 'Yes,' said Herr Lehmann, wiping away the tears. 'Bingo! All over!' That promptly set him off again. 'By the way,' he said between two paroxysms of mirth, 'what's your name?'

'Rainer,' said the wheat-beer drinker, and went on laughing.

7 A LATE SNACK

THEY GOT A big welcome when they entered the *Abfall*. Jürgen and Marko, for whom the night was only just beginning, listened entranced to Karl's extravagant account of Herr Lehmann's heroic defence of his employer. Karl also prevailed on Erwin, who had been somewhat sobered up by the whole alarming incident and surprised everyone by standing drinks all round, to demonstrate what Herr Lehmann had done with his opponent's ear. Jürgen and Marko watched in awe as Erwin took hold of Karl's ear and led him, waddling and whimpering, across the bar room.

'That's great, Herr Lehmann, really great.'

'I must make a note of it. We ought to call it the "Kreuzberg Twist" and patent it.'

Herr Lehmann felt uncomfortable. For one thing, it was only thanks to his best friend Karl that he'd come off relatively unscathed; for another, he hated fighting and disliked watching other people engaged in it. Not only did it look repellent; it was embarrassing and, above all, completely pointless. The fact that he had been forced into it – for that was how he viewed the matter – cast a dark shadow over his existence. Until now his only knowledge of such unpleasantnesses had derived from descriptions given by people who worked in tougher bars than the *Einfall*. In the *Einfall*, troublemakers had always been easy to eject. They usually turned up during the day and mainly towards the end of winter, when everyone in Wiener Strasse was stressed in any case. Physical resistance was rare and negligible: you simply hustled them out and that was that. But now, if they were starting to fight in earnest . . . Perhaps Katrin the beautiful chef had been right after all – perhaps it wouldn't be right for him to stand behind a bar-room counter for evermore. But that would mean changing his life, and he didn't want to do that. He liked his life and enjoyed standing behind a counter – in fact there was nothing he enjoyed more. He briefly tried to imagine what it would be like to work as a forwarding agent, the job he'd trained for. It seemed so absurd, he couldn't help laughing.

'Look, he's laughing again,' his best friend Karl said to Erwin, slapping Herr Lehmann on the back. The three of them were sitting at a table in the gloom at the back of the bar. 'Herr Lehmann's a tough customer. No matter what happens, give him a beer and he's back on top form in no time.'

'Top or bottom, who cares?' Erwin said jocularly. 'I'm going to buy him another beer.'

'No you don't!' Karl said firmly, getting to his feet. He swayed a little but steadied himself quite well for someone who hadn't slept for thirty-six hours. 'This is on me. We've got something to celebrate.'

He went over to the bar. Erwin put his mouth close to Herr Lehmann's ear. The music in the *Abfall* was rock of some kind, not the boom-boom stuff Erwin called Acid House, but just as loud.

'Who's that guy drinking wheat beer?' Erwin yelled. 'The one at the bar, but don't look now. He's been hanging round our place the last couple of weeks.'

'His name's Rainer,' said Herr Lehmann.

'How do you know?'

'He told me earlier on. And stop yelling in my ear, it's bugging me.'

'Funny fish.'

'Sure he's a funny fish, the world's full of them.' Karl returned with two beers, a brandy, and a bag of crisps. 'Karl,' said Herr Lehmann, 'do you remember—'

'Here,' said Karl, tossing the crisps on to the table. 'Eat up like good boys. Think of the electrolytes. Electrolyte deficiency is the drinker's greatest enemy – apart from dehydration.' He took a big swallow of beer. 'You'll be grateful to me tomorrow morning.'

'Karl,' Herr Lehmann began again, 'do you remember the guy that used to sit in the *Treibsand* every night, putting away one wheat beer after the other? What was his name?'

'"Schneider" Jürgen, you mean. What about him?'

'"Schneider" Jürgen,' Herr Lehmann said to Erwin. 'He was the same.' He turned back to Karl. 'What's become of him?'

'He's dead,' Erwin cut in without looking at the man at the bar.

'How'd it happen?'

'I don't know, exactly,' said Erwin. 'It's immaterial. Anyway, there's something wrong with him.'

'What was that?' Karl called from across the table. 'What was that about Schneider Jürgen? What's wrong with him?'

'He's dead,' said Herr Lehmann.

'Have some crisps,' shouted Karl, who'd stopped listening already, and stuffed a fistful into his mouth.

'What's so funny about him?' Herr Lehmann asked Erwin. 'There's nothing unusual about a guy who sits there drinking. After all, that's what keeps you in groceries.'

'No,' said Erwin, 'there's something wrong with the guy. We must keep an eye on him.'

'Erwin,' said Herr Lehmann, 'if you're really such a good judge of human nature, how come you took a punch on the hooter?'

'He's an undercover cop, take it from me. He's checking the place out.'

'Hey, Frank,' said Karl, 'are you and that Katrin girl an item already?'

'Why bring *her* up?' Herr Lehmann protested rather too indignantly – almost suspiciously, even to his own ears. He felt himself going red. '*You* were the one that took her to the Prinzenbad today, weren't you?' he added, and instantly felt he'd made matters worse. Sheer annoyance prompted him to eat some crisps.

'I know a funny fish when I see one,' said Erwin. 'We'll have to watch him. It wouldn't surprise me if he was a plain-clothes cop checking all the bars for drugs.'

'Relax, Herr Lehmann,' Karl said cheerfully, reaching across the table and patting him on the shoulder. 'No offence, but you at the Prinzenbad?' He gestured like someone screwing in a light bulb. 'Very suspicious, Herr Lehmann.'

'You bet it is,' Erwin chimed in from the other side. 'Something smells. This guy isn't like Schneider Jürgen.'

'No,' Herr Lehmann said sardonically, 'he's still alive.'

'Very suspicious,' Karl insisted. '*You* swimming, of all people? Nobody would believe you go swimming voluntarily.'

'I didn't mean that,' said Erwin. 'This is no joking matter.'

'Everyone knows your attitude to physical exercise,' said Karl. 'It's notorious.'

'What do you mean, notorious? What's notorious about it?'

'He isn't the Schneider Jürgen type,' said Erwin, 'they're just not comparable. It'd never have occurred to anyone that Schneider Jürgen was an undercover cop.'

'Erwin!' Herr Lehmann said firmly. 'You're the only one who's taken it into his head that he's an undercover cop. It's baloney, all this stuff about drugs. Nobody gives a damn if someone smokes a spliff on your premises.'

'That's what *you* think.'

'By "notorious" I mean it's common knowledge.' Karl gave Herr Lehmann another slap on the shoulder.

Meantime, Herr Lehmann had turned back to Erwin. 'And even if they did close the *Einfall* down, what then? You own another nine or ten bars. The *Einfall* would stay shut for a while, that's all. You're filthy rich anyway. Why get worked up over a fleabite?'

'Boy-oh-boy, fancy a guy like you going swimming,' mused Karl. 'How long have we known each other, Herr Lehmann?'

'You don't have a clue!' cried Erwin. 'Not a clue! They're worth nothing. If they're shut, they aren't worth a bean.'

'Must be six or seven years – no, more like eight or nine. When did you get here? 1980?'

'If you lose your licence, you've lost it for good. I don't have any money, it's all tied up in the bars.'

'Nine years . . . I know you, my lad. If you go swimming it can only be because of that girl, but there's nothing wrong with that. She's just your type. On the other hand, what *is* your type? I've known you nine years, and I still don't have the slightest idea what your type is. Aside from the fact that they tend to be a bit big round the hips.'

'You can't sell them if they're shut – if they aren't a going concern. Once they're shut, I'll get nothing for them. Nothing!' Erwin went into tearful mode. 'I'm sick of the whole business. I've a good mind to chuck it in.'

'She goes for you, honestly. You shouldn't waste any time, the two of you. She fancies you – wanted to know all kinds of things about you, what else you do and so on. It really bugged me, the way she went on pumping me.'

'What did you tell her?'

'Only good things.' Karl checked off Herr Lehmann's assets on his fingers. 'Like you're a really well-educated, cultured guy who's into movies, books, museums, the works – she likes that kind of thing, I'm sure – and you trained for a proper profession, and you're destined for great things—'

'Oh, stop it.'

'No,' cried Erwin, 'I mean it. I'm going to sell the whole caboodle. I ask you, what do I get out of it? Nothing!'

'What's his problem?' asked Karl.

'He wants to sell up,' said Herr Lehmann.

'Who does?' asked Jürgen, who had just sat down at their table.

'Erwin, according to Herr Lehmann,' said Karl.

'Really?' Jürgen turned to Erwin. 'Well, I'd take the *Einfall* off your hands.'

'I bet you would.' Erwin grinned bitterly. 'I'd sooner burn the place down than let you have it, you bastard.'

'Ouch,' Jürgen said with a laugh, flapping his hands as if he'd scalded himself. 'Hard words, Erwin, hard words. So what else is new?' he asked the others.

'Erwin thinks that guy at the bar is an undercover cop,' Herr Lehmann said maliciously. 'He thinks they're checking on his joints with a view to raiding them for drugs and so on.'

'That guy there? All he does is sit there drinking Kristall,' said Karl. 'He comes to the *Markthalle* too, sometimes.'

'Exactly!' cried Erwin. 'That's just what I'm saying.'

Jürgen turned and looked at the man. 'I don't know. He's often in here too. Reminds me vaguely of Schneider Jürgen, except that he drinks Kristall instead of Hefe. What's become of him, by the way?'

'Who?' asked Karl.

'Schneider Jürgen.'

'He's dead,' said Erwin.

'Really? How'd he die?'

'No idea.'

'Hm, well . . . An undercover cop, huh? In that case he must have a nice fat expense account. Never asks for a receipt, either.'

'*Are* they allowed to drink on duty?' asked Karl.

'Undercover cops? Sure.'

'Funny customer,' said Karl. 'I don't understand, though. How does a guy like him get to be an undercover cop?'

'Just a minute,' Herr Lehmann broke in. 'What makes you all so sure he's an undercover cop?'

'I don't know,' said Karl. 'He's a funny customer, somehow. Always drinks Kristall without lemon.'

'But drugs?' Jürgen said dubiously.

'They've already closed down two joints in Schöneberg,' Erwin whispered during a lull in the music. 'There's something going on.'

'I thought it was only the *Loch*,' Herr Lehmann objected.

'What do you mean, only the *Loch*?'

'Erwin, a couple of hours ago you told me they'd closed the *Loch*. Now they've closed down *two* bars in Schöneberg.'

'One, two, what's the difference? Stop staring at him like that, Herr Lehmann.'

'Frank, if you don't mind.'

'Careful,' said Karl, 'he's looking in our direction.' He turned away and took a big swig of beer. Very inconspicuous, thought Herr Lehmann.

'He can't see us, he's blind drunk,' he said. Somehow he felt sorry for the man because he always drank on his own and made himself look suspicious into the bargain. 'Besides, it's dark where we're sitting.'

'That's just it,' Erwin said mysteriously.

'Well I don't get it,' said Herr Lehmann. He was bored. He would sooner have gone on talking about the beautiful chef with Karl and found out precisely what she'd asked him, but Karl had probably covered that already.

'If he did drugs he wouldn't get drunk so quickly,' Jürgen said, and went off to get some more beers.

'I just don't understand that,' said Herr Lehmann, who well remembered how hard he'd found it, years ago, to climb aboard the late-night bus when he'd taken one drag at a joint after sinking ten bottles of Beck's.

'No need for you to understand,' said his best friend Karl, patting him on the shoulder. 'That's the nice thing about you: you don't know the first thing about drugs, but you understand everything all the same – and by everything I mean the truth.'

'Maybe someone ought to have a word with him,' mused Erwin. 'Unobtrusively, I mean. Maybe we'd get something out of him.'

'Could be tricky,' said Karl.

'Very tricky,' said Erwin.

'Herr Lehmann ought to do it – he's a hundred per cent unobtrusive,' said Karl. 'With men, at least. Women find him nice and obtrusive,' he added with a wink, and gave Herr Lehmann, who was getting thoroughly sick of this, another slap on the shoulder.

'But not now,' Erwin said conspiratorially.

'Yes, yes,' said Karl, 'now's the ideal time. Herr Lehmann's on top form tonight.'

Jürgen returned with the beers. 'Herr Lehmann's going to straighten things out,' Erwin told him.

'You're all crazy,' said Herr Lehmann.

'I don't want a beer,' Erwin said. 'I want one of your shitty brandies, but not the piss you usually serve.'

'Right away,' said Jürgen. 'As soon as Herr Lehmann's straightened things out.'

'I'm not straightening anything out. You're crazy, the lot of you.'

'Herr Lehmann's a hero,' said Jürgen.

'Herr Lehmann's hungry,' said his best friend Karl. 'We need some more crisps. For the electrolytes.' He raised his bottle. 'To Herr Lehmann, the hero of the hour.'

'To Herr Lehmann!' they chorused, clinking bottles. Herr Lehmann didn't protest, but he was sceptical.

'Mind you,' said Erwin, 'he'll have to tread carefully.'

'How do you mean?'

'When he's interrogating him. The man's a pro. Actually, you can't interrogate a guy like that, he'll only act dumb.'

'Maybe he *is* dumb,' said Karl.

'We could christen him "Kristall" Rainer,' Jürgen suggested. 'In memory of "Schneider" Jürgen.'

'What's he doing these days?' asked Karl.

'He's dead.'

'How'd he die?'

'No idea.'

'Aids, maybe,' hazarded Karl.

'I don't think he was gay,' said Jürgen. 'He wasn't anything at all, I reckon. Can you imagine Schneider Jürgen having sex with someone?'

'I've lost the ability to imagine anyone having sex with anyone,' said Erwin.

'You must catch him at just the right moment,' Jürgen told Herr Lehmann.

Herr Lehmann was already feeling better, now that he was off duty in the *Abfall*'s cosy atmosphere with a few beers inside him. He ate some more crisps and turned cocky.

'Well, here goes,' he said.

'No,' said Erwin, 'he'll smell a rat.'

'What's it all about?' asked Karl.

'I'm going to tackle him right now,' said Herr Lehmann, who was keen to make the most of his sudden and surprising momentum. 'You're being paranoid, all of you.'

'Well,' said Karl, 'I think you should take her to the movies.'

'The movies?'

'Of course. Couples always go to the movies when they're in love.'

'Who said I was in—'

'The movies, that's the ticket. Culture, darkness, togetherness – what could be better?'

Jürgen pricked up his ears. 'What was that about movies?'

'Herr Lehmann should pay a romantic visit to the movies.'

'There's a Lubitsch retrospective on at the Notausgang,' said Jürgen, who fancied himself a film buff. '*Ninotchka*, *To Be or Not To Be* – they don't make movies like that any more.'

'You can't do it now,' Erwin hissed, 'it'd be too obvious.' Herr Lehmann ignored him.

'But I hardly know her,' he objected. 'I can't just ask her if she'd like to go to a movie with me.'

'It was only a suggestion,' said his best friend Karl. 'Happiness is a warm gun.'

Herr Lehmann reinforced his original intention. 'I'm going over there right now.'

'I'll take care of it,' said his best friend Karl.

'Be careful, though,' Erwin insisted. 'Look casual, so to speak.'

'I wouldn't if I were you,' said Jürgen.

'That trip to the movies,' said Karl, 'leave it to me.'

Herr Lehmann was already working on his secret agent's legend. 'I'll simply order drinks all round,' he said, rising. He made his slow and unobtrusive way to the counter, sensing that they were all staring at him and unpleasantly aware what a tight fit Erwin's new T-shirt was. Then he sat down on the bar stool beside Kristall Rainer, who should really have been called 'Kristall-But-No-Lemon' Rainer, and addressed himself to Marko.

'Give me another three beers, a brandy for Erwin, and some crisps.'

Marko said something about Erwin and his predilections, but Herr Lehmann ignored him. He tried to establish eye contact with Kristall Rainer, but the latter was dreamily contemplating the bottles behind the counter.

'Why does the rain stop when it makes bubbles?' was Herr Lehmann's opening gambit. Kristall Rainer didn't react. Herr Lehmann tugged him gently by the sleeve. 'No, be honest: why does the rain stop when it makes bubbles?'

Kristall Rainer stared at him. Meantime, Marko was depositing the drinks on the counter. 'Put them on Erwin's tab,' Herr Lehmann told him without looking. Marko said something about Erwin and his tab. Herr Lehmann took no notice. He gazed into Kristall Rainer's eyes, uncertain whether the man had registered his presence at all. 'There seems to be some truth in it,' he said.

Kristall Rainer grinned. There was something mask-like about his grin, as if it were the product of lengthy deliberation. 'It's what my granny used to say.'

'Ah yes, grannies,' said Herr Lehmann. 'They've got a saying to fit any occasion.'

'If the rain makes bubbles it'll soon be over, that's what she always said.' Kristall Rainer chuckled. 'It's only logical,' he added.

'Why?'

'Can't you work it out?'

'No,' said Herr Lehmann, who found the question rather presumptuous in view of Kristall Rainer's condition. Erwin's right, he thought. Not about him being an undercover cop, but he shouldn't be underestimated.

'If it rains for a long time, puddles form,' said Kristall Rainer. It struck Herr Lehmann that his speech never became slurred in spite of the vast quantities of wheat beer he imbibed, and he caught himself wondering, quite irrelevantly, whether it was only the lemon that made someone slur his words. That, he thought, is the silliest idea I've had in the last ten years. Unless he secretly pours it away, he amended, looking on the dark side. I mustn't start thinking like Erwin, he commanded himself, or I'll get nowhere.

'It can't make bubbles before puddles have formed,' Kristall Rainer pursued. 'That's logical, isn't it? And if it's rained long enough . . .' – he paused for effect and swigged at his wheat beer, spilling some down his chin – '. . . long enough for puddles to form, it won't be long before it stops.'

'I see,' said Herr Lehmann, who'd been expecting something less banal. 'But it can't make bubbles unless the raindrops are really big,' he objected. 'I mean, if it's only drizzling, there can be as many puddles as you like but it won't make any bubbles. Maybe that's the reason. Maybe it's a particular size or weight of raindrop that's responsible for making bubbles which indicate that the rain will soon stop.'

'Your guess is as good as mine,' said Kristall Rainer.

Herr Lehmann was disappointed. Kristall Rainer isn't making an effort, he thought. First he gets fresh and now he clams up. He started this bubble business, after all. He can't just wash his hands of it.

'By the way,' he said, changing the subject, 'what do you do for a living?'

'Why do you ask?'

'You aren't in the police, are you?'

Kristall Rainer seemed unsurprised. He merely stared past Herr Lehmann and into the gloomy bar room.

'No,' he said after quite a time.

'So what *do* you do?'

'Computer technician.' Kristall Rainer enunciated each syllable carefully, as if first having to call them to mind.

That, Herr Lehmann instantly decided, is the truth. Nobody with something to hide would dream that up. He couldn't conceive of anything more boring and perverse, dreary and unglamorous than being a computer technician.

'My name's Frank, by the way,' he said, raising one of the beer bottles standing on the counter in front of him.

'Mine's Rainer.' Kristall Rainer smiled with such genuine warmth that Herr Lehmann felt thoroughly mean. The man's glass was almost empty. Lucky there isn't any lemon in it, Herr Lehmann reflected. It makes the last mouthful taste sour and leaves you with bits of fruit in your mouth. 'Like another?' he asked.

'I wouldn't say no,' said Rainer.

'Another Kristall,' Herr Lehmann told Marko. 'Without lemon.'

'Right first time,' said Rainer.

'It's on Erwin,' Herr Lehmann said to Marko. And to Kristall Rainer, 'Well, I'd better be going . . .' He gestured vaguely at the drinks and the bag of crisps. 'I'm with the guys over there.'

'Sure.'

'They're waiting.'

'Of course.'

'I'll be off, then.'

'Okay.'

'Well, how'd it go?' Erwin asked eagerly when Herr Lehmann returned to the table. 'What did you talk about?'

'Just stuff,' said Herr Lehmann, opening the bag of crisps.

'To Herr Lehmann,' said Jürgen, and raised his bottle.

'Herr Lehmann,' they chorused, clinking bottles.

'Well, go on,' said Jürgen. 'You were talking together for ages.'

'I wanted to tell you why there's something to celebrate,' said Karl.

'Come on, what did he say?' asked Erwin.

'I've landed an exhibition in Charlottenburg.'

'What should he have said?' Herr Lehmann retorted, leaning back with a handful of crisps.

'In Knesebeckstrasse. At the gallery there.'

'You mean it?' said Herr Lehmann, genuinely impressed.

'Then we must all go,' said Jürgen. 'To Charlottenburg.'

'But what did he say?' Erwin persisted.

'Just stuff. About rain and so on.'

'About rain?'

'I'll tell you this much, Erwin,' Herr Lehmann said cruelly. 'He's a funny fish, that man.'

'I told you so.'

'A very funny fish.'

'Well, go on . . .'

'It's hard to say,' said Herr Lehmann. 'A very funny fish.'

'I reckon so too,' said Jürgen. 'He isn't kosher, somehow.'

'But seriously,' said Erwin, 'is he a cop?'

'Sure,' said Herr Lehmann. 'If he isn't a cop, my name's . . . oh, I don't know . . . Frank, probably.'

'I knew it!' Erwin said triumphantly. 'I knew it!'

'In Knesebeckstrasse, you assholes,' said Karl. 'Knesebeckstrasse. In November. You'll all be calling me Herr Schmidt before long.'

'To Herr Lehmann,' cried Jürgen.

'To Herr Lehmann,' the others chimed in, clinking bottles.

8 STAR WARS

WHEN HERR LEHMANN woke up, Luke Skywalker was soaring across the Death Star before finally – as far as he could recall, and it irked him that he could – putting two aerial torpedoes into the Death Star's weak spot, some kind of ventilator shaft that led to the power source or something. There he goes, thought Herr Lehmann. The Empire's troops had just boarded Princess Leia's spaceship when he fell asleep, and a fair amount had happened since then. He glanced sideways at Katrin and Karl, then watched Katrin gazing spellbound at the screen and eating salted popcorn, and his love for her at that moment was so strong, it made him feel utterly and completely at a loss. He shuffled around in the sagging cinema seat to ease his stiff limbs and wondered how much longer he could go on watching her before she noticed. He also wondered how much longer the performance would last. A long time yet, he told himself, because this was *Star Wars* night at the Minoa Cinema, when all three *Star Wars* films were shown in succession. It formed the backbone of the romantic night out organised for him by his best friend Karl, and if he recalled correctly – and it irked him that he did – the battle for the Death Star was only the finale of the first film.

I should never have gone along with the idea, he told himself, it's no good letting Karl have a free hand in these things. But that was exactly what he'd done, worn down by four long weeks during which he'd vainly hoped to forge some kind of closer relationship with Katrin, the *Markthalle*'s beautiful chef. There were few stones he'd left unturned. He now knew a lot more about her, for instance that she was twenty-seven years old, that she'd come to Berlin to study industrial design, and that she hoped to spend the next year compiling a portfolio that would gain her admission to the relevant college. He knew her life story and that of her parents, and he knew much more about Achim than ever before. They had talked and laughed together. More importantly, they had argued together as they alone knew how, but nothing had happened that would really have constituted progress: no chance physical contact that transcended the purely friendly or fortuitous, no goodnight kisses that might have become protracted and developed into something more serious, no verbal intimacies. Above all, no twosomes. Now that autumn had finally come, there was no question of suggesting an excursion to the Wannsee or the Tegeler See or a boat trip on the Landwehr Canal on the innocuous pretext of relaxing or exploring the city, and he simply hadn't plucked up the courage to ask her to go to a movie. 'Inviting her to go to a movie,' he'd been forced to explain to his best friend Karl, 'would be pushing my luck. It's still too soon for that.' Karl had bombarded him with repeated offers to take the matter in hand and organise a romantic evening *à trois*, a threesome being less obvious. 'I'll fix it for you,' Karl had told him. 'You've got lover's block. Everyone needs a little help now and then – we can't always handle things by ourselves. Least of all a girl like that,' he added, slapping Herr Lehmann on the back. 'Culture,' said Karl, ' – culture and romance, they're the only things that work in the autumn.' And, in his dire predicament, Herr Lehmann had finally consented. 'I'll fix it for you,' Karl had promised, and fix it he had – you had to give him that much.

They'd begun by going to an early evening session by Marko's and Klaus's new combo, because 'Music opens the heart', his best friend Karl had asserted. 'We've got to make the most of a Friday evening like this. First music, then a movie.' The *Star Wars* film night had been Katrin's idea. She'd always wanted to see all the *Star Wars* films at a sitting, she told Karl, and Herr Lehmann was doubly fascinated by the fact that she was an inveterate sci-fi fan because it was the last thing he would have expected of her. So there they were, and Luke Skywalker was just being urged by Obi Wan, who was really dead but refused to bow out, to put his faith in the Force. Luke Skywalker thereupon switched off his targeting computer and took aim in the old-fashioned way, and Herr Lehmann knew – and hated himself for knowing – that this was the method destined to succeed. Culture's the main thing, Karl had said; the rest will come by itself. Karl trusts the Force too, thought Herr Lehmann. Katrin, the beautiful chef, was mean-time consuming popcorn as if it were the last form of nourish-ment she would ever get. Still, he had got into conversation with her once in the course of the evening, if only briefly and only on the subject of why the devil salted popcorn existed at all, a circumstance which would forever remain a mystery to him. He'd told her so, too, but she had disagreed, and here they now were.

'I'm going to get myself a beer,' Karl called across Katrin. 'How about you two? Want one too?'

'Sure,' Herr Lehmann called back.

'Be quiet, can't you?' said a voice behind them. This was bull-shit, because the whole auditorium was alive with whispers, catcalls, and the rustle of crisp bags. It also reeked of grass, and a lot of people were laughing in the wrong places. There were even dogs present. Just then, Herr Lehmann caught sight of one that reminded him of the animal he'd encountered in Lausitzer Platz some weeks ago. He couldn't make out any details, it was too dark, and the dog made only one brief foray past the screen from left to right, but it had the same physique as the one in Lausitzer Platz, a sausage-shaped body with spindly legs attached, and it moved in a way he found vaguely familiar. Not knowing what to make of this, he looked back at Katrin, who was just lighting a cigarette although her mouth was full of popcorn. Bugger the dog, he thought, and concentrated on looking at her until he was so in love it became too much for him.

'I'll come too, I need a pee anyway,' he said. But Karl had already gone.

'Very interesting,' said the voice behind them. It was a woman's voice. Doubtless a *Star Wars* buff, Herr Lehmann thought bitterly – the kind that hates to miss a single word of dialogue. 'Shut up, I want to watch the film,' he snapped. He got up and made his way out under cover of the numerous explosions that were currently putting paid to the Death Star.

Karl was already at the kiosk beside the box office. He was in great form, his massive body positively radiating vigour as he genially rocked to and fro while paying with small change. Arrayed in front of him were three bags of crisps and three bottles of beer.

'What do you want with those crisps?' Herr Lehmann demanded acidly. 'She's already got popcorn.'

His best friend Karl raised an admonitory forefinger. 'Salted popcorn,' he amended. 'You've picked yourself a smart cookie there, my friend. She thinks of her electrolytes!'

'I didn't pick her, you can't say that.'

'True, you don't pick girls, they pick themselves. Love is a divine force, et cetera,' said Karl, handing him a beer.

'I don't want to go back inside, it's pointless. Why didn't we go to see *Rumble Fish*? It's showing next door.'

'Oh, Frank,' said Karl, '*Rumble Fish* is a turkey.'

'It's a great movie,' Herr Lehmann said defensively. 'Absolutely first-rate, it is.'

'But you've seen it umpteen times, old son. I wouldn't be surprised if it's the one and only movie you've seen in the last ten years. 'You're a great lover, Rusty James,' Karl misquoted. 'That appeals to you, of course, being the Rusty James of Eisenbahnstrasse. But women aren't like that, believe me. They don't think sex is so great.'

'That's not the point. And what was all that shit you gave me about Marko's and Klaus's combo? They were the grottiest bunch I've ever heard.'

'They always were grotty,' said Karl. 'Their old combo was just as bad. And the one before that.'

'That's no excuse. Some lousy night out, this is.'

'Yes, a person has to go through hell sometimes, but you wouldn't understand that. You've always had it too easy with women.'

'But this is teenager stuff. Besides, it's kind of embarrassing, you playing Cupid.'

'Come on, no need to be embarrassed about anything with me. But okay, okay,' said Karl, raising his hands in surrender, 'I'm to blame, it was a rotten idea. Drink up your beer. The girl's stupid, that's all.'

'Oh? Why this change of tune?'

'Well, the *Star Wars* night was down to her. Only an absolute nut would come up with an idea like that, especially when *Rumble Fish* is showing next door. You're a genuine movie buff, Frank. I'm sure *Johnny Guitar* is on somewhere too.'

'I've nothing against it as such – *Star Wars*, I mean. It's just a question of taste. And *Star Wars* has kind of . . .' – Herr Lehmann faltered in his search for telling arguments – '. . . kind of got something.'

'Aha!' said his best friend Karl.

Herr Lehmann felt caught out. 'Not that it isn't crap, of course,' he added.

'What are you two up to?' asked Katrin, who had suddenly appeared beside them.

'We got talking,' said Karl. 'Is the first part over?'

'Yes, the second one's just starting,' she said. 'But I don't think it's as good, somehow.'

'Why not?' Herr Lehmann asked belligerently. 'The second part is the best, actually. If you'd only give it some thought, you'd—' He got no further because Karl kicked him on the shin.

'What Herr Lehmann means is this: the second part is definitely the best time to nip round the corner for a drink.'

'Why do you always call him Herr Lehmann?' asked Katrin, eyeing Herr Lehmann dubiously. 'I've been meaning to ask you for ages.'

'Because there's something so . . .' – Karl groped for the right turn of phrase – '. . . so different about him. He isn't like the common herd. He's wrapped in mystery.'

'What sort of mystery?'

'Ah!' Karl threw up his arms. 'If only one knew. Let's go to the *Blase*.'

'Why the *Blase*?' Herr Lehmann demanded angrily. 'Why go to a gay bar, on top of everything else?'

'Have you got something against people like that?' Katrin inquired suspiciously.

Herr Lehmann inwardly cast his eyes up to heaven. People like that . . . She said 'people like that' when referring to gays. 'Why should I have anything against gays? I merely said it was a gay bar, and are we gay? Are *you* gay?' Rather too aggressively, as he himself conceded, but so badly in need of catharsis that he couldn't do otherwise, he addressed the last question to his best friend Karl and prodded him in the chest with his forefinger. 'Are *you* gay? No. Am *I* gay? No.' He turned to Katrin. 'Are *you* gay?'

'Now look—'

'Why in God's name should we go to a gay bar if we aren't gay? Why don't we leave the gay bars to the gays and go to a straight bar instead? Why should we go to a gay bar with a woman in tow?'

'Now look!'

'Take it easy, Frank, just take it easy. The *Blase* is okay. Besides, Sylvio's working there tonight.'

'Oh, very well,' said Herr Lehmann. He felt uneasy about the idea, but that was an argument he couldn't counter.

Nothing much was happening when they walked into the *Blase*. Even gays aren't what they used to be, Herr Lehmann reflected. Karl headed straight for a central table and sat the other two down at it. Then, with three bags of crisps clamped under his arm, he went over to Sylvio, who was chatting with a leather-clad gay behind the bar, and had a word with him. Herr Lehmann was still feeling uneasy about the whole situation.

'Are they all gays in here?' asked Katrin.

'Yes.'

'They look quite nice, though.'

Herr Lehmann, who found this reminiscent of a conversation with his mother, tried to change the subject.

'Whereabouts in Bremen did you live?' he inquired.

'Oh,' she said, lighting a cigarette, 'in Hastedt.'

'Where in Hastedt?'

'Herzberger Strasse. With a girlfriend.'

'Really,' said Herr Lehmann. 'What's it like there?'

'Much the same as anywhere else,' she said listlessly. Karl came back and deposited three bottles of beer on the table.

'Sylvio isn't happy to see us,' he said contentedly, helping himself to one of Katrin's cigarettes. 'And his boss even less so. They don't want us eating our crisps in here.'

'Who's his boss?'

'The bogus biker he's standing around with,' said Karl. 'They wondered if we wouldn't like to drink up our beers and take the lady somewhere else. They even stood us the beers. I gave them our crisps in exchange.'

'Well,' said Herr Lehmann, 'if that's what Sylvio said, maybe we should take the hint.'

'Nonsense,' said Karl, 'he didn't mean it. He only said it for his boss's benefit. Sylvio's new here, he needs the money.'

'Is it because I'm a woman, or what?' Katrin demanded indignantly. 'That would be the limit.'

'Sure it is,' said Herr Lehmann. 'On the other hand, it's a gay bar, isn't it? I mean, that's the whole point of a gay bar, so gays can be with their own kind.'

'But they can't throw us out just because I'm a woman.'

'Easy,' said Karl, draining his beer. 'No one's going to throw anyone out. Hey, look who's just come in!'

Herr Lehmann turned to look at the entrance and saw Kristall Rainer, who recognised him and raised a hand in greeting.

'Can he be gay too?' Herr Lehmann wondered aloud.

'I know him,' said Katrin. 'I've seen him before.'

'Yes,' Karl said with a laugh, 'he's a gay undercover cop.'

Kristall Rainer walked up to the bar and bought himself a wheat beer. Then Herr Lehmann's worst fears were realised: he came over to them.

'Hello,' he said, and he sounded so diffident that Herr Lehmann promptly felt rather sorry for him.

'Hello,' Herr Lehmann replied. 'Why don't you join us?' he added reluctantly.

'Oh, how nice of you. My name's Rainer, by the way.'

'Sure,' said Karl. 'Do you come here often?'

'No, why?'

'Just asking,' Karl replied with an enigmatic smile. 'We need someone to go to the bar and get us some more beers. I'll pay for them, but somebody else'll have to go.'

'Leave it to me,' said Rainer. 'No problem.' He got up and went over to the bar, taking his wheat beer with him.

'Where have I seen him before?' Katrin asked when he was out of earshot.

'He tours all the bars,' said Karl. 'Drinks nothing but wheat beer. Kristall.'

'Without lemon,' Herr Lehmann added glumly. The whole night out was an unmitigated fiasco.

'Hey, look at Herr Lehmann,' Karl said to Katrin. 'He badly needs cheering up.'

'Why, what's the matter with him?' Katrin asked solicitously.

'No idea. What's the matter, Herr Lehmann? What's eating you?'

Herr Lehmann quoted the next-best problem that occurred to him. 'My parents are coming here soon,' he said. 'On a coach. Package deal, Kurfürstendamm hotel included. Staying over the weekend.'

'That's tough,' said Karl. 'When did you hear?'

'I don't know. Weeks ago.'

'And that's what's been eating you all this time?'

'But why?' said Katrin. 'It could be quite nice.'

'I'll have to go to the Kudamm and pick them up and take them on a guided tour of Berlin.'

'You poor sod,' said Karl. 'When is it?'

'And then they want to see the restaurant where I work.'

'Restaurant?' Karl guffawed.

'I told them I was the manager of a restaurant.'

'But that's a lie,' said Katrin, 'isn't it?'

'Depends which way you look at it,' Karl said with a laugh. 'The *Einfall* does at least serve Verena's super sandwiches, Herr Lehmann insists on that.'

'Very funny.'

'Well I don't know, fancy lying to his parents like that . . .' Katrin shook her head disapprovingly.

'It makes them feel happier,' said Herr Lehmann. 'If I told them I worked in a bar, they'd be unhappy. I said I worked in a restaurant – told them I was the manager, in fact – so they're happy. They can live with that. "Manager" sounds good, too. It sounds better when the neighbours ask about me.'

'True,' said Katrin, 'it does sound better.'

'That makes me a manager too,' said Karl, and he laughed so hard he choked.

'Manager isn't better at all,' said Herr Lehmann, slapping him on the back. 'It's bullshit.'

'You're right,' Karl said, still laughing, 'but why say so? You shouldn't bite the hand that rescues you.'

'You've got that wrong,' said Herr Lehmann, but then it occurred to him that this was precisely what the dog in Lausitzer Platz had done when it bit the policeman. But he'd never told Karl about that. For some reason unknown even to himself, he'd told no one about it, not even Karl. 'Besides, why shouldn't I?'

'Don't act dumb. I know why you're telling us all this. You want me to be on duty at the *Markthalle* that day. Then you'll waltz in with your parents, have something nice to eat, and I'll tell them what an A-1 boss you are. That's logical, isn't it? When are they coming, anyway?'

'The end of October.'

'The end of October! You really are a doom merchant, Herr Lehmann. There's still a whole month to go till then. You used to be such a *carpe diem* type. What's wrong with you? And where's Kristall Rainer with our beers? What's he blathering about with Sylvio and Leather Pants? Are they fixing up a threesome, or what?'

They looked over at the bar. Kristall Rainer was deep in conversation with the boss and Sylvio, who was pouring him a wheat beer. Their own three beers were already on the counter.

'Sylvio's losing his grip,' said Karl. 'How much longer is it going to take him to pour a glass of beer? And how come Rainer's getting another when he's only just had one?'

Kristall Rainer returned, but with Sylvio at his heels. Herr Lehmann didn't like the look of things. Kristall Rainer sat down, handed round the bottles of beer, and retired into his shell.

'Listen, folks,' said Sylvio. He broke off, looking embarrassed. They all stared at him. 'Look, it's nothing to do with me,' he went on eventually, 'but Detlev, that's my boss, he—'

'Detlev? Is that his name?' boomed Karl. 'You mean that nancy boy's actually called Detlev? Fantastic!'

'Put a sock in it, Karl,' Sylvio entreated. 'It's like this: he says you must go after these beers. Alternatively, you can take them with you if you care to go sooner – in fact that would be preferable. This is a gay bar, he says, and he doesn't want any straights making themselves at home in here.'

'I'm sorry, Sylvio,' said Herr Lehmann, 'we'll go right away.'

'We'll go when we're good and ready,' said Karl. 'I mean, we aren't amateurs. I know my licensed-premises law, and it doesn't make any special provision for gays. I wouldn't chuck your friend Detlev out of the *Markthalle*.'

'We'll go right away,' said Herr Lehmann.

'We'll go when we feel like it.'

'Well,' said Katrin, 'I'd never have thought my gender was a problem.'

'Thinking doesn't come into it,' Karl shouted to the bar room at large. 'Leather Pants hasn't thought of anything for years, apart from where his next buttfuck's coming from.'

'Karl,' Sylvio said desperately, 'for Christ's sake cut it out.' But it was too late.

The leather–clad gay at the counter stood up and came over to them. He was at least as tall as Karl and even heavier. His belly overhung his tight leather pants like a massive bolster.

'That's it, folks,' he said. 'Take your bottles and get out, all of you. The glass of wheat beer stays. And take your fat tart with you.'

That made Herr Lehmann mad, really mad. Mad at the entire world, at the pitfalls that lurked everywhere, at all the shit you had to bear in mind, at his own presentiments and his own considerateness, mad at Luke Skywalker, mad at Kristall Rainer, mad at Karl for provoking the whole imbroglio, but mad above all at Detlev for insulting Katrin, the woman he loved. He felt cold fury welling up inside him like vomit. He knew it wouldn't be good if he spoke – knew it would create problems rather than solve them – but he had to do something, let it out, put Detlev in his place.

'Piss off, you asshole, or I'll land you in deep shit with the licensing authorities,' he blurted out. His breathing had speeded up and his pulse was racing. This is madness, he thought, but what else can I do?

Detlev laughed and looked down at him as if he were something the cat had brought in. 'Who's this, the cunt-sucker in chief, or what?'

It'll end in tears, thought Herr Lehmann, it really will. He stood up and punched Detlev on the nose with all his might. Detlev didn't flinch. He took the blow in his stride, then leisurely extended a massive paw in the direction of Herr Lehmann's throat. This is bad, thought Herr Lehmann, really bad. He grabbed Detlev's hand, selected a finger, and sank his teeth in it. The sensation of biting gave him pleasure. He felt his jaw muscles straining as he bit deeper and deeper, and it seemed to him, as the big, fleshy hand flapped and jerked around in front of his face and he was hurled to and fro by the superior strength of the man named Detlev, that his teeth had grated on something hard. I've reached the bone, he thought dully, quite unconscious of the hectic activity in progress around him. People sprang to their feet, tables fell over, Detlev screamed like a stuck pig, Karl, Katrin, Sylvio and others tried to separate them. The whole bar became engulfed in a milling, swaying throng centred on Herr Lehmann and Detlev, but none of this mattered to the former as he went on biting. He was alone with his teeth and his jaw muscles and a taste of blood in his mouth he would never forget.

'Let go, let go!' Karl shouted in his ear. 'He's had enough, let go!'

So he let go, and suddenly it was all over. They were outside in the street, fists were shaken, and Detlev's cries faded as Herr Lehmann and his friends hurried along Oranienstrasse towards Adalbertstrasse. He heard a man yell something and run after Karl, who flung him into a doorway, and then they were around the corner, and everyone paused to catch their breath and he spat and went on spitting to rid himself of the metallic taste of Detlev's blood.

'Not bad, not bad,' he heard Karl say. Looking up, he saw them all in the glow from a doner kebab stall: Karl, Sylvio, Katrin, who was crying gently, and Kristall Rainer, who was comforting her, which he didn't like the look of at all.

'Shit, shit, shit,' said Sylvio, putting an arm round his shoulder. 'You're okay,' he added – a strange remark, coming from him, but Herr Lehmann felt very grateful for it.

'Drinks all round, we can't go on like this,' cried his best friend Karl, who was quite unshaken by it all. On the contrary, he was in high spirits: he had a plan. 'Off we go, no dawdling. All hands to the pumps. I've got an idea. Follow me, everyone.'

They followed him. The exercise did them all good. They walked fast, panting with mingled exertion and excitement. Walking differs from running, Herr Lehmann reflected to take his mind off things. You've always got one foot on the ground when you're walking, never both feet in the air at once the way you have when you're running. That's the crucial difference, it's got nothing to do with speed, he thought as his best friend Karl urged them all along. They hurried after him, first down Adalbertstrasse, then along Skalitzer Strasse, straight on down Admiralstrasse, across the dark, gleaming waters of the Landwehr Canal, and into Grimmstrasse, where they turned left at Karl's behest into the *Savoy*, a bar Herr Lehmann hadn't been in for years and had never liked, if only because it boasted a billiard table, which he couldn't abide, and wall-to-wall carpet, which he considered the biggest mistake of all. But Karl must know what he's doing, thought Herr Lehmann – Karl has everything under control. The next thing he knew he was sitting at a table, and Karl was talking to a woman behind the bar whom he seemed to know well, and they were are all out of breath and sweating, and Katrin had stopped crying, and Kristall Rainer had stopped comforting her or whatever he'd thought he was doing, and that, thought Herr Lehmann, is something at least.

'Drink up,' said Karl, plonking some schnapps glasses on the table. 'Bottoms up, everyone!'

They knocked them back.

'My God,' said Karl, 'I'm getting too old for these group activities.'

'I'm sorry,' Herr Lehmann said to Sylvio. 'I'm really sorry, Sylvio, I didn't want it to end that way.'

'It's okay,' said Sylvio, who was looking rather pale. 'The guy deserved it. He's a complete asshole.'

Looking at Sylvio, Herr Lehmann saw how wrung out he was and, at that moment, loved him dearly. He'd never had much to do with him. They'd worked together now and then, but Sylvio normally shared his shifts at the *Einfall* with Stefan, so they'd never had much to do with each other, but all the same, thought Herr Lehmann, he's a real pal, and gutsy too. 'I'm really sorry,' he repeated, not knowing what else to say. 'We should simply have gone somewhere else.'

'It's all my fault,' Karl put in loudly. 'I'm a dead loss.'

Nobody contradicted him. 'Okay, okay,' said Karl, putting his hands up. 'Who wants to kick me in the ass?' He jumped up, turned round, bent down, and presented his massive rump. 'Go on! Now or never!'

They all relaxed a little, Katrin included. Herr Lehmann looked at her, and she returned his gaze with a strange expression. 'You're crazy,' she said in a low voice. He suddenly felt her hand on his thigh, but only for a moment.

'We've no need to worry about Herr Lehmann from now on,' said Karl. 'A bottle of fizz!' he called to the woman behind the bar. 'Right away!'

The woman popped the cork and came over to their table bearing a tray with five glasses on it. 'I'll be mother,' Karl told her. She put the tray on the table and gave his head an affectionate stroke before departing.

'Well, one thing's for sure,' Karl repeated as he filled the glasses, 'we've no need to worry about Herr Lehmann.'

'Why not?' asked Kristall Rainer, who had no business butting in, or so it seemed to Herr Lehmann.

Karl, too, seemed faintly surprised at this interjection. He eyed Kristall Rainer as if he were a cold sausage. 'Because Herr Lehmann has patented a new form of martial art, you dummy. First he invents the Kreuzberg Twist, and now he's come up with the antidote. Fantastic.' He doled out the glasses. 'I only hope that asshole hasn't got Aids or anything.'

They all froze. Herr Lehmann himself felt a pang of fear.

'He hasn't,' said Sylvio. 'He just had himself tested again.'

'Are you sure?' asked Karl, a question Herr Lehmann found uncalled for.

Sylvio seemed unmoved. 'He once got hepatitis B – I mean, in the days when people didn't know too much about it – so he took good care from then on. It's saved his life, he says.'

Karl raised his glass. 'Well then,' he said, 'here's to hepatitis B. At least it's some use!'

They could all agree on that, but Herr Lehmann felt dejected nonetheless. Whatever constitutes a romantic night out, it shouldn't culminate in my biting a gay bar-owner's finger. We couldn't have got off to a worse start, he thought, looking across at Katrin, who returned his gaze with a smile. He felt her hand on his thigh again. She's an odd girl, he thought. Very odd.

'Cheer up, Frank,' Karl boomed at him across the table. 'The night is young. It's still too early, but later we must all go on to the *Orbit* for some proper boom-boom music, as Herr Lehmann calls it, and mineral water at five marks a throw.' He laughed. 'Ah, culture, there's nothing to beat it.' He turned to Sylvio. 'Don't worry, I'll have a word with Erwin. He'll give you a few extra shifts, and that'll be that – people are always walking out on him anyway.' He ruffled Sylvio's hair, thoroughly in command of the situation.

'I'm hungry,' Katrin said, looking at Herr Lehmann. 'Really hungry. Funny thing, at this hour . . .'

'Me too,' Herr Lehmann said quickly. 'I know a place where we can still get something, down by the canal.'

'That's right,' Karl chimed in, 'you two go off and get a bite to eat. Sylvio and Rainer' – he slapped Rainer on the back – 'will stay here and keep me company. Later on we'll go to the *Orbit*, but first we'll have another bottle of fizz and a wheat beer for you, eh, Rainer?' He almost felled the man with an even harder slap on the back.

'Actually,' said Kristall Rainer, 'I'm hungry too.'

'No,' Karl said quickly, 'you stay here like a good boy. They've got tasty cheese snacks and shit like that.' He rolled his eyes in exasperation. 'You stay here like a good boy. When in doubt, have another beer. It's as good as half a loaf.'

'True,' said Sylvio.

Herr Lehmann and Katrin went on drinking with the others for a while. Meantime, as if by chance and without moving it around, she rested her hand on his knee. Then they were outside at last, and she slipped her arm through his as they walked along the canal. She looked at him as she did so, and he looked back at her, and she smiled, and he smiled back at her, and everything was fine. We aren't walking in step but precisely the other way round, he reflected. When she puts out her right leg, I put my out left leg, that way we don't sway to and fro. We would if we walked in step, but if she puts out her left leg when I put out my right leg and vice versa, we keep steady. Either Karl's a genius, he thought, or he's an idiot with the right instincts. Still, he reflected gratefully, it probably amounts to the same thing.

9 SMOKING IN BED

HERR LEHMANN LAY beside her smoking a cigarette. He didn't really like cigarettes, which always made his head swim, but it didn't matter, his head was swimming anyway, and she was also smoking a cigarette, and if he smoked one too at least his hands had something to do instead of incessantly roaming over her naked body, which was just what they would otherwise have been doing at this moment, if only because he found it so incredible to be lying naked beside her, he had to keep reassuring himself that it was true. So a cigarette was just what he needed, and it made him even dizzier than he was already — a pleasant kind of dizziness that took his mind off the magnitude of his simultaneous feelings of happiness and anxiety.

He bent over her and tapped his ash into the ashtray, which was lying between her breasts. She screwed up her eyes, blew some smoke into his face, and smiled.

'Do you always get what you want?'

'No, why?'

'I don't know, you strike me as someone who always gets what he wants.'

'Well, I don't want much.'

'Not much?' She put the ashtray down beside her on the floor and turned to face him. 'Not much? You mean this isn't much, or what? And don't pretend you didn't want it!'

Herr Lehmann looked at her and said nothing. There are questions better left unanswered, he thought, especially when you don't know what they're getting at.

'You *did* want it, didn't you?' she said teasingly, and boxed him on the chest. 'You planned it from the outset.'

'Well,' Herr Lehmann said warily, 'I wouldn't say "planned". "Planned" sounds so calculating . . .'

'I think everyone underestimates you.'

'I love you, that's what matters.' There, Herr Lehmann thought as he stroked her forehead and patted some stray hairs into place, I've said it now.

'They think you aren't really with it,' she went on. 'That's your secret weapon.'

'What is?'

'The fact that everyone underestimates you.'

'I don't have anything to underestimate, I'm exactly what I am. What you see is what you get.'

'Yes, but what *are* you? That's what I'd like to find out.'

'Can I have the ashtray?'

She handed it to him and he stubbed out his cigarette. 'I hate to disappoint you,' he said cautiously, 'but perhaps I really am what you can see, nothing more.'

'Haven't you ever considered doing something different from what you do now? I think you're the type of person who could become anything he chose.'

'What do you mean, become? Becoming something means you aren't anything to start with. I don't see myself that way.'

'Did you really mean that just now?'

'What?'

'That you love me?'

'Yes, of course. I don't say it to every woman I meet.'

'I should hope not,' she said with a smile, and boxed him on the chest again. They tussled awhile, then kissed, and she climbed on top of him. He found it a trifle hard to breathe, but it didn't matter.

'I don't know if I love you,' she said. 'I mean,' she amended swiftly, 'I think I love you but I'm not in love with you, if you know what I mean.'

'No, I don't.'

'Well, I love you all right, but I'm not really in love. That's something else.'

'No it isn't, not at all. If you love someone you're in love with them as well.'

'You're wrong.' She sat up and looked down at him gravely. Her hair tickled his eyelids. 'If you love someone it's a general emotion, whereas if you're in love with them it's urgent and instant.'

'I see,' said Herr Lehmann. 'One is acute and the other's chronic, is that what you mean?'

She thought for a moment. 'Yes, kind of.'

'So one is like pneumonia and the other like chronic bronchitis?'

'You make it sound so unromantic.' She bent down and gave him a love bite. 'There,' she said, 'now I've branded you.'

'Do you always do that?'

'Yes.'

'That *is* unromantic,' said Herr Lehmann. They smooched a bit longer, then she climbed off him and pulled on her bathrobe.

'Are you hungry?' she asked. 'I'm famished. I'll fix us something.'

She disappeared into the kitchen. Herr Lehmann sat up and looked around. The TV, which she'd turned on as soon as they came in, was still on. At least they'd found time at some stage to zap the sound, and that was a good thing because Herr Lehmann found it hard to concentrate on sex while listening to the dialogue from a medical soap opera.

He was fascinated by her room, which was the same shape as the larger of his own one and a half rooms. The whole apartment, or as much as he'd seen of it, was almost identical architecturally but as different as chalk and cheese in other respects. Everything here was just so. The decor had been lovingly assembled. There were even lampshades suspended from the ceiling, and vases with flowers in them, and a proper bed, and everything was clean and tidy. The few but elegant pieces of furniture went well together, and the books were neatly arranged in a bookcase worthy of the name. She's in command of her own life, thought Herr Lehmann, and he found that notion not only fascinating but slightly disheartening. Whenever he tried to imagine living with her, he was struck by the contrast between their respective lives: hers, which had or at least tried to have some meaning and purpose, a well-ordered existence with many important facets; and his, in which none of these things played a role. He couldn't have said where its meaning and purpose resided – and, just to make matters worse, the question didn't interest him in the least.

He put something on and went over to the bookcase to inspect her reading matter. It was just what it should have been: books on design and designers, art books, exhibition catalogues, and a few novels and collections of stories by those German and American authors whom everyone read if they read anything at all. They all went well together somehow, and he found that perturbing.

A scent of fried potatoes drifted in from the kitchen. Perhaps she always saves her left-over boiled potatoes with a view to frying them later, thought Herr Lehmann, and the idea pleased him because that was what he himself always did when he cooked for once and potatoes were involved, except that this hardly ever happened because he seldom did any cooking and potatoes were seldom involved, and, even if they were, the ones he'd saved turned mouldy in the refrigerator as the days went by, and sooner or later he threw them away and resolved not to save any in the future. On removing a couple of big art books from the bookcase, he found, nestling in the space behind them, some garish, well-thumbed paperbacks with gold-embossed lettering on the covers. They were romances. 'Bruce Atkinson is a successful man, tall, well-built and in the prime of life,' Herr Lehmann read on the back of one of them. 'He has everything a man could desire: a wonderful job, a luxurious residence in Santa Monica, and a yacht in a Palm Beach marina. No one would suspect that he has been haunted by dark thoughts of suicide since his wife's death two years ago. Then Sandra comes into his life, a young, vital woman with a dark secret of her own . . .' Herr Lehmann heard Katrin coming and replaced the books in a hurry. He felt immensely relieved.

'Where do you want to eat,' she asked, 'in bed or in the kitchen?' She had a plate in each hand.

'In bed,' he said. 'At this hour, I'd say in bed.'

She laughed. 'Yes, it's late. What time will you have to leave?'

'I won't, actually,' he said. 'I never start work till the evening.'

'I'm on duty at the *Markthalle* tomorrow morning, but you can stay here.'

'Yes,' he said, rather surprised. She handed him his plate and they ate in bed. It was a kind of farmer's breakfast, and very good. She wasn't offended when he asked for some ketchup, just sent him off to the kitchen. 'Bring the Turkish stuff,' she told him. 'It's the best, it's really spicy.'

Katrin set her alarm clock when they'd finished, then lay in his arms for a while with one leg draped across him. All that now lit the room was the TV's flickering glow. Herr Lehmann was already dozing off when he suddenly noticed she was weeping.

'Hey, what's the matter?' he asked tenderly.

'You're a wonderful person, Frank,' she said between two sobs. 'Really you are. A wonderful lover too, honestly. But . . .' She sniffed and sat up.

'But what?'

'Somehow . . . I don't know why, but I feel it's bound to go wrong. I think you're expecting a bit too much, maybe.'

'I wasn't even expecting something to eat. Looked at from that angle——'

'Maybe we should try it, the two of us,' she said. 'But would it work?'

'Sure it would,' said Herr Lehmann. 'Why wouldn't it?'

'Because you're so different. And because you don't save potatoes.'

'That doesn't matter,' he said.

'Yes, it does!' she shouted, punching him. 'It does!'

'Oh shit,' he said, and woke up. A news broadcast on the TV was featuring demonstrations of some kind. Katrin lay on her back beside him, snoring gently.

That's all right, then, he thought, and fell asleep again.

10 THE KUDAMM

SOME WEEKS LATER, when Herr Lehmann got to Wittenberg-platz, where he maintained that the Kurfürstendamm began, although at that point it was still called Tauenzienstrasse, his spirits were at a low ebb. He was on the way to see his parents, who were waiting for him at their Kudamm hotel. It didn't matter too much that he was rather hung-over and had slept very little; that was a normal problem. No, what mattered was that he had been compelled to leave Katrin asleep in bed, and that had hit him hard because he didn't see her as often as he would have wished and was invited to spend the night with her less often still, and he'd have liked to spend the morning with her as well. 'Pity,' she'd said when he told her he had to go out early to visit his parents in the Kudamm. 'We might have been able to do something together in the morning,' she'd added, but not with any real regret. Herr Lehmann, who regretted it very much, had – not for the first time – pricked up his ears at this, and he would gladly have spent the trip from Görlitzer Bahnhof subway station to Wittenbergplatz subway station debating what on earth he could do to transform Katrin and himself into genuine lovers and not just participants in a casual affair, which was what they'd really been for some weeks. It was as if nothing at all had happened between them, which Herr Lehmann found almost worse. After all, he'd briefly reflected in the subway train from Görlitzer Bahnhof to Wittenbergplatz, who likes to starve with a well-stocked refrigerator within reach? But he promptly discarded that metaphor. It's an unromantic way of looking it, he told himself, and was forced to concentrate once more on other matters.

Because everything was going wrong on other fronts as well. He hadn't had time to buy a subway ticket because the train was pulling in just as he got to Görlitzer Bahnhof, which meant that he'd been compelled to travel without one, and that he thoroughly disliked. He was always unlucky on such occasions and already had one minor conviction for evading payment, but he'd had to board the train at once, it being essential for him to get there on time, not because his parents would have minded his being late, as they naturally would have, but because he was always on time. He hated being late, he hated it even more than travelling illegally, and he hated it even more when other people were late, not that it really mattered to him. What mattered was to be punctual himself, and he always was. So he'd had to board the train at once, even though it was early – too early, strictly speaking, because he'd got to Görlitzer Bahnhof just before ten and his parents weren't expecting him until eleven. That gave him plenty of time to get to the Kudamm, even by way of Line No. 1, which in his opinion was a rotten line, unbearably slow and crowded with psychopaths and nutters who jostled him even more unpleasantly than usual today, of all days, when he not only had a hangover but was bound for the Kudamm, of all places. Travelling without a ticket made him nervous. He'd promised himself never, never again to be humiliated by those intolerably loquacious men in ill-fitting uniforms who periodically blocked the station exits or threaded their way through jam-packed subway trains travelling at a snail's pace, checking tickets, and if he hadn't cherished an even greater loathing for Berlin's equally loquacious, tabloid-reading, topographically ignorant and inefficient cab drivers, he would happily have spared himself the tribulations of the subway system by taking a cab.

When he finally reached Wittenbergplatz and, thus, what he considered to be the mouth of the Kurfürstendamm, he got out and emerged as quickly as possible from the subterranean crush into the open air, be it only the air of Wittenbergplatz. This was where the horrors of the Kudamm began, and where you could already obtain a one-mark bus ticket that would take you along that thoroughfare. He crossed the street and joined the queue at the bus stop, which was, as usual, thronged with the kind of people who were always – for reasons that surpassed his comprehension – attracted to the Kudamm in droves on Saturdays.

A bus came along at once. It was pretty full, and he dreaded the prospect of travelling in such a crowded vehicle, but it never came to that because, just as he was about to get in, the driver waved him away with a peremptory gesture and shut the door. Looking at the nearest clock, Herr Lehmann saw that it was twenty past ten. There's still time, he thought, and settled down to wait for the next bus. He had to get to the Kudamm-Schlüterstrasse intersection. It's not that far, he told himself, at a pinch I could walk it, and he found that thought very comforting. He knew precisely where he had to go, fortunately, having checked the location of his parents' hotel with the aid of the Yellow Pages and a street map. He had also phoned the hotel for safety's sake, because one never knew, and the Kudamm was as long as it was unattractive. Then the next bus came along and he climbed aboard, but the driver refused to accept his twenty-mark note.

'You'll get nothing from me for that,' said the driver. 'I don't have to give change for twenty marks.'

'It's perfectly good money,' said Herr Lehmann. 'Twenty Bundesbank marks.'

'I don't have to give change for it.'

'Who says?'

'The public transport regulations. All right, either produce some small change or get off.'

'But the public transport regulations also state that, if you can't give me change, you must give me a receipt for the balance, which I can cash at the depot,' said Herr Lehmann, who had once whiled away a bout of acute boredom at Möckernbrücke subway station by reading the Berlin public transport regulations from beginning to end.

'I don't have time for that,' said the driver. 'It's small change or nothing.'

'You're violating your own public transport regulations,' said Herr Lehmann.

The bus driver turned off the engine and folded his arms. 'I've got time. If you don't get off at once I'll call the police.'

'But you just said you *didn't* have time. So what happens now?'

'Off, or I'll call the police.'

Complaints began to issue from the interior of the bus. 'Get rid of the silly bugger!' and 'We haven't got all day!'

This is pointless, thought Herr Lehmann, there's no defence against stupidity. Besides, it occurred to him just in time that his ban on using public transport was still in force, so it wouldn't, however legally impeccable his case, be wise to fight it to a finish.

'Shall I tell you what you are?' he called when he was outside.

'No,' said the driver. He shut the door and drove off.

'You're a monumental asshole!' Herr Lehmann shouted over the hiss of the pneumatic door, but it didn't achieve much.

He might have known it. Even now he wasn't in the Kudamm proper, just in Wittenbergplatz, and the shit had already started to hit the fan. He toyed with the idea of changing some money somewhere, or of taking the No. 3 subway train to Uhlandstrasse, but he promptly dismissed it. There was something terribly wrong with Berlin's public transport system. It was five minutes before half past ten. If I walk fast, he told himself, I can still get to the hotel in time. A good thing I was so early, he thought, and set off. He'd really been hoping to relax on the way to see his parents, if not thereafter. He'd pictured himself arriving at the hotel too early, taking in a coffee somewhere nearby, and then, on the stroke of eleven, strolling casually into the hotel's breakfast room, where his parents would be eagerly awaiting him, because he was just as averse to being too early and knew when to slow down.

But he also knew when to put on speed, so he hurried down Tauenzienstrasse. It was difficult, if not fundamentally impossible, to proceed any faster than the rest of humanity, who seemed to have gathered in Tauenzienstrasse en masse for the purpose of exasperating him with their sluggish rate of progress. He broke out in a sweat and swore under his breath as he skipped to and fro between his fellow mortals, evaded obstructive groups of strolling, rubbernecking, chattering tourists who always walked seven abreast at least, swerved around old ladies in fur coats, and blundered into huge, unpredictable gaggles of youngsters who abruptly halted or changed direction just as he endeavoured to overtake them. There were a lot of these youngsters, and Herr Lehmann noticed despite his haste that most of them were wearing identical tracksuits emblazoned on the back with the words 'German Gymnastics Festival – Berlin 1989', a circumstance that did nothing to improve his mood. If their gymnastics are anything like the way they walk, he thought grimly, the German

Gymnastics Festival may as well shut up shop right now. They'll all fall off the asymmetric bars, they couldn't even play leapfrog, they're all on the pill, they're all on dope, but the wrong kind, thought Herr Lehmann. By the time he got to Breitscheidplatz, his nerves were in shreds.

I can't go on like this, he thought, I'll have to take a bus or there'll be mass murder. He found a kiosk, bought some cigarettes, and paused to smoke one. This not only provided him with some small change but enabled him, while smoking with far more aplomb than he'd displayed when he started four weeks ago at Katrin's place, to think of her in peace and of how good it was with her in spite of everything – or could be, at least. He had kissed her before leaving, and she'd given a contented little grunt in her sleep, which had heartened him. A coffee would go down well now, he thought, but he couldn't see any realistic possibility of getting one quickly. It was twenty-five to eleven when he stubbed out his cigarette and stationed himself at the bus stop in Breitscheidplatz. This time the boarding operation went smoothly and he got his Kudamm ticket.

'But it's only valid as far as Adenauerplatz,' the driver couldn't resist calling after him.

'Yes, yes,' Herr Lehmann said grumpily, refusing to be provoked although he felt like adding that it was a goddamned public rip-off because the Kudamm extended well beyond Adenauerplatz, so why was the damned thing called a Kudamm ticket or whatever? – but by this time he didn't care. The lower deck was chock-full, so he went upstairs, where he had to walk along at a crouch in search of a non-existent empty seat, and where he also felt sick because the bus had moved off and was lurching around. Aware that standing on the upper deck was prohibited, Herr Lehmann made his way to the stairs at the rear, but other passengers were already occupying them, so he was compelled to maintain his crouching stance until the bus stopped at Joachimsthaler Strasse and he could at last descend the stairs. Promptly sluiced out on to the pavement by exiting passengers who shoved him in the back, he waited until they'd all got off and then got in again.

'You there,' came a voice from the loudspeaker, 'board the bus at the front.' Herr Lehmann couldn't take it in.

'I'm not moving till you get off,' the voice announced. 'Board the bus at the front.'

By now past caring, Herr Lehmann got off and made his way to the front. When he showed the driver his Kudamm ticket, the man shook his head.

'It's only valid for one journey,' he said.

'But I just bought it from you.'

'That's your story.'

'But I only got out for a moment to make way for the others. I was here on board the bus. I only just bought this ticket from you.'

'Anyone could say that. One mark.'

Herr Lehmann had had enough. Time to play a different tune, he thought grimly. Time to clear the decks and make a clean sweep, fun's over. He smiled at the driver and deposited his ticket on the little cash desk.

'There you are, my good man,' he said.

'What is it now?'

'Well,' Herr Lehmann said amiably, 'I don't have any further use for your nice ticket, if you'd kindly dispose of it. A new one will cost me another mark, correct?'

The driver nodded. 'One mark.'

'Here are two, my good man,' said Herr Lehmann, putting a two-mark coin beside the old ticket. 'Take them and have a nice day. No,' he went on, raising his hand, 'I don't want any more of your tickets, thanks all the same.'

So saying, Herr Lehmann got off the bus. He turned and waved to the driver. 'You've more than earned the two marks,' he called genially. 'You're a brilliant strategist. Now drive on, you don't have all day.'

The driver stared at the money and at Herr Lehmann in turn, groping for words. This delighted Herr Lehmann, who made a gesture of dismissal. 'Chop-chop,' he called. He left the man and his bus standing there and walked on in a better mood.

The battle wasn't lost yet, but time was getting short. The clock across the way said twenty to eleven. Herr Lehmann crossed Joachimsthaler Strasse, firmly resolved not to allow his better mood to be spoiled by the sight of the Café Kranzler, which to him symbolised all that made the Kurfürstendamm so intolerable. He strode swiftly along the extreme outer edge of the pavement, where dogshit proliferated and no one else cared to tread, and made for his destination past hotels and motor show-rooms, steak houses and cafés, souvenir stalls and kitsch shops, thimbleriggers and three-card tricksters. His victory over the bus driver had bred a sense of euphoria. More than that, he felt confident of making it to his parents' hotel not only punctually but even, perhaps, with a minute or two in hand. This isn't such a bad day after all, he reflected, and he devoted the time to thinking a bit more positively about Katrin and recalling what she looked like in the nude.

Then he saw the dog. Somewhere between Knesebeckstrasse and Bleibtreustrasse, the door of a jeweller's opened and the dog came tumbling out on to the pavement, yowling, presumably because someone had kicked it. Although Herr Lehmann didn't actually see this, the animal's hindquarters slewed round in a funny way as it landed among the old ladies window-shopping outside. No sooner had the dog scrambled to its feet than it looked Herr Lehmann in the eye. Why me, he thought, coming to a stop, why me? Undeniably the same dog he'd encountered in Lausitzer Platz, it propelled its fat, sausage-shaped form in his direction. Herr Lehmann prepared to call for help – there may be some cops around, he thought, they're always patrolling the area because of the thimbleriggers and so on – but the dog was already at his side. It sat down and looked at him.

'Not again,' he said softly, 'not again.'

But the dog didn't growl, it just looked at him placidly with its head on one side – a posture which in any other dog would have made a cute, friendly impression.

'Out of luck today, huh?' said Herr Lehmann.

The dog cocked its head at a different angle and emitted a whimpering sound.

'Well,' said Herr Lehmann, 'got to press on. I'm in a hurry.'

He slowly walked off. The dog did absolutely nothing. After a few steps he turned to look. It was simply sitting there, staring at him.

'Sorry,' he called, 'I'm in a hurry.' A look at the nearest clock told him it was eight minutes to eleven, so he knew he could still make it.

11 THE HOTEL LOBBY

'BUT YOU'RE SWEATING, Frank. And in this awful weather, too. You'll catch your death.'

'Yes,' said Herr Lehmann, flopping down in an armchair. 'I had to run, the bus didn't come.'

'So that's why you're in this state. You pong a bit, too.'

His parents weren't in the breakfast room, which made sense somehow, because they'd only set off that morning. Instead, they were sitting in their overcoats – his father was even wearing a hat – amid the garish cushions and rattan furniture in the hotel lobby. They looked as forlorn as two refugees hoping to catch the last train to the West. Herr Lehmann, who hadn't seen them for a long time, had trouble remembering the last occasion. He'd missed last Christmas, so it must have been his father's sixtieth birthday, and that was eighteen months ago.

'Did you have a good trip?'

'Well,' his father said with a smile. Herr Lehmann noticed how grey his hair had gone, though it suited him. He'd lost weight, too, but he was looking tired. 'Depends how you look at it. We've been up since half past three.'

'They took ages to pick up the rest of the party,' said his mother. 'We had to trail all the way across Bremen, when the autobahn's only a stone's throw from home. As for those GDR border guards, checking on every last thing . . . Really terrible, the time it took . . .'

'Maybe I should get us some coffee,' Herr Lehmann suggested. 'Would you like some?' They both nodded.

'White for me,' said his father.

Herr Lehmann went over to the reception desk. They wouldn't have had any coffee once upon a time, he thought, not in a million years. They're going soft. 'Can we get some coffee here?' he asked the woman at the desk.

She replied in the negative but said she could send out for some coffees from next door. Herr Lehmann, who promptly took to the woman because her response and general manner were so completely unlike the Kudamm, ordered three coffees and went back to his parents.

'You really do pong a bit,' his mother said when he sat down again.

'I'm sorry,' said Herr Lehmann, who hadn't showered that morning and was still wearing the clothes he'd worn last night at the *Einfall*. 'It must be because I'm sweating. I had to do some work first, and everything went wrong on the way. But why are you sitting in the lobby – I mean, all dressed up and so on?' he asked, changing the subject. 'Why not up in your room?'

'It wasn't worth it,' his father said with a gesture of resignation. 'Anyway, our room is no great shakes.'

'Maybe not,' said his mother, 'but it isn't expensive. The whole thing, here and back in the coach and the overnight accommodation, all for a hundred marks – fantastic. Then there's the sight-seeing tour as well.'

'That starts at midday,' his father amplified with a faint smile. 'We can't miss that, of course.'

'What sight-seeing tour?' said Herr Lehmann.

'Like I told you,' said his mother. 'It's all thrown in – takes three hours.'

'So you'll be off again almost at once,' said Herr Lehmann, who didn't know whether to feel relieved or piqued.

'I thought you'd be coming with us,' said his mother. 'That would be lovely.'

'Well,' said Herr Lehmann, inwardly shuddering at the idea. 'Sight-seeing tours aren't really my—'

'He knows it all,' his father interrupted. 'He's been living here so long. I wouldn't go on a sight-seeing tour of Bremen.'

'Why not? It could be interesting.'

'Well, I don't know,' said Herr Lehmann, panic-stricken at the thought of lurching through the city in a double-decker bus on a tour of Checkpoint Charlie and similar delights. 'It's more for tourists and visitors et cetera.'

'Don't badger the boy,' said his father. 'He doesn't need to come.'

'Surely we can do something together for once?' his mother said stubbornly.

Looking at her, Herr Lehmann felt as indefinably sad as he always did, sooner or later, whenever he saw his parents. She wants things to be the way they used to be, he thought. 'But we'll be having dinner together this evening,' he said. 'I've reserved a table for us specially. Then you can see the restaurant where I work.'

'This evening?' his mother said. She sounded puzzled. 'But there's the variety show.'

'What variety show?' Herr Lehmann's mood abruptly changed.

'Stop asking silly questions,' said his mother. 'You can't come with us, I'm afraid, it's only for the coach party. The seats are all reserved in advance – it's a block booking and all that.'

'Just a minute,' said Herr Lehmann, no longer sure if he'd

gauged her feelings correctly. 'We discussed your visit on the phone more than once. You were absolutely set on seeing where I work – you wanted to have a meal there with me, so what's all this about a variety show?'

'He's right, Martha,' said his father. 'I told you so. That was the arrangement.'

'This evening?'

'Yes, of course, we leave tomorrow evening.'

'I'd completely forgotten.'

'He's booked a table, so that settles it. We must go,' his father said firmly. 'Anyway, Frank, how are things?'

'Pretty good,' said Herr Lehmann.

'Yes, of course we can go and have a meal together,' said his mother, 'it's better that way. We'll forget about the show, then.'

'How's the firm doing?'

'I only thought, if it's all included . . .'

Herr Lehmann's father made the gesture of resignation he'd noticed before. It was new. 'Everything's so different these days – you wouldn't recognise the place. A lot of people have left.'

Herr Lehmann, who had trained as a forwarding agent in the firm where his father had worked for forty years, gave a knowing nod. 'Times have changed, eh?'

His father, who was sitting by himself in a two-seater, draped his arms over the back and nodded likewise. 'They've just offered me early retirement.'

'And? Are you taking it?'

'No fear.' His father glanced briefly at his wife. 'I'm not insane.'

'I'd have him under my feet all day long,' said Herr Lehmann's mother. 'You need time to get used to these things.'

'I'll only be working twenty-five hours a week before long. We'll see . . .'

'Well,' said Herr Lehmann, to whom all this sounded like

information beamed from another planet, 'at least that's better than forty.'

At that moment a smartly dressed waiter entered the lobby bearing a large silver tray. He looked inquiringly at the receptionist, who pointed to Herr Lehmann, and then came over to them.

'Three coffees,' said the man. 'Were they for you?'

'Yes, yes,' Herr Lehmann said, gratified. Very classy, he thought, and quickly appropriated the bill while the waiter was still manoeuvring the tray on to the low table. He didn't want his mother seeing what sort of prices they charged here.

'There you go,' said the waiter, making some final adjustments to the contents of his tray: three coffee pots of solid silver, Herr Lehmann was quick to note, plus three good or good-looking china cups and saucers, three silver spoons, a sugar bowl equipped with tongs, and a small cream jug. Maybe the Kudamm isn't so bad after all, he reflected.

'That looks nice,' his mother said happily.

The waiter, a dapper, tanned young man, looked equally nice. He gave them an amiable smile, and Herr Lehmann tipped him liberally. Meantime, his parents were busying themselves with the cream and sugar. Herr Lehmann took his coffee black.

'But Frank,' his mother exclaimed, 'since when have you smoked?'

'I don't smoke often,' said Herr Lehmann. 'Only when I'm drinking coffee.'

'Anyway,' said his father, 'we'll be eating with him tonight. That's much nicer. Who needs that variety show rubbish?'

'Except that you don't get it anywhere else,' said his mother. 'It's with transvestites and suchlike.'

'What do you mean, transvestites?' Herr Lehmann demanded. 'I thought you said Harald Juhnke was in it.'

'Harald Juhnke?' His mother looked puzzled. 'What's he got to do with transvestites?'

His father laughed.

'You told me on the phone it was something with Harald Juhnke in it.'

'Oh, that,' said his mother. 'No, it's with transvestites.'

'By the way,' said his father, 'someone sends their regards: Frau Brandt.'

'Who's Frau Brandt?'

'Oh yes, she used to be . . . One moment, yes, she used to be Fräulein Dormann, that's it. She remembers you from the old days – works in the accounts department.'

'Oh,' said Herr Lehmann, whose principal memory of Fräulein Dormann was of losing his virginity to her. 'You mean she's still with the firm?'

'Yes, yes, she's married now. No children, though.'

Herr Lehmann cast a suspicious glance at his father, who was again wearing that faint smile. He's an enigma – I probably underestimate him all the time, he reflected, and there was something comforting about the thought.

'What good coffee this is,' said his mother. She turned to her husband. 'And the boy paid for it. It's come to that already.'

'Many thanks, Frank,' his father said. 'Nice of you.'

'Yes, really nice,' said his mother.

Herr Lehmann felt uncomfortable. He didn't want his parents to feel they had to thank him, it seemed wrong somehow.

'Have you got a girlfriend at the moment?'

'Stop that, Martha,' said his father, and turned to Herr Lehmann. 'She's been bending my ear all the way from Helmstedt: I wonder if he's got a girlfriend, I wonder if he'll introduce her to us . . .'

'What's so wrong with that? It isn't as if he's the other way inclined.'

'Nobody said he was.'

'Did *I*, then?'

'I didn't say that, but you started it.'

'We might ask him sometime, that's all I meant.'

'No, it's out of order.'

'Please don't argue,' said Herr Lehmann, who had noticed that the lobby was steadily filling up with people, all of them around his parents' age. From this he inferred that midday was approaching and the sight-seeing tour was imminent. He seized the initiative.

'Listen,' he said, 'I think I'll give the sight-seeing tour a miss if you're coming to have dinner with me. It's at my restaurant – the one I manage, at least.' My God, he thought, how stilted that sounds, they must think I'm cracked. 'Besides, that was what we arranged.'

'You're right,' said his mother.

His father nodded. 'I'd like to have a bit of a lie-down before then. This sight-seeing tour will finish me. The last thing I need is a nice bus ride.'

'I've booked the table for eight.'

'So late?' said his mother. 'A hot meal at that hour?'

'Now stop it,' said his father. 'We don't eat any earlier at home.'

'Of course we do, supper's always over by news time.'

'Yes, but we don't live in Berlin.'

'That's true.'

Herr Lehmann sighed. 'I'll write down the address for you.' He went to the reception desk and asked for a pencil and paper. The woman behind it smiled at him in a way that gave him gooseflesh. The Kudamm does have its points, he thought as he rejoined his parents.

'Here's the address,' he said, putting the slip of paper on the table. 'It's in Kreuzberg.'

'Oh dear,' said his mother, 'what if there's a riot?'

'Don't be silly,' said his father. 'That was years ago.'

'These things can happen any time,' his mother said with a knowing air.

'Yes, you're right,' Herr Lehmann said brutally. 'But look at it this way: Kreuzberg covers a wide area. The chances of your running into a riot are pretty remote.'

'If you say so.'

'Just tell the cabby the address and everything'll be fine.'

The lobby was really full now, and Herr Lehmann couldn't shake off the unpleasant feeling that they were being watched by the other members of the coach party. They aren't used to people knowing someone someplace they've gone on a coach, he thought. They now regard my parents as experts. With a failure for a son. But with coffee.

'Fancy you smoking so much!'

'Let the boy smoke if he wants to.'

'You'll pick up a taxi anywhere.'

'Don't worry,' said his father, 'it won't be the first time we've taken a taxi.'

They lapsed into silence for a while. Herr Lehmann noticed that his parents were getting fidgety, so presumably the bus was going soon. His father looked at the clock.

'What time is it?' asked Herr Lehmann.

'Twenty to,' said his father.

'Sorry I'm not coming with you,' said Herr Lehmann, 'but it really isn't my scene.'

'Forget it,' said his father. 'I wouldn't come either.'

'They show you everything,' his mother said helplessly. 'We shouldn't miss the opportunity.'

'All right, we'll take a look at it all,' said his father. 'You'll see,' he went on, patting his wife on the knee, 'we'll know more 'about Berlin than Frank and his brother combined.'

'How is he, by the way?' asked Herr Lehmann.

'Ah, Manfred,' said his mother. 'I wonder how happy he is, over there in New York . . .'

'He may be coming for Christmas,' said his father.

'Will you be coming for Christmas too?' asked his mother. 'I mean, if Manfred comes over?'

'Of course,' said Herr Lehmann.

'I think it's time,' said his father. The people round about had stopped staring at them and were crowding towards the exit. His parents rose. So did he.

'Eight o'clock, okay?' he said. 'I'm relying on you.'

'You can, you can,' said his father. His mother put her arms round him. 'I still haven't really said hello,' she said, giving him a hug, 'and now we're going our separate ways again.'

'We'll be seeing each other this evening,' Herr Lehmann reminded her.

'Sure thing,' said his father, patting him on the shoulder.

Herr Lehmann allowed his parents and their fellow tourists to go on ahead. Then, after a lingering, reciprocated look at the woman behind the reception desk, who gave him a parting smile, he went out into the street himself. His mother, seated at a window on the upper deck of the bus, tapped on the glass and waved as he walked past.

Herr Lehmann waved back, feeling suddenly sad that he wasn't going too. It wasn't that he had any desire to see Checkpoint Charlie and the Brandenburg Gate and the Wall and whatever else was on offer, but still, he felt sad somehow. I'm getting soft, he told himself, and lit a cigarette before crossing the street to the nearest bus stop.

12 THE BANQUET

WHEN HERR LEHMANN walked into the *Markthalle* at eight o'clock precisely, his parents were already there. Seated at a good table not too near the kitchen, not too near the toilets, and not too near the entrance, they were chatting animatedly with his best friend Karl, who seemed to have primped himself for the occasion. He was wearing a second- or third-hand dark suit far too big even for him – Herr Lehmann had never seen it before – together with a white shirt and a bow tie. He looked quite grotesque, like a monstrous spin-dried penguin. Herr Lehmann felt tempted to turn and run.

'Ah, there he is,' said his mother when he came over to the table.

'Hello, boss,' said his best friend Karl, shaking hands.

'Cut it out,' Herr Lehmann said acidly, and sat down.

'We wondered where you'd got to,' said his mother.

'It's spot on eight,' Herr Lehmann retorted. 'You were early.'

'The taxi drove so fast.'

'How was the sight-seeing tour?'

'Tiring,' said his father.

'The sight of that Wall . . .' his mother said, shaking her head sadly.

'Here's the menu, boss,' Karl broke in, handing it to him. His

145

parents already had theirs. Karl proceeded to light a candle, the only one in the entire establishment. Herr Lehmann, who noticed that Karl's fingernails were dirty, wondered if this had struck him only now, in his pseudo-managerial capacity, or whether his best friend was letting himself go.

'No need to say "boss",' he said. 'These are my parents, by the way, and this is Karl Schmidt.'

'We know,' said his mother. 'We've been having a nice chat.'

'That's good,' said Herr Lehmann. He surveyed the menu. 'What would you like to drink?'

'We've ordered already,' said his mother. 'Herr Schmidt recommended something.'

Herr Lehmann looked round inquiringly at his best friend Karl, who was standing just behind him, his massive form blotting out the light. Karl grinned. 'I recommended a bottle of the best, boss.'

'The best what?' Herr Lehmann was getting annoyed. He had no objection to a little fun, but this wasn't subtle, it was laid on with a trowel.

'The red.' Karl winked with his right eye. 'The one there's hardly any left of. The 'eighty-five.'

'Oh, that,' said Herr Lehmann. 'All right, and let's have some mineral water as well.' He turned to his parents. 'What about food? Have you chosen yet?'

'No,' his father said irritably, 'we haven't had time.'

'I'll go and decant the wine,' said Karl, and disappeared.

'Nice young man,' said Herr Lehmann's mother. 'What would you recommend?'

'The roast pork is good.'

'Roast pork? I can cook roast pork myself. Isn't there anything more exciting?'

'This restaurant is famous for its roast pork,' Herr Lehmann said sternly. 'People come here from all over the city, just to eat our roast pork. You won't find better roast pork anywhere.'

'Yes, but roast pork . . .' His mother laughed. 'They might as well come to me.'

'Our roast pork is first-class. Alternatively,' he said, trying to regain the initiative, 'have some fish. There!' He reached across the table and indicated the fish section on his mother's menu. 'Trout, cod, sea bream, the works. Or,' he added maliciously, 'have something vegetarian, mother.'

'I think I'll have the pork,' said his father.

'So will I,' said Herr Lehmann.

'I will too, then,' said his mother. 'I think. I don't know a thing about vegetarian dishes.'

'How about a nut cutlet with curry sauce?' Herr Lehmann suggested.

'No, no, if you say the roast pork—'

'Here we are,' Karl butted in. He bent over, his open jacket billowing around in Herr Lehmann's face, and deposited a bottle of red wine on the table. 'This is a very, very nice drop of stuff.'

'Glasses, water,' said Herr Lehmann.

'Right away, boss,' said Karl, and disappeared again.

'Hm,' his father put in, 'this hasn't been decanted. It isn't an 'eighty-five, either.'

Herr Lehmann felt tempted to ask his father how long he'd been an expert on wine, but he managed to restrain himself. Karl returned with the glasses and water.

'Is the roast pork good?' Herr Lehmann's mother asked him.

'Good isn't the word,' Karl replied. 'It's a dream – everyone says so.'

'Does it come with crackling?'

'One moment,' said Karl, and went off again. Watching him disappear into the kitchen, Herr Lehmann had a nasty premonition. Sure enough, he emerged with Katrin at his heels.

Katrin came over to the table. 'May I help you?' she inquired.

'Does the roast pork come with crackling?' asked Herr Lehmann's mother.

'With crackling? Of course it does.'

'Why of course? I never make crackling, it's too much trouble.'

'You're right,' Katrin said with a smile. 'Crackling is generally overrated.'

'This is Katrin Warmers, by the way,' said Herr Lehmann, 'our chef. And these are my parents.'

'Your son is a really great expert on roast pork,' Katrin said earnestly.

'Won't you join us?' said Herr Lehmann's mother, pulling up a chair from the next table. My parents would make great Kreuzbergers, thought Herr Lehmann. It had never occurred to him before.

'I don't have much time, though.' Katrin sat down beside his mother and brushed a strand of hair out of her eyes.

'I never make crackling,' his mother resumed.

'Neither would I, for choice,' said Katrin. Herr Lehmann, who wasn't sure of the nature and extent of the embarrassment he should be feeling at all this, decided to relax. He poured the red wine.

'I'll have a drop too,' said Katrin.

Karl, who was hovering nearby, listening, darted forward with another glass.

'Can you be spared from the kitchen for so long?' asked Herr Lehmann's mother.

'When the boss is involved,' Karl put in.

Herr Lehmann drained his glass in a hurry and promptly refilled it. Alcohol was the only answer.

'In that case,' said his mother.

'If I don't make crackling, half the customers complain they want it,' said Katrin, looking at Herr Lehmann as she spoke. 'You've no idea what a fuss they make sometimes.'

'You poor dear,' said Herr Lehmann's mother, patting her arm. 'I can well imagine. It can't be easy, cooking for a bunch of total strangers.'

'The roast pork people are the worst,' said Katrin.

'Oh my, I shouldn't have asked!'

'No, no, you're welcome.'

'Can I take your orders now?' Karl was still hovering.

'What's the point?' Herr Lehmann demanded belligerently. 'What do you plan to do with them, take them to the kitchen? Is there anyone there at the moment?'

'I'm only doing things by the book. After all, boss, that's your cast-iron rule.'

'As he's always telling us,' Katrin confirmed.

'Well then,' said Herr Lehmann's mother, 'I'll have the roast pork.'

'So will I,' said his father.

'Roast pork for three,' said Herr Lehmann. 'Complete with overrated crackling.'

'I always stud my pork with cloves of garlic,' said his mother.

'I do too,' said Katrin. 'That's far more important than crackling.'

Herr Lehmann clinked glasses with his father. Meanwhile, the woman he loved and the woman who was his mother immersed themselves in a detailed discussion of garlic and all the dishes it went with.

'Is business always so slack?' asked Herr Lehmann's father.

'No, it doesn't really get busy till later,' Herr Lehmann told him. 'The place is bursting at the seams by nine.'

'But they don't all eat,' said his father.

'No,' he conceded. He'd just noticed that Kristall Rainer had settled down at the bar. 'And even if they do, it's the booze that makes the real money.'

'I thought as much,' said his father. 'Well,' he added, 'drinking never goes out of fashion. From that point of view, you're on to a good thing here.'

'Right,' said Katrin, rising, 'I'd better go back to the kitchen.'

'It was nice talking to you,' said Herr Lehmann's mother.

'Your son,' Katrin repeated, 'is a really great expert. On everything.' And she went.

'What did she mean?' Herr Lehmann's mother asked him.

'No idea,' he said. 'I sometimes think I ought to fire them all.'

'I don't know about restaurant,' said his mother, leaning forward for a better look at the premises. 'It looks more like a bar to me. They aren't all eating – far from it.'

'You can't force people to eat.' Wine, especially when drunk quickly, tended to make Herr Lehmann rather silly. 'Besides,' he added, 'alcohol has a high calorific value.'

'Hi there!' His best friend Karl had reappeared. He put a basketful of bread and a little pot of dripping on the table. 'Here's something to nibble. Put plenty of salt on it. Remember your electrolytes.'

'A really nice young man, that,' said Herr Lehmann's mother, staring after him. 'A bit odd, though. Is he all there?'

'Hard to say,' said Herr Lehmann. 'How was the sight-seeing tour?'

'Terrible.' His mother tucked into the bread. 'I don't know how you can live here, with that frightful Wall all around you. It's really terrible. I couldn't stand it.'

'It's not that bad, not for us. We can always get out.'

'But one feels so completely shut in.'

'Nonsense.' Herr Lehmann didn't feel like this Wall crap. It was always the same when outsiders visited Berlin. 'If a street in Bremen ends in a wall, you don't immediately think: Oh dear, I'm shut in.'

'That's quite different.'

'Yes, but it's the others who have the problem, the ones in East Berlin. The purpose of the thing isn't to stop us getting out, it's to stop them getting in. Except, of course, that they would regard it as getting out.'

'Yes,' said his mother. 'They'd all like to get out, from the sound of it.'

'It's tough, what's going on there at present,' said his father. 'The whole place is falling apart.'

'True,' said Herr Lehmann, 'but it doesn't have any bearing on life in West Berlin. We aren't affected in the least.'

'Well, I couldn't live here,' his mother insisted. 'I'd feel completely shut in.'

And so it went on until the arrival of the roast pork, which Karl served in a surprisingly civilised manner and without any fooling around. This was probably related to the fact that Erwin had appeared and exchanged a few words with him before sitting down at the bar as far away as possible from Kristall Rainer.

'It's really good, this roast pork,' said Herr Lehmann's mother.

'Yes, very good,' said his father. 'There aren't many restaurants that serve good roast pork.'

'I told you so,' said Herr Lehmann.

'Do they pay you well?' his father asked. 'You being the manager, I mean,' he added with another of his faint smiles.

Herr Lehmann glanced at him before replying. There was something different about him. He looked tired, but he also made a more knowing impression. Perhaps I really have always underestimated him, thought Herr Lehmann.

'Manager doesn't mean much,' he said.

Karl, who had reappeared, was just putting another bottle of red wine on the table. 'Come, come,' he said as he withdrew.

'It doesn't mean much,' Herr Lehmann repeated. 'I take care of the outside orders, keep the books and so on. It's more of a sideline.'

His mother pricked up her ears. 'What do you mean?'

'I mean,' he said, feeling annoyed – mainly with himself – for having dreamed up this manager story in the first place, 'that I'm really just another guy who stands behind the bar and dishes out drinks. At least it's better than waiting at table and so on.'

'But Frank,' his mother protested, 'no need to get so hot under the collar. It's not my fault you're a barman.'

'I never said it was.'

'You're getting by, that's the main thing,' said his mother. 'Anyway, I think it's lovely here. So much nicer than it usually is in restaurants, where everything's so stiff and formal and you don't feel comfortable. And the people here are all so nice as well.'

'Yes, sure.'

'I think so too,' said his father. 'As long as one's enjoying oneself . . .' He laid his fork aside and topped up the glasses. 'Good wine, this, but it isn't an 'eighty-five.'

'Why does it have to be an 'eighty-five?' said Herr Lehmann, whose mood had suddenly brightened. It's all the same to them, he thought, they don't give a damn what I do. 'I only kept on about me being a manager so you had something to tell Frau Dunekamp,' he said to his mother. 'You told me Frau Dunekamp had asked you what I did, and you didn't know what to say.'

'I didn't, either,' said his mother.

'Enjoying your meal?' asked Erwin, who had materialised beside them.

'This is Erwin Kächele,' said Herr Lehmann. 'Erwin, my parents.'

'Yes, hello there,' said Erwin.

'Erwin owns this place,' said Herr Lehmann.

'Really first-class roast pork,' said his mother. 'The crackling, too.'

'I hate to intrude,' said Erwin, 'but can I have a quick word with you, Herr Lehmann – I mean, when you've finished your meal?'

'Yes, of course,' said Herr Lehmann, feeling rather surprised. 'Be with you right away.'

'How come he calls you "Herr Lehmann" when you call him "Erwin"?' his mother asked. 'It seems odd.'

'I know, mother, I know.'

They went on eating in silence for a while. 'It's good to see you again,' his father said abruptly. 'I don't know exactly what goes on here, but you seem to be doing pretty well.'

'I think so too,' said his mother. 'Nice people, they are.'

'Very nice,' said his father.

'If only it wasn't for the Wall. Which reminds me,' his mother said suddenly, 'there's something we wanted to discuss with you.'

'Just a moment.' Herr Lehmann was feeling rather uneasy about whatever it was that Erwin wanted to speak to him about. He wanted to get it over with, so he rose, picked up his glass of wine and went over to his boss, who was once more seated at the bar drinking mint tea with milk and keeping an unremitting watch on Kristall Rainer. The latter said a friendly hello as Herr Lehmann passed him, so he had no choice but to respond in kind. The man's sudden irruption into his life puzzled him.

'That guy Rainer is starting to get on my nerves,' Erwin said when Herr Lehmann reached him. 'Yes,' said Herr Lehmann, 'mine too.'

'I'd like to know what he's after,' Erwin went on. Herr Lehmann watched him watching Kristall Rainer. Erwin looked kind of old and grouchy, but he always did when he was sober.

'Here, Erwin,' said Heidi, who had suddenly appeared beside them. 'Found this near the trash can. Is it yours?' She was waving a fifty-mark note. Erwin's putting his prices up, thought Herr Lehmann.

'Eh? Yes,' said Erwin, swiftly pocketing it.

'So how's the manager doing?' Heidi asked Herr Lehmann. 'Nice folk, your parents.'

Erwin looked baffled. 'What manager?'

'My lips are sealed,' said Heidi, and walked on.

'You wanted a word with me about something,' Herr Lehmann said.

'Since when have you been a smoker?'

Herr Lehmann looked at the cigarette he'd just lit. 'Get to the point, Erwin.'

'It's Karl,' said Erwin, rubbing his eyes. 'I'm worried about him. Any idea what's the matter with him?'

'Nothing's the matter with him. Karl's okay.'

'I don't know, he's losing his grip, kind of. It can't go on like this.'

'What can't?'

'Oh, hell,' said Erwin. 'Of all the people who still work for me, Karl's been here the longest. Karl and you,' he amended.

Herr Lehmann was perturbed by the turn their conversation was taking. He disliked it when Erwin got confidential.

'How long have we been working together?' Erwin asked.

'I don't know, nine years maybe.' Working together isn't quite the right way of putting it, thought Herr Lehmann, but this wasn't the moment for an excursion into the class struggle. 'Just tell me what's wrong, Erwin. We can always get sentimental later.'

'It's Karl,' Erwin repeated. 'There's something wrong with him. He forgot the deliveries the day before yesterday – he simply wasn't there when they came – and the books haven't added up lately.'

'Karl isn't diddling you, Erwin,' said Herr Lehmann. 'You can forget that for a start.'

'No, I didn't mean that. Boy-oh-boy-oh-boy . . .' Erwin rubbed his eyes again as if his life depended on it. 'I'm worried about him, though – I can't have him running this place any longer. He's going to pieces. All he does is mooch around. I mean, get a load of the way he looks.'

'Oh, you mean the suit,' Herr Lehmann said soothingly. 'He only did that to make me look good in front of my parents – it really isn't important. Or do you think it worries people?'

'I don't give a damn about the suit,' said Erwin, 'although it really does look like shit. But have you seen his fingernails? And half the customers don't have anything to drink because he forgets everything et cetera. You think I don't notice things like that?'

'Come on, Erwin,' Herr Lehmann said for want of a better idea, 'how long have we been working together?' Now *I'm* getting sentimental, he thought. 'You know Karl. He's got a lot on his plate at the moment, with this exhibition in Charlottenburg coming up. It's only natural he's a bit absent-minded.'

'Yes, sure, I thought of that myself,' said Erwin. 'That's all very well, but things can't go on like this. I don't want to give him the boot. I simply wondered if you could look after this place for the next few weeks while he works at the *Einfall*.'

'No, no,' Herr Lehmann said firmly. 'No, it doesn't appeal to me. I mean, it's okay with me if Karl works at the *Einfall* – that's fine – but this manager business isn't my scene. Besides, there are plenty of other people. What about Heidi?' Herr Lehmann caught her eye, and she came over to them again.

'What is it?' she asked.

'I'd like a large beer,' said Herr Lehmann, sliding his wine glass towards her. 'I can't take wine, it goes to my head.'

'Draught?'

'Yes, for once,' said Herr Lehmann. 'But make it a big one.'

'There aren't any big glasses left,' said Heidi, and went off again.

'Heidi won't do,' Erwin said when she was out of earshot. 'She couldn't handle it.'

'Oh, come now, Erwin,' said Herr Lehmann. 'This is the twentieth century.'

'Anyway, I already asked her,' said Erwin. 'She doesn't want to.'

'Then ask Stefan or Sylvio,' Herr Lehmann suggested. 'Let one of them swap with Karl or run the place yourself. Then I'll share the night shifts with Karl at the *Einfall* and everything'll be fine.'

'I don't know,' said Erwin. 'There's something wrong with him. I'm worried about him, somehow.'

Herr Lehmann failed to detect any duplicity in his eyes, but appearances could be deceptive. Although he'd never regarded Erwin as a person who genuinely worried about anyone whose name didn't happen to be Erwin Kächele, he seemed to be in earnest.

'In that case,' he said, 'it's doubly important for me to work with him. And Stefan has always set his sights on becoming a manager.'

'Yes, that might work. Maybe it's time you went back to your parents.' Erwin jerked his head in their direction. Looking over at their table, Herr Lehmann couldn't believe his eyes: not only was Katrin sitting beside his mother again, but Kristall Rainer had joined the party. The man was sitting on *his* chair and chatting to *his* father.

'Maybe it is,' he said.

'I'll have a word with Karl,' said Erwin.

'Yes, but don't mess him about,' said Herr Lehmann. 'He doesn't deserve it.'

He went back to his parents' table. 'You're sitting in my place,' he said to Kristall Rainer, who looked up at him guilelessly.

'Oh, so sorry, I didn't realise,' said Kristall Rainer, getting up.

Herr Lehmann sat down on his chair. It's warm, he thought irritably — my chair has been warmed by that man's buttocks. 'Don't forget your beer,' he said, holding it out. Kristall Rainer lingered there irresolutely. 'It makes me kind of nervous if someone stands over me when I'm sitting down,' he added, but Kristall Rainer still didn't go. He nodded, pulled up a chair from the next table, and sat down. Thick-skinned bugger, thought Herr Lehmann.

'It's really nice here, Frank,' his father said. 'What was all that about?'

'Oh, just a staff problem,' said Herr Lehmann.

'Anything I can do?' asked Karl, who had suddenly appeared and was looking down at Kristall Rainer. 'Hey, that's nearly empty,' he said, snatching the beer glass from his hand. 'Just dishwater, that is. Come to the bar with me and get another. Besides, I wanted to ask you something.'

Kristall Rainer rose and followed him.

'Where's he off to?' Katrin asked from the other side of the table.

'No idea,' Herr Lehmann said tetchily.

'Oh well,' Katrin said, getting up, 'I'd better be going.'

'The pork was really wonderful,' Herr Lehmann's mother called after her.

This is the strangest night out I've had in ages, he thought.

'What a jolly night out we're having,' said his mother. 'It must be really nice for you, working here with all your friends.'

'Sure, sure,' he said.

'But there's something we've got to talk to you about,' she said.

'What is it now?'

'Well,' said his father, 'we've a favour to ask. You must do something on our behalf for Granny.'

'For Granny?'

'We can't manage it,' said his mother. 'We'd have to do it tomorrow, and there simply wouldn't be time, with the coach leaving tomorrow evening.'

'It would be really good of you to do it for us,' his father added. 'It's nothing much.'

'So what is it?' asked Herr Lehmann. He signalled to Karl, who was fiddling with the till, to bring liqueurs all round.

'A quick trip to East Berlin.'

13 ART

'WHAT WAS THAT you said?' Karl hadn't been listening. Rather at a loss, Herr Lehmann stood there in his best friend's studio, a defunct shop in Cuvrystrasse whose steel shutters were permanently lowered because Karl preferred to work by artificial light and 'didn't give a shit' about the time of day, as he'd once put it. It was hot in there, thanks to the naked bulbs dangling everywhere, and the whole place was crammed with Karl's latest sculptures or *objets*, or whatever he called them, which were welded together out of all kinds of bits of scrap metal. Herr Lehmann didn't quite know where to stand because Karl kept darting around among his works of art and making minor improvements to them with a hissing blowtorch, which rendered conversation almost impossible. Added to that, Herr Lehmann couldn't see an ashtray anywhere and he wasn't sure it would be right to drop his ash on the floor.

'Perhaps I'd better come back another time,' he called, although he was happy to see his best friend again. Karl hadn't shown his face anywhere since that night at the *Markthalle* with Herr Lehmann's parents, which was five days ago. Since then he'd been closeted in his studio, putting the final touches to his stuff for the Charlottenburg exhibition.

'Oh, shit!' Karl extinguished the blowtorch, then tore off his welder's goggles and hurled them into a corner. 'It's all so pointless.'

'You've finished off some good stuff there,' said Herr Lehmann. The things Karl made meant nothing to him in themselves, and Karl knew it. That was why he could never say what he thought of them, which was fine with him. His brother had once turned out some quite similar pieces, albeit — initially, at least — with more success, and Herr Lehmann had never been able to make anything of them either. Art in general left him cold, but he cherished as much respect for people who devoted themselves to it as he did for anyone capable of getting enthusiastic about anything.

'Oh, shit.' Karl ran his fingers through his hair, and Herr Lehmann noticed for the first time how profusely he was sweating. His hair was wringing wet, and fat beads of perspiration were following various routes down his cheeks from forehead to chin. 'It's rubbish, the whole shooting match,' he said. 'You can take it all away.' He proceeded to kick one of his works, which teetered perilously despite its ponderous metallic bulk.

'Balls,' said Herr Lehmann, who knew Karl's mood swings of old. 'Impressive stuff, this is.'

'Stuff!' Karl said bitterly. 'That's just what it is: stuff. You've hit the nail on the head.'

'When is the exhibition, in fact?'

'November the eleventh — only another flaming week to go. The woman from the gallery was here yesterday. She thought everything was great. "Just as I'd imagined it" — that's what she said, the silly cow.'

'You should be glad.'

'You don't understand these things. What was that you said just now? What have you got to do?'

'Make a trip to East Berlin.'

'Why?'

'For my granny. She's suddenly developed a soft spot for our relations in the east.'

'You've got relations in the east?'

'It was news to me too. Some cousin of my mother's – she's going to be sixty, and my granny insists on sending her five hundred marks.'

'Couldn't she send them by post?'

'I don't know, she wants them delivered by hand for some reason. She doesn't trust the communists, she says, and things are in chaos over there, et cetera. My parents didn't feel like going when they were here.'

'Hm, East Berlin,' Karl said thoughtfully. He took two bottles of beer from a crate beneath his workbench, levered off the caps with a screwdriver, and handed one to Herr Lehmann. 'I wouldn't feel like it either. When are you going?'

'Sunday. The day after tomorrow.'

'You'll have to change some D-marks, it's compulsory. Did your parents at least give you some cash to change?'

'You're kidding. They don't have a clue about things like that.'

'Things are pretty tough there at the moment,' said Karl. 'You'll be needing a multiple-entry permit, or whatever it's called.'

'I've already got that. All I have to do now is phone her,' said Herr Lehmann, ' – this relation, I mean. She lives somewhere in the east. It'll probably be best if I meet her in Alexanderplatz or somewhere like that. Then I can hand over the money and come straight back.'

'But not before you've got rid of your East German marks – you can't bring those back with you. That's a problem. You'll have to be in good shape if you want to blow them all on booze. I'd come with you if I didn't have to work.'

'Katrin wants to come – thinks it'll be interesting. She's really looking forward to it.' Herr Lehmann had spent the previous night with her, and his account of the forthcoming trip to East Berlin had filled her with enthusiasm. At last she would see the other half of the city, she said, and Herr Lehmann was glad she was glad, which was why he'd refrained from pointing out that she still didn't know *this* half of the city. Although he was pleased to be able to give her a treat, her enthusiasm was such that the whole East Berlin trip was threatening to get out of hand. She had even asked whether Herr Lehmann's aunt – or whatever one called a mother's cousin – could give them a guided tour of the city.

'I went there once,' said Karl. He picked up a file and rasped away at a piece of metal, creating a din that set Herr Lehmann's teeth on edge. 'It's about as exciting as Spandau on a Sunday.'

'Ever been to Spandau on a Sunday?'

'You're joking! I know what it's like, though: exactly like East Berlin. I went there once with your brother, not long before you turned up here. How is he, by the way?'

'I don't know. He wasn't doing too well in the art line, last time I heard. He said Germans are so out of fashion in New York, he was thinking of starting again from scratch – as a Dutchman.'

'But business was booming, wasn't it?'

'Seemed so, what with his gallery and all.'

'A gallery in New York – that's saying something. Must be hell, though, when it goes down the tubes.'

'I guess so.'

'So how does he make a living?'

'As a plumber or heating engineer or something.'

'A plumber?' Karl looked shocked. 'A plumber? I don't believe it. Manfred a *plumber*?'

'More of a heating engineer, I think,' said Herr Lehmann. 'He knows how to weld, after all. They don't look down on that kind of job over there.'

'But Herr Lehmann!' With a sweeping gesture, Karl hurled his file into a corner. 'Do you know what you're saying? Your brother a plumber? I always thought he was the greatest.'

'It's not so bad, he says. I think the money's good.'

'Frank!' Karl took him by the shoulders and gazed dramatically into his eyes. He's exaggerating, thought Herr Lehmann. His best friend's eyes were bloodshot and he hadn't had a bath for days, to judge by the smell he gave off. He works too hard, thought Herr Lehmann. 'Frank!' Karl repeated. 'Your brother is one of the greatest artists in existence. That's my honest opinion, and if one of the greatest artists in existence has to work as a heating engineer to make ends meet, it's one of the lousiest things I've ever heard.'

'Well,' Herr Lehmann said soothingly, 'at least he's still doing something. And he doesn't have to work all the time. He paints a lot too, these days.'

'He paints? Manfred *paints*?'

'Yes, I think so. In oils and so on. More for fun, he says.'

'He paints for *fun*?' Karl shook his head.

'Why get so worked up? I mean, you've got this Charlottenburg exhibition coming up soon. You may even make some real money out of it, so what's the problem?'

'I'm talking about your brother, Herr Lehmann.'

'I know,' said Herr Lehmann, suddenly aware that he missed his brother. Everything would be better if Manfred were here, he thought without knowing why. 'Maybe I ought to call him sometime. Maybe things are going better with him again.'

'But painting! In oils! I just can't believe it.'

'Why not?'

'Your brother is the greatest living sculptor of *objets*, no shit. Remember how I knocked over that thing of his?'

'I wasn't here in those days. I moved here shortly after he left.'

'So you did.' Karl fetched another two bottles of beer and opened them. 'It was at an exhibition in that funny gallery in Admiralstrasse. The thing was standing on a block of concrete or something – it wasn't attached in any way. At some stage, when we were all smashed, I blundered into it. Priced at five thousand marks, it was – had a label on it saying so. That was when Manfred was just starting to become a really hot property. Five thousand marks, and I knocked it over – smashed it to smithereens. Five thousand marks . . . And, just to make matters worse, the thing was really good. Really good. But all he said was, "The hell with it, I'll make another." That was Manfred for you.'

'Yes,' Herr Lehmann conceded, 'he was cool.'

'Cool isn't the word. And to think he's welding radiators in New York.'

'Perhaps he enjoys it,' said Herr Lehmann. 'I mean, if he's really cool he may not get worked up over shit like that. Anyway, he was doing okay when we spoke. If he could pass for a Dutchman, he said, he could turn out some shitty paintings on the side.' He laughed. Karl did not.

'That's a really sad story, Herr Lehmann.'

'I don't know. Perhaps it's worse for you than for Manfred.'

'Meaning what?'

'No idea, it was just a thought. I'm surprised you're so het up.'

'Here, I'll show you something.' Karl went over to the work-bench, picked up a large scrap-metal artefact standing on it, and hurled it at the floor. It disintegrated into numerous pieces. 'I've spent two days on that, and it's not worth a damn.'

'Why not?'

'Because it's crap. And so is that.' Karl went to an object standing on the floor and kicked it over, then turned to Herr Lehmann and looked at him with a strange expression, as if close to tears.

'Stop that, lay off this shit!' cried Herr Lehmann, who was terribly alarmed by now. 'It's crazy, plain crazy!' He went over to Karl and gripped his arm.

'I'll tell you something, Herr Lehmann. If your brother really is welding pipes together, or whatever, it's worth more than all this crap here combined.'

'Now wait a minute!' Herr Lehmann couldn't stand histrionics, and the tearful note in his friend's voice was getting him down. This isn't the Karl I know, he thought. 'Your nerves are shot, that's all,' he said. 'You should have a good sleep or a decent meal or get laid or something. You've produced some great stuff here.'

'Says who? You don't know the first thing about it.'

'Of course I don't, but neither do you. You're probably less qualified to judge your own stuff than anyone else in the world. You're too close to it. Leave it as it is – put it out of your mind for a couple of days. Besides, we've got to go soon.'

'Go? Go where?'

'To work, you dummy. We've got a shift at the *Einfall*. There are times when I think Erwin's right, and we ought to be worried about you.'

'Is that what he says?'

'Yes.'

'He'd do better to worry about his liver.' Karl looked suddenly relaxed and cheerful. 'A shift at the *Einfall*?'

Herr Lehmann sighed. 'Yes, at the *Einfall*.'

'I'd completely forgotten.'

'That's obvious.'

'I really ought to carry on working here.'

'No! Better come to the *Einfall* with me. It'll blow the shit out of your head, doing something sensible for once.'

'Oh, Frank.' Karl sighed and draped a heavy arm around Herr Lehmann's shoulders. 'Know why I like you so much?'

'No.'

'Because you've no connection with art and all that crap. You're so . . . so . . .' Karl waved his free hand in the air as if trying to capture the appropriate word.

'Boring?' Herr Lehmann suggested.

'No, not boring. Just so . . . so refreshingly naive.'

'Yes,' Herr Lehmann said, amused. 'So say a lot of people. Incidentally, Herr Schmidt, you ought to take a shower. You stink.'

'See? That's what I mean.'

'I know.'

14 THE REUNION

IT GLADDENED HERR Lehmann's heart to be working with his best friend again. That's what I've been missing, he thought as he stood behind the counter and watched Karl stowing bottles of beer in the refrigerator with his fat backside in the air. The shift had got off to a normal start. Although nothing much was happening, it was enough to warm them up for the Friday night turmoil to come. The pleasantest thing about working with Karl had always been their unspoken agreement about what was to be done and who should do it. They were like two pistons in the same well-tuned engine, and everything went smoothly when they worked together. That had been so in the past, at least, and it seemed to be so again, even though it was two years since they'd last manned the bar together. That's how it ought to be with friends, thought Herr Lehmann. When you see them or work with them again, no matter how long it's been, it ought to seem as if no time at all has gone by. Such were his thoughts as they opened bottles of beer, frothed white coffees, and filled shot glasses.

The place filled up after ten o'clock. It being Friday night, the usual suspects rubbed shoulders with numerous weekend or amateur drinkers, as Karl always called them, who were duly exhilarated by the prospect of the weekend ahead and enlivened the atmosphere with their cheerful exuberance. A lot of wise-cracks and laughter mingled with the all-encompassing musical din which Klaus and Marko referred to as avant-garde rock. Karl had put it on after hiding 'Sylvio's shit', as he termed it, in one of the fridges. Herr Lehmann had only just stopped him from throwing the cassettes into the trash can.

'You can't do that,' he said, faintly puzzled for the first time that night. It wasn't like Karl to get worked up over music of any kind.

'But it's a load of crap.'

'What? You're always going to the *Orbit*, where they play nothing but that boom-boom stuff. Erwin says it's the music of the future.'

'Erwin hasn't a clue. Anyway, it's not all the same, just because it goes boom-boom. There are different kinds.'

'Maybe, but Sylvio recorded those tapes specially. You can't just chuck them away.'

'Sylvio can get stuffed. It's rubbish.'

'Karl! Stop it!'

So the upshot had been that Karl hid the cassettes in the fridge. Although unusually childish of him, this wasn't wholly out of character, and Herr Lehmann quickly dismissed the incident from his mind. When the place became really full, however, other things happened that made him think twice. For a start, Karl drank an exceptional amount of beer while working. Then he dropped a bottle. Then he flew off the handle because the trash can wouldn't open properly when he stepped on the pedal, becoming so infuriated on one occasion that he simply dumped the ashtray he'd been endeavouring to empty. Then he kept disappearing into the cellar, but not before giving Herr Lehmann a detailed explanation of why he was going – ostensibly to fetch something they needed, like wheat beer or glasses or whatever

— and this was mostly absurd, because Herr Lehmann hadn't asked him for an explanation and never would have. None of these things was really out of the ordinary, but taken together they made him smell a rat. To crown it all, Erwin turned up at some stage and wanted a word with Karl. So they went upstairs to Erwin's apartment when the joint was already jumping, and Herr Lehmann started to wonder if everyone had gone mad.

But then Katrin came in and greeted him with a kiss on the lips, and she put her arms round his neck as she did so, which was something she'd never done before in front of other people, and which she'd never wanted him to do to her in public, and this made him so happy, he gave away the next five bottles of beer at random. She remained standing at the counter for a while, watching him at work, and he tried to keep the conversation going but there was simply too much to do, and after they'd smilingly exchanged a few trivial remarks they both realised that, under the present circumstances, there was nothing that absolutely had to be said.

The conversation between Erwin and Karl seemed to have been of an equally trivial nature. It certainly couldn't have been about anything unpleasant, because they were both in high spirits when they came downstairs again. Karl went straight back to work, and Herr Lehmann couldn't resist asking what he and Erwin so often found to discuss.

'Oh . . .' Karl swiftly opened a bottle of beer for himself, grinning. 'You'll never believe it, but Erwin's become an art buyer. He wants to acquire a piece of mine for his new joint in Charlottenburg.'

Funny way of putting it, thought Herr Lehmann. Karl would have phrased it differently once upon a time. He'd have said, 'That asshole wants to buy something from me.' What's all this about 'you'll never believe it' and 'art buyer'? Why is he talking so oddly? But all he said was, 'Looks like Charlottenburg is your big chance.'

'So it does, so it does.'

Herr Lehmann would have liked to speak to Katrin about Karl. Maybe she's spotted something I've missed, he thought, women are like that sometimes, but she'd vanished into the throng. Later on he saw her in the distance with Klaus and Marko, and the insistent way they were talking to her suggested that she'd got involved in a conversation about music. She settles in quickly, he thought. She gets on well with everyone, she's more outgoing than I am. To her all this seems new and exciting, and she's right, of course. He remembered how it had been for him when he first came to Berlin. That was a long time ago – he'd only just turned twenty-one, and now he'd soon be thirty – and he resolved to be a bit more outgoing and upbeat himself. Otherwise you grow old before your time, he thought, and he treated himself to a beer.

Then the Poles appeared. There were five of them, and all Herr Lehmann saw of them at first was the neck of an enormous double bass that seemed to be propelling itself across the crowded bar under its own steam. Then a pretty blonde came up to him and asked, in heavily accented German, whether they might play a little music. This was all right with Herr Lehmann, so he turned off the tape and the universal hubbub subsided considerably. Then the crowd parted a little at one point and the musicians – there were four: an accordionist and two guitarists in addition to the bass player – began to play. The music they played was strange and kind of folksy, and Herr Lehmann wondered if it was a polka, and if the word 'polka' had some connection with the name Poland. Whatever the truth, it was very unusual music for the *Einfall*, but no one minded. On the contrary, people seemed to welcome the change. They talked less, and some of them even nodded their heads to the rhythm. It must be great to play music just like that, thought Herr Lehmann; it must really be fun. Katrin suddenly appeared beside him. She smiled at him and slipped her arm through his.

'How about a dance?' she said.

'No,' he said dismissively, 'no, it's no good, I don't know the first thing about dancing.' He quailed at the thought of trying to dance in front of all those people.

'Oh, come on,' she said.

Herr Lehmann fought a hard battle with himself. He wished he was capable of engaging in such a nonsensical activity, but he didn't have the least idea how to go about it.

'I can't, really I can't, I'm a total zilch when it comes to dancing.' He briefly paused for thought, then added, 'I'm sorry, I know it's sad and disappointing and so on, and I don't want to be a drag, but that's the way it is.'

'Oh, come on,' she said, putting her arms round his waist. 'It's quite simple, just sway to and fro a bit.'

Herr Lehmann had always wanted to be able to dance, but he couldn't. Even wiggling his hips was beyond him, and as for moving his feet or legs in time, not only simultaneously but in front of everyone, that transcended the bounds of his imagination. As luck would have it, several people on the other side of the counter were waving money at him and doing their best to attract his attention, so he had a valid pretext for copping out.

'Duty calls,' he said, feeling relieved. He picked her up, spun her round once, and put her down again. 'That'll have to do for now,' he said. 'I really must get back to work.'

'All right,' she said with a smile, 'in that case . . .' She didn't seem to take it too hard. This reassured Herr Lehmann, who really had to get stuck in because Karl had disappeared again.

The Poles were loudly applauded. They played another

number, and another. Already faintly annoyed because Karl failed to reappear, Herr Lehmann began to tire of them and felt that the novelty had lost its charm. Many of the customers seemed to share his sentiments, because the majority redirected their attention to more important matters and clamoured for beer. When Herr Lehmann finally spotted Karl, he was dancing with Katrin. It was a strange spectacle. Having clamped her to his chest with one arm and hoisted her off the floor, he was reeling across the bar with his free hand waving around in the air. That's a minor refinement of my own technique, Herr Lehmann thought resentfully. Karl can't dance either, but he's dancing all the same. He was impressed despite himself. I ought to take a leaf out of his book, he thought. When the Poles stopped playing and Karl put Katrin down, they laughed and patted each other on the back. Herr Lehmann disliked this, but he didn't show it when Karl rejoined him behind the bar, opened another bottle of beer, and ceremoniously raised it.

'No lightweight, your honeybun,' he said with a wink. 'You must be stronger than I thought.'

Herr Lehmann gave him a searching look. Karl wasn't given to making suggestive remarks, but he couldn't detect anything sly or malicious in his best friend's expression. The only odd thing was that he persisted in winking and pulling faces. He was also sweating like a pig and breathing heavily.

'Okay,' said Herr Lehmann, 'but please don't call her my "honeybun", or at least, not when she's within earshot. I don't think she'd like it, and she'd take it out on me.'

'Silent as the grave, that's me,' his best friend said dramatically, putting two fingers to his lips. 'See? Sealed.'

Herr Lehmann didn't know what to make of this. 'Look Karl,' he said, 'are you feeling okay? I mean, is something wrong?'

'Wrong?' said Karl, still grinning. 'Everything's absolutely fine.'

Then he gave a strange, rather constrained laugh, or so it seemed to Herr Lehmann, whose annoyance gave way to faint concern. Karl's overtired and physically below par, he thought. It's not his day, I guess.

At that moment the blonde, who was going around with a hat, came over to him and asked for some money for the musicians. Herr Lehmann gave her ten marks from the till. She asked if he'd ever thought of taking a vacation in Poland. He smilingly shook his head and said he hadn't taken a vacation for years. 'I'm not the vacation type,' he added.

'Everyone is vacation type,' she said looking him straight in the eye with a strange expression. 'You must also rest sometime. Look tired.' She smiled at him and produced a looseleaf binder. 'You can rent. Many houses, everything is possible.' She opened the binder, and Herr Lehmann inspected the photographs it contained, which were stuck to sheets of cardboard. They depicted various houses situated in fields or on the edge of woods.

'Very nice,' he said, not knowing what else to say. He had resolved to be less inhibited in future, and this seemed a good place to start. He offered the woman a cigarette, but she declined it.

'Have cigarettes, better cigarettes,' she said, and lit one of her own. 'Beautiful houses, beautiful scenery. You can take vacation with friends, with girlfriend.'

'Well,' said Herr Lehmann, 'it's autumn now, and that's not the ideal time for a vacation. I mean, rotten weather and so on.'

'In winter is beautiful,' she said. 'Beautiful snow. I give you my number.'

She took a beer mat and wrote a long telephone number on it. 'My number in Poland,' she said. 'I am there often. You must only call and say Elzbietta.'

Herr Lehmann was rather surprised to hear one could simply

pick up a phone and call Poland, it being behind the Iron Curtain and all that. Which reminded him that he still had to call his relation in the east. 'Doesn't one need a visa?' he asked.

'Visa no problem,' she said with a smile, looking him straight in the eye again. She was standing so close he thought he could smell her hair. 'Is not so bad like GDR.'

'Well, then,' said Herr Lehmann, who didn't know what else he could talk to her about, 'I'll have to see.'

She planted a finger on his chest. 'You should come. You look tired. Poland not far.'

'No,' he conceded, suddenly aware that he had never given Poland a second thought, 'it's not far.'

'You should do something different sometime,' she said, fixing him with the same strange expression as before, which gave him butterflies in the stomach.

Erwin suddenly appeared beside them. 'Give Karl a hand, Herr Lehmann, he's making a hash of things.'

'Why?'

'No idea. Boy-oh-boy, I'm getting really worried about that guy.'

'You must take vacation,' the Polish woman told Erwin. 'Look tired.'

Herr Lehmann left them to it and looked around for Karl. He was calmly cleaning the espresso machine with a whole crowd of people clamouring for drinks behind his back.

'What's the matter with you, Karl?' Herr Lehmann demanded. 'Why clean it now? You can do that later.'

'It's all gummed up,' Karl said without raising his head. 'I'll have it finished in no time.' He continued to polish away as if everything depended on it. Herr Lehmann didn't feel like arguing, so he devoted himself to the customers, but that was no good because the Beck's had run out.

'Karl, we need more beer.'

'Got to get this finished. You can't have cleaned it for years.' Herr Lehmann was baffled.

'Beer, Karl. We need more beer.'

'Yes, yes,' said his best friend, and went on polishing.

This, thought Herr Lehmann as he quickly lit a cigarette, is like an ambulance driver washing his vehicle with crash victims bleeding to death around him. This, he thought as he raced down the steps to the cellar, is like a security guard brushing his uniform in the middle of a bank raid. This, he thought as he pounded back up the steps with a crate of beer in each hand, is like a sailor scrubbing the deck while his ship sinks under him.

Once upstairs again he sold the beer straight from the crates. Needless to say, one or two wise guys promptly complained that it wasn't cold enough. 'Beer doesn't have to be cold, it has to be drunk,' he told them, a ritual retort from the days when he and Karl had worked as a team – the days when Erwin had, on principle, dispensed with the luxury of refrigerators and similar refinements. Although this cheered him up a little, he felt worried nonetheless. Karl was still polishing the espresso machine with manic intensity, his fat posterior restricting freedom of movement behind the counter. In the old days it had always been Karl who restocked the bar – he enjoyed doing it. Their supplies of beer should have been replenished long ago, but Karl had neglected to do this all night, even though he'd kept going down to the cellar for no good reason. It was worrying, genuinely worrying. We aren't on the same wavelength any more, Herr Lehmann reflected, and the realisation saddened him. We used to be a good team, he thought, but that was in the old days. We made a perfect team, like Bonnie and Clyde or Laurel and Hardy or Simon and Garfunkel or Sacco and Vanzetti. Turning thirty is hell, he reflected: it's when you begin to have a past and maunder on about the good old days and all that shit.

He went straight back down to the cellar to fetch some more beer. When he resurfaced Karl had started polishing glasses. Polishing glasses was fair enough, but doing it now was plain daft. Herr Lehmann found time to put some bottles in the fridge. Most of the customers already had their beers, warm or not, and the place was beginning to empty. The *Einfall* had passed its nocturnal zenith, and people were moving on to other bars and clubs and discos and whatever. All that remained were the twenty or thirty regulars for whom no other bars or clubs or discos would do. The Poles, too, were still there. They sat together at a table, relaxing, while the blonde tried to convince Erwin and Katrin of the advantages of taking a vacation in her native land. At this point, Kristall Rainer walked in. Herr Lehmann merely put a bottle and a glass in front of him. That's good enough for Rainer, he thought, treating himself to another warm beer.

'How's life?' Kristall Rainer inquired. He certainly knew how to pour a wheat beer, Herr Lehmann had to admit.

'I can't complain,' Herr Lehmann replied, although he felt like asking the man what business it was of his. He proceeded to help his best friend polish the glasses, a daft occupation but better than being drawn into conversation by Kristall Rainer.

'What goes on over there?' Karl asked, nodding at the Polish woman and Katrin and Erwin, who had now been joined by Kristall Rainer. They were all poring over the photographs.

'She rents houses,' said Herr Lehmann. 'For vacations in Poland.'

'Great country, Poland,' Karl said earnestly.

'What makes you say that?'

Karl pondered this briefly, then grinned. 'No idea.'

'Why did you say it's a great country?'

'How should I know? Why not?'

'If you say something's great you've got to have a reason.'

'What's the matter with you, old son? Since when have you been so pedantic?'

'I'm not being pedantic,' said Herr Lehmann, not knowing why he didn't let the subject drop. 'I simply want to know why Poland's such a great country. I mean, if someone says something's great they've got to have a reason.'

'Frank!' His best friend put down the glass he'd been polishing. 'Hang loose. I said it, that's all.'

'Yes, but why?'

'Frank,' said Karl with a pensive shake of the head, 'you really worry me sometimes.'

'That's great,' said Herr Lehmann. 'That's just great. I don't know if Poland's great, but that is. *You* worry about *me*?'

'Somebody has to,' said his best friend Karl, patting him on the head. 'Joking apart, though, it's fun working with you again.'

'Yes,' said Herr Lehmann. 'It is.'

15 THE CAPITAL OF THE GDR

THE DOOR CLOSED, and Herr Lehmann was on his own. He realised that things didn't look good for him at the moment — in fact they looked rather ominous. I'm in the shit, he thought — I'm in it up to my elbows. He yearned for a cigarette but didn't know if smoking was allowed. It seemed unlikely. There was no sign of an ashtray in this small, bare room, whose only contents were a table, two chairs and a neon tube, and he strongly suspected that it would be better not to provoke these people. There were no windows either, and the door had no handle on the inside.

So that's that, he thought. He tried to remember how things had come to such a pass. Everything had gone quite smoothly at first. They had accepted his Berlin ID, approved his multiple-entry permit, and changed his own few marks. Katrin had passed through another checkpoint, thank God. She only possessed a West German passport, which had exempted her from the multiple-entry palaver but rendered her liable to a visa charge or something — Herr Lehmann wasn't altogether sure, but that was pretty immaterial at this stage. Now she was probably hanging around up there in East Berlin, waiting for him, while he was sitting down here in a windowless room in Friedrichstrasse station, awaiting whatever lay in store for him. I hope she won't go and ask them where I've got to, he thought – if she really *is* up there. Maybe I'm up top and she's down below. He seemed to be in a basement, but it was hard to tell. Friedrichstrasse station was on so many levels that he'd lost his bearings.

Anyway, he'd almost completed the formalities when a man in uniform came up and asked if he had anything to declare. 'No, not that I know of,' he replied, whereupon the man in uniform, a fat, amiable individual, asked him to step into the room next door. There he was made to turn out his pockets and put their contents on the table. The five hundred marks wouldn't have been a problem by themselves, he reflected grimly. Money wasn't incriminating in itself. The trouble was, the five hundred marks were still in the envelope given him by his parents, on which his grandmother had not only written the name and address of her relative in the east but underlined the words 'East Berlin'. And that, in the uniformed circles of which Herr Lehmann had fallen foul, was a really monumental booboo.

For my stupidity, Herr Lehmann told himself, they should sentence me to twenty years. Stupidity deserves to be punished, he thought, and I'm stupid, stupid, stupid. The man in uniform had betrayed no emotion – he hadn't roared with laughter or anything. All he'd said was, 'Aha, what have we here?' Then he'd disappeared, come back, shepherded Herr Lehmann into this room, sat him down on this chair, and shut the door. So here he now was, trying to work out a plan of campaign. No point in beating about the bush, he thought, better to come clean right away. Telling the truth disarms people. It's the simplest policy, and anyway, anything else would be stupider still. He was less afraid of being clapped in irons and carted off to Siberia, which was pretty unlikely, than depressed by the embarrassing nature of his situation. I'm dependent on their goodwill, he reflected, so I'd better play dumb. I won't even need to put on an act.

The door opened and another man in uniform came in bearing an enormous typewriter, which he deposited on the table. 'Stay there,' he said. He went out again and returned with several sheets of paper, the envelope containing the money, and Herr Lehmann's documents. Having arranged these neatly on the table, side by side, he sat down and looked at Herr Lehmann.

'Right,' he said, 'let's get started.'

'Sure.'

'What have you got to say about this money?'

'It's my grandmother's. I'm supposed to take it to a relative of hers who lives in East . . . that's to say, in the capital of the German Democratic Republic.'

'So this woman . . .' The official behaved as if he were seeing the envelope for the first time. 'This handwriting is almost illegible. Whose is it?'

'My grandmother's.'

'The name appears to be Helga Bergner. Is she a citizen of the GDR?'

'Yes, I think so.'

'What do you mean, you think so?'

'Well, she lives in the GDR, so she's probably a citizen of the GDR.'

'Don't be impertinent. How are you related to this woman?'

'She's a cousin of my mother's, I think.'

'You think she is?'

'Yes.'

'What do you mean, you think she is?'

'I know she is, in fact.'

'And your grandmother, what's her name?'

'Margarete Bick.'

'And your name is Lehmann?'

'Yes.'

'So how are you related to this Bergner woman?'

'Well, my mother's maiden name was Bick, and my grandmother's maiden name was Schmidt, and a sister of hers married a man named Bergner. At least, I assume so.'

'You assume so?'

'Well, that's the only explanation. Unless my mother's cousin is the daughter of one of my grandmother's brothers, in which case her maiden name would have been Schmidt. In order to be called Bergner she'd have had to marry someone of that name, otherwise we wouldn't be related.'

'Are you trying to make a fool of me?'

'No, no, certainly not.'

'Do you think this is some kind of joke?'

'Of course not.'

'Do you think I'm fooling around? Do you think this is a coffee party and we're merely having a little chat? Do you think . . .' The official's voice rose and his face turned puce. He's only young, thought Herr Lehmann, but he ought to watch his blood pressure. 'Do you think you can *flout the customs and foreign exchange regulations of the German Democratic Republic and laugh it off, or something?*'

'But you did ask,' said Herr Lehmann. He resolved to sound slightly less dumb from now on. They're a thin-skinned bunch, he thought. It's getting on their nerves a bit, what's happening over here.

'Did you hide this envelope in the inner pocket of your coat deliberately, so we wouldn't find it if we searched you?'

'Certainly not,' Herr Lehmann protested indignantly. 'That really isn't so. Ask your colleague. I put everything on the table right away. I wasn't to know the money could be a problem.'

'Why didn't you declare it when the customs officer asked if you had anything to declare?'

'I wasn't aware I had to. I don't know anything about your customs regulations.'

'If you don't know anything about our customs regulations, why did you try to smuggle the money through customs and into the GDR?'

'I didn't try to smuggle it through customs. All I said, when asked if I had anything to declare, was, "Not that I know of." That's all I said, and I *didn't* know, either. It never occurred to me that I had anything to declare. I mean, let's be honest . . .' Herr Lehmann leant forward, trying to create a somewhat more informal atmosphere. 'If I'd wanted to smuggle something I had absolutely no need to smuggle, do you think I'd have smuggled it in an envelope on which my granny had written the recipient's name, complete with her address and everything?'

'Don't get cocky,' the official said sternly. 'Kindly leave the interpretation of the facts to us. You still haven't grasped what a position you've landed yourself in, have you?'

'But I haven't done anything.'

'Stay here, I'll be right back.'

'May I smoke?'

'No.'

After some five minutes the official reappeared. He returned to the attack at once.

'Why, when asked if you had anything to declare, didn't you ask the customs officer what the regulations were? In other words, why didn't you leave the question open and make inquiries before you replied in the negative?'

'Just a moment,' Herr Lehmann said, bewildered. 'Could you repeat that?'

'Why, when asked if you had anything to declare, didn't you ask the customs officer what the regulations were? In other words, why didn't you leave the question open and make inquiries before you replied in the negative?'

Herr Lehmann was beginning to like the man. He's quite something, he thought.

'I didn't answer the question in the negative in *that* sense,' he replied. 'I said, "Not that I know of." That could even be construed as an indirect question, or at least as an indication that I wasn't familiar with the regulations, so it's quite wrong to assume that I'm guilty of deliberate deception or anything of that kind. I made absolutely no attempt to conceal—'

'No!' the official broke in.

'What do you mean, no?'

'"No, not that I know of." That's what you said. You said, "No, not that I know of." Not just, "Not that I know of." You said, "*No*, not that I know of."'

'Yes, well, of course that's what I said. I mean, it's only natural to begin a sentence with "No" when you're going on to say "not that I know of", but it shouldn't be interpreted as an unqualified negative. That would be absurd.'

'What do you mean, absurd? Are you accusing the customs authorities of the German Democratic Republic of absurdity?'

'Of course not.'

'So why use the word?'

'I was using it in a general sense.'

'Herr Lehmann!'

'Yes?'

'You're talking drivel.'

'Yes, well, this is an exceptional situation. It's not the sort of thing that happens every day. Anyone would get confused and talk drivel.'

'No one in your position should talk drivel, it's out of keeping with the gravity of the matter.'

'That's one way of looking at it, naturally.'

'Did you come here alone?'

'Yes, of course.'

'Why of course? Didn't any friends accompany you? A girl-friend, perhaps?'

'No.'

'You came without accomplices, in other words?'

'With respect, you're drawing a false inference from my reply to your question. Even if I were visiting the capital of the GDR with friends or a girlfriend, that wouldn't mean they're accomplices – far from it. I haven't knowingly or deliberately broken your laws – I'd like to stress that. Therefore, if I don't qualify as someone who has knowingly broken your laws, I can't have any accomplices. It wouldn't make any sense.'

'No companions, then?'

'Not that I know of.'

'Don't start that again.'

'Start what?'

The official sighed. 'Forget it,' he said. 'We'd better take down your statement.' He pulled the typewriter towards him and screwed a sheet of paper into it. Then he proceeded to type – with two fingers, Herr Lehmann noticed. From time to time the type bars got stuck and had to be prised apart, but that didn't seem to worry the man. He's used to it, thought Herr Lehmann. This is going to take some time.

'Right. Record of the interrogation of Lehmann, Frank, citizen of the independent political entity of West Berlin,' the official read aloud. 'Date?'

'Fifth of the eleventh,' Herr Lehmann said helpfully.

'Correct. Name?'

'You already put that.'

'Lehmann, Frank,' the official said imperturbably, and tapped away.

Then they got down to the statement itself, every sentence of which was the product of hard bargaining. In its eventual form, the document to be signed by Herr Lehmann was very brief and boiled down to an admission that he had infringed the customs regulations and exchange control laws of the German Democratic Republic, coupled with a rider to the effect that he had done so unwittingly.

'Ignorance of the law is no defence,' the official could not resist pointing out, when Herr Lehmann had signed.

'If you say so,' said Herr Lehmann.

'Wait here,' said the official, and disappeared.

He returned after half an hour, or so it seemed to Herr Lehmann, but not alone. Accompanying him was a somewhat older man whose epaulettes were laden with somewhat more braid, and the latter injected a certain chill into the proceedings.

'Stand up,' he said.

Herr Lehmann stood up. The newcomer proceeded to read aloud from a sheet of paper in his hand.

'The following executive decision is taken in respect of Frank Lehmann, citizen of the independent political entity of West Berlin, born in Bremen, Federal Republic of Germany, on 9 November 1959: for having infringed the customs and foreign exchange regulations of the German Democratic Republic, and, in particular, Sections . . .'

He rattled off several sections followed by the decision itself, which Herr Lehmann had difficulty in understanding, it was couched in such esoteric language.

'Is that clear?' the man demanded when he had finished. The one who had questioned Herr Lehmann stood motionless alongside, staring past him at the wall.

'Yes, well,' said Herr Lehmann, 'I suppose I can kiss my granny's five hundred marks goodbye.'

'The undeclared sum of money you attempted to import into the capital of the GDR has been confiscated,' the man confirmed, 'and the capital of the GDR will dispense with your presence for today.'

'Very well.'

'Here's a carbon copy. You can lodge an appeal against this decision with the relevant GDR court – it's all down there. My colleague will escort you back to the subway to West Berlin. Your GDR marks will be changed back into D-marks at par. Your multiple-entry permit is cancelled. In case of need, you'll have to reapply for one.'

'I'll see,' said Herr Lehmann, who thought this highly unlikely.

'You may go now.'

'Come with me,' said the other man, holding the door open. Herr Lehmann went back the way he'd come – hours ago, it seemed. It was a bit like a film running in reverse. He had to change his East German money back into West German at a loss, though this was a fleabite compared to the five hundred marks he'd just lost. The official channelled him back through customs and passport control in the opposite direction, then came to a halt. Herr Lehmann halted likewise.

'Just keep going,' the official said, pointing straight ahead. 'You'll find the subway to West Berlin at the bottom of the stairs.'

'Yes,' said Herr Lehmann. 'So long, then.' He walked on. The official stayed where he was and said nothing. When Herr Lehmann looked back he was still standing there, staring after him. He waved, but the man didn't respond. He simply stood there, watching him go. Poor devil, Herr Lehmann thought as he descended the stairs to the subway.

16 PLAIN SPEAKING

HERR LEHMANN HAD fixed himself up with a shift at the *Einfall*
on the evening of his excursion to East Berlin, just in case his
East Berlin relative invited him to dinner. An evening shift would
have made a nice excuse. Now, as things had turned out, it was
only three o'clock when he got home. He couldn't think of a
better way of using the time he'd gained than to have a bit of
a lie-down, and he'd already got undressed when the phone
rang. He thought it would be Katrin, back from East Berlin and
wondering what had happened to him, but it was only Erwin
calling from the *Einfall* to ask if he could come into work earlier.

'I'm really still in the east,' said Herr Lehmann, who didn't
feel like working overtime and was anxious to be available if
Katrin called. She's bound to be worried, he thought. She'll be
back from the east at any moment, looking for me.

'But I need you badly,' said Erwin. 'I'm here all by myself. I
don't know what's the matter. Sylvio's sick and not even Rudi
can come.'

'Who's Rudi?' Herr Lehmann asked.

'It doesn't matter,' said Erwin. 'He never can come anyway.
They're all sick. Verena will be on this evening, but that's all.'

'Why Verena? I thought Karl was on tonight.'

'Forget it,' said Erwin. 'He won't be coming any more.'

'What?'

'It's a long story.'

'Karl won't be coming any more?'

'I can't explain on the phone.'

'Stay there, then,' said Herr Lehmann. 'I'll be right over.'

He got dressed again, pinned a note for Katrin to the door, and went off to the *Einfall*. Erwin was standing behind the counter frothing white coffees for the single mothers who liked to meet up there in the afternoons. Their children kicked up a diabolical din while they soothed their nerves with cappuccinos and a shot.

'What's the matter with Karl?' Herr Lehmann asked.

'Good question,' said Erwin. 'Good question. He turned up at the *Markthalle* this morning. I was there myself, having a bite to eat. Walked straight up to me, the crazy bugger, and picked a fight. I don't know if he was drunk, or what. Boy-oh-boy!' He wiped some imaginary sweat from his brow. 'I've never seen him in such a state. Said something about me owing him money and whether I'd ever worked out how much of a profit he'd made me and shit like that. I couldn't understand what he was on about.'

'Yes, well, it happens sometimes when he's drunk.'

'How do I know if he was drunk? Then he went berserk.'

'Karl did?'

'You bet he did. Started swearing at people.'

'And then?'

'And then?' Erwin stopped frothing milk for a moment and looked Herr Lehmann in the eye. His face was a mask of exhaustion. 'Then he clouted me.'

'No!'

'Yes he did! Here!' Erwin pointed to his cheek, but there was nothing to be seen.

'He actually hit you, you mean?'

'What else? And then he stormed out.'

'I don't believe it.'

'Ask Heidi, she was there – ask Heidi if you don't believe me. Honestly, Frank' – they always call me Frank when things get serious, thought Herr Lehmann –'I think he's going nuts. He's cracking up.'

'Not Karl. He's a bit overwrought because of his exhibition and so on, that's all.'

'But he clouted me, Frank! *Me!*'

'Sure, Erwin,' said Herr Lehmann, 'that's not on, of course.'

'Stop taking the piss, this is serious. I'm not just thinking of myself. He's lost his marbles.'

'That's a daft expression, Erwin.'

'What is?'

'Lost his marbles.'

Erwin shrugged. 'I couldn't care less, he's not working for me any more. If all that bothers you is my choice of words, fair enough, no problem, I couldn't care less, he's your friend, but he's not working for me any more.'

'Come on, Erwin, don't make a big thing out of it.'

'No, no, I couldn't care less. I'm not the only one, though. You can ask around – ask those cretins at the *Abfall*, if you like. There's definitely something wrong with him.'

'Okay, Erwin, listen,' said Herr Lehmann. 'I can't work now, I must look in on Karl first. I'll be back by eight. Can you hold the fort against these dangerous young mothers?'

'I don't know,' Erwin said resignedly. 'I've got . . .' – he broke off and proceeded to count on his fingers – 'eight bars at the moment. Three in Kreuzberg, two in Schöneberg, the new one in Charlottenburg, that makes six, plus – no, wait a minute, four in Kreuzberg, the *Eimer*'s in Kreuzberg too . . . anyway, I always have hassles here. Always here, nowhere else. Whenever something goes wrong, it's always here at the *Einfall* or the *Markthalle*. Can anyone tell me why?'

'It's probably because trouble only crops up where your trouble-shooting influence is at its strongest, Erwin.'

'I don't follow you.'

'You spend more time here than elsewhere. At the other places you've got partners who cope with the shit, but not here.'

'Well,' said Erwin, 'this is where it always starts.'

'Yes,' said Herr Lehmann, 'this is where it always starts. I've got to take care of Karl now, okay?'

'Weren't you going to the east today?'

'Yes, but I didn't stay.'

'How was it?'

'Okay.'

'Was there another demo et cetera?'

'Not that I saw.'

'Things are really hotting up over there.'

'I'm off then, Erwin. I'll be back by eight. Hang loose.'

'That's right,' said Erwin, 'go and see to that lunatic. I mean, what do *I* matter? Don't show any consideration for *me*.'

'Have a peppermint tea, Erwin. With milk.'

'Go on, piss off.'

Herr Lehmann made his way across Görlitzer Park to Cuvrystrasse. Karl's derelict shop cum studio apartment was locked, and the steel shutters were down as usual. There was no bell that worked. He hammered on the door for a while, though he didn't think his best friend would be home in any case. Karl must be prowling around somewhere, he thought. If he's in this state he won't be simply taking a nap or filing away at some piece of scrap metal. He tried to remember when his best friend's exhibition was, the tenth or the eleventh or thereabouts. I only hope, he thought as he crossed over into Schlesische Strasse, that he's finished off his stuff, because if he's in this state he probably wouldn't be capable of finishing anything.

The first bar Herr Lehmann checked on was the *Goldener Anker*, a bar Karl liked to patronise when he was in one of his extreme moods. He stationed himself in front of the window and tried to make out what was going on inside, and if Karl was there, but it was no use, he couldn't see a thing, although the *Goldener Anker* – and this was the only thing Herr Lehmann could say in its favour – had no lace curtains over its windows even though it ought, by its very nature, to have had some. Bars like the *Goldener Anker* always have lace curtains over their windows, Herr Lehmann thought whenever he saw the place. The *Goldener Anker* was the only one that hadn't, and not just because it was always so dark inside that it didn't need any lace curtains to shield the interior from everyone's gaze. So he had to go in. All he saw, once his eyes became accustomed to the prevailing gloom, were a few forlorn figures, old age pensioners and other idlers, who sat scattered around the big room staring into bottles of Schultheiss beer, which the *Goldener Anker* sold for only two marks, a form of dumping rendered acceptable – in Herr Lehmann's opinion – by its infinitely dreary atmosphere. Karl wasn't there, and he didn't feel like asking the fat woman behind the counter if she'd seen him. This wasn't one of Herr Lehmann's stamping grounds, and besides, he would have had to drink a Schultheiss for form's sake, and that, he thought, would be expecting too much of himself.

So he walked on and worked his way down Schlesische Strasse to the Schlesisches Tor. He checked the Greek restaurant where Karl sometimes shovelled huge helpings of *gyros* down his throat, and the Italian restaurant next door, and an independent bar whose name he neither knew nor wanted to know. Then he went into the *Klausur*, a cavernous establishment with red plush curtains, and spoke to the barmaid on afternoon shift, a girl named Sabine, but she barely knew Karl and hadn't seen him either, and because none of this yielded any results he eventually, without further digressions, made his way to the *Markthalle*, where he had a word with Heidi. She confirmed what Erwin had told him.

'But what was the matter? What was it all about?' Herr Lehmann asked when she'd served him a coffee and an ouzo, something he never drank as a rule, if only because it was spirits, but this was an exceptional day and the Greek restaurant had reminded him of the drink. 'How did he get into such a state?'

'I don't know. He acted really weird — it was awful,' she said, perching on the stool she always put behind the counter. 'You wouldn't have recognised him. Hey, weren't you supposed to be going east with Katrin today?' she asked abruptly.

'I'm back again,' said Herr Lehmann. 'Any idea where he could have gone?'

'Not a clue. How are things between you and Katrin?'

Herr Lehmann looked at her inquiringly. 'Why do you ask?'

'Are you an item these days?'

'Did you ask Katrin that?'

'Oh, her . . .' Heidi made a dismissive gesture. 'She hardly talks to me, so I wouldn't know.'

'That makes two of us,' said Herr Lehmann. 'Which reminds me: got to make a phone call.'

He went to the toilets and called Katrin. There was no reply. He told her answerphone what had happened, said he was okay and hoped she was the same. Then he went back to the counter. Heidi was still sitting on her stool, staring out at the dismal afternoon through the window opposite.

'I'm going away this winter,' she said. 'I can't take it any more. To Bali.'

'On your own?'

'No, with a couple of friends. It isn't expensive once you're there. They're taking me with them – they've got an agency for Balinese gear, so they're always going there. I may even get a job with them. I'll have to see.'

'That wouldn't be bad,' said Herr Lehmann. 'I mean, Bali and all that.'

'Yes. I'm sick of the winters here, honestly. They get me down every time.'

'I know what you mean,' said Herr Lehmann. 'About Karl, though: any idea where he could be right now?'

'No. He's been a mystery to me for ages.'

'You mean he's struck you as odd for a long time? Erwin thinks he's losing his marbles or something.'

'Oh, Erwin. Erwin likes the sound of his own voice. Karl is Karl, that's all, but today was something else. The way he clouted Erwin . . .'

'With his fist?'

'No, but he slapped him hard. Sounded like a pistol shot.'

'What's he got against Erwin all of a sudden?'

'I've no idea, honestly, he wasn't making much sense. He was drunk, too, and he stank . . .'

'Hm . . .'

'I think he's got a girlfriend somewhere. I don't know her name, but she runs a bar.'

Herr Lehmann had a sudden recollection of the night they'd all gone to the *Savoy*, and of the woman who had stroked Karl's head. I should have thought of that right away, he thought. He knocked back his ouzo and shuddered.

'Since when have you been drinking stuff like that?' asked Heidi.

'It was just an idea.' Herr Lehmann chased the ouzo with the rest of his coffee and got up.

'Put it on the slate?'

'I can't, not now,' said Heidi.

'Why not now?'

'Erwin says, even people that work for him have to pay on the nail from now on. He can't afford to keep us all, he says. Free drinks are only for when we're working.'

'Since when?'

'He said so earlier on, after Karl had gone. That was when he looked through the bar chits, yours included.'

'What *is* all this shit?'

Heidi shrugged. 'I can't help it, you'll have to ask Erwin. Tell you what, though!' she added with a smile.

'What?'

'I simply won't write it down. It's as simple as that.'

'You're okay, Heidi.'

'Nice of you to notice.'

'I've always thought so.'

'All the nicer of you to say so.'

'I'm going to look for Karl now, okay?'

'Sure. How is it with you and Katrin? You still haven't told me.'

'It's hard to say.'

'I don't think she's the woman for you.'

'All the nicer of you to say so.'

'Now push off and go look for Karl.'

It was quite a trek to the *Savoy*, but it wasn't worth taking the subway and Herr Lehmann disliked taking taxis. Besides, it was quite possible that Karl was roaming the streets, so he might run him to earth if he went there on foot. The long walk did him good. It gave him plenty of time to think, and the more he pondered the situation the less he liked it. Things aren't the way they used to be, he reflected. There's something wrong somewhere, he thought, but he found it hard to put his finger on it. On the other hand, he rebuked himself, the fact that things aren't the way they used to be isn't a valid argument, it's the kind of thing people say when they're on the verge of thirty. It doesn't matter that things aren't the way they used to be; what matters is whether they're good or not. But there's something wrong somewhere, he thought, and the mystery surrounding Karl struck him as symptomatic of the whole business, whatever the whole business was. Something isn't functioning any more, so how can Karl be expected to function any more? — but he promptly rejected that idea as being too cheap and easy, too simple.

He thereupon tried to devise an explanation for his malaise about things in general by compiling a mental inventory of the various snags he'd encountered in recent weeks. So many things had gone wrong lately, and he wasn't sure if his affair with Katrin, at its present stage of development, was a ray of hope that could make him forget all the other stuff. Everything's gone sour, he thought: the fight with Detlev, Luke Skywalker, Erwin's bullshit, Kristall Rainer, Karl's sculptures, the Charlottenburg exhibition, Katrin's plan to study industrial design, the capital of the GDR (which had dispensed with his presence), his work at the *Einfall*, the customers there . . . Somehow, he thought, the fire has gone out, and he spent the rest of his walk brooding on whether everything had really changed, or whether it only seemed so because he himself had. But why, he wondered, should I have changed when it's the last thing I want to do? And that brought him back to Karl, who had certainly changed in some way, and who had lately become so odd and so bitter, which was quite unlike him because Karl had always been the rock he could depend on. Karl and fun had been synonymous. They'd always had fun together, and as long as you had fun,

195

everything was all right. Perhaps it's the other way round, he thought – perhaps it isn't that Karl has ceased to function because everything else has, but that nothing else functions because Karl himself has ceased to do so. But he rejected that idea as well. It's too simple, he decided. Things don't work like that.

He wasn't much the wiser by the time he reached the *Savoy*, but at least he now knew that everything was wrong, and that what was getting him down so much was more than just a bunch of trivialities or unfortunate coincidences. If everything's wrong, he thought as he entered the *Savoy*, it enlarges your range of alternatives.

There was a woman behind the bar, and he thought he recognised her as the one who had recently stroked Karl's head. Now, in daylight, she looked older than he had thought at the time – he put her at thirty-five or forty – and he remembered that Karl had always had a weakness for women older than himself. 'Never go for the young things,' he'd once told Herr Lehmann. 'They're always wanting to change their lives, and suddenly you don't fit in any more.' Karl has his own special recipes for living, thought Herr Lehmann. He sat down opposite the woman and began by ordering himself a beer, which he felt he'd earned. They only had draught beer. Oh well, he thought, at least having to draw it will keep her here for a while.

'Any idea where Karl is?' he asked at length, while she was busy with his beer. The question cost him quite an effort. He disliked talking to people he didn't know, especially about things they might have in common.

'Oh, yes,' she said with a smile – a wry smile, or so it seemed to him. 'You're Herr Lehmann, aren't you?'

'Yes. How did you know?'

'You were here a few weeks ago, and he's talked about you

a lot lately. More than he does about me, that's for sure. I'm Christine. Has he told you about me?'

'Of course,' Herr Lehmann lied.

'I'm surprised,' she said. 'It isn't like him to talk about me.'

'Why not?' said Herr Lehmann. 'We were in here together, after all.'

'So what? Did I sit down at your table?'

'No. Why didn't you?'

'Good question.'

Herr Lehmann wasn't enjoying this conversation, but she seemed to have been waiting for it for a long time. He covertly watched her as she went on speaking. She looked nice – sad too, somehow. There was something tragic about her eyes that reminded him of Romy Schneider, but he liked her, unlike Romy Schneider. He couldn't stand Romy Schneider except in *What's New, Pussycat?*, not that he'd ever admitted as much.

'For Karl there are two worlds,' she said. 'You're in one and I'm in the other, and he takes damned good care they never come into contact. The only question is, which world is the right one for him?'

'You tell me,' said Herr Lehmann, trying to keep the ball rolling.

'Your world, of course,' she said. 'I've given it a lot of thought. When he tells me I'm his one and only, he means it as a compliment, and he means every word.' She was about to put Herr Lehmann's beer down on the counter, but he took it from her hand. 'The trouble is, it only applies in our world. That's the hard part. It means there's only the two of us in our world, and he doesn't find that very exciting. That's why he tells me about you but doesn't tell you about me.'

'I see.'

'And he only comes here when he's reached the end of his

rope in your world – when he needs to relax. In practical terms, I'm his inflatable mattress.'

'Steady on,' said Herr Lehmann, who thought this was going a bit too far and found it rather embarrassing as well. She hardly knows me, he thought, and she's telling me things like this. Meantime, the woman called Christine was pouring herself a brandy.

'But even that's an exaggeration,' she went on, sipping her drink. 'Being his inflatable mattress would at least mean he lay on me from time to time, but there hasn't been much of that either, not lately.'

'Hm, well,' Herr Lehmann said helplessly. 'Do you get the feeling that he's changed in some way? That he's kind of going off the rails?'

'Not specially. You could be right, but that's your problem. It's all the same to me. Like to see him? Then you'll know what I mean.'

'Please.'

The woman said something to her colleague behind the bar and went outside with Herr Lehmann, then in at another door around the corner. From the look of it, she lived above the bar itself. It struck Herr Lehmann, not for the first time, that people who owned bars never had trouble finding somewhere to live. Unlocking the door was an elaborate operation. She fumbled with her bunch of keys, bending low over the lock and inserting one of them as carefully as if all depended on doing so in a particular way. Herr Lehmann could hear Karl snoring as soon as they entered the hallway.

'Feel free,' said the woman. 'Take a look at the poor devil, then you'll know why he comes here.'

Herr Lehmann followed her along the passage to the living room, where Karl was lying asleep on a capacious sofa. He lay sprawled in a strangely contorted position, half on his side with his legs trailing on the floor. His T-shirt had ridden up, exposing his big belly, which sagged sideways like bulging sack. He was snoring fit to shake the walls, and the room stank of drink, sweaty armpits, dirty socks, and stale cigarette smoke.

'Get the picture?'

'Yes.' It dawned on Herr Lehmann that he didn't like Christine after all – in fact he disliked her quite as much as Romy Schneider. 'Can you tell him to come and see me when he wakes up?'

'When he wakes up he'll probably beat it right away,' she said. 'He usually does. I don't know why I still give him houseroom.'

'No,' said Herr Lehmann, 'it is a little hard to fathom.'

'What do you mean?'

'Just that.'

'Well, I'm not going to stand for it any longer,' she said. Meanwhile, Karl's snores rose in volume. 'If you speak to him before I do, you can tell him he needn't come back.'

'Okay.'

'I've had it up to here.'

'Okay.' Herr Lehmann made for the exit. She followed him.

'You can tell him that from me. Never again. He needn't bother. He won't find that a problem – he won't even trouble to phone me any more.'

'How long have you known each other?'

'How long have we been going together, you mean? How long have we been screwing, or what?'

'Something like that.'

Christine gave a little bark of laughter. She caught him up, opened the door, and held it for him. 'Two years. Two years for nothing.'

'What can I say?'

'Don't say anything.'

'I won't.'

'I'd sooner you took him with you right now,' she said.

Already outside, Herr Lehmann lingered there, unsure. She stood in the doorway, looking at him. 'Maybe I should do that,' he said.

'You won't be able to wake him,' she said. 'I've often tried in the past.'

'In that case . . .' he said. 'I mean, I couldn't carry him.'

'No,' she said with a mirthless smile, 'you couldn't.'

'So long, then,' said Herr Lehmann, and walked off. She continued to stand in the doorway, staring after him as if he were an old acquaintance who had shown up again after many years but had, alas, been compelled to leave almost at once.

17 A SURPRISE

HERR LEHMANN ESTIMATED that it was only half past five when he left Christine's apartment, and he had absolutely no desire to put Erwin out of his misery before time. I should simply have had a lie-down earlier on, he thought. If I hadn't answered the phone, which I should never have done, I'd be asleep like Karl. But it was too late for that now, and besides, he was hungry, so he decided to have something to eat at the *Kottbusser Tor*. It wasn't far, and there were several good Turkish restaurants there. First he went into a phone booth and called Katrin, but only got her answerphone as before, which started to worry him. Then he repaired to a nearby Turkish restaurant of the stricter kind, one with quotations from the Koran on the walls and no alcohol and so on. He'd discovered the place only a few weeks ago. It was really more of a snack bar, but a snack bar with a handful of tables you could sit at, and the food was the best Turkish food in the city, of that Herr Lehmann was convinced. He'd gone there with Katrin as soon as he discovered it. Like him, she had taken to the funny little restaurant that was really more of a snack bar, and it had, at least in Herr Lehmann's opinion, proved very effective from the romantic angle as well.

That's the good thing about Katrin, Herr Lehmann thought

as he walked into the small establishment, which was tucked away in a rather inconspicuous position: at least where eating is concerned, she doesn't let herself be deluded by falderals like candlelight and snooty waiters in aprons; she concentrates on the matter in hand and the food in particular. The same applies from the romantic point of view, he thought as he studied the dishes displayed in the window. What matters to Katrin is what she's eating and who she's eating it with, not superficial frills like subdued lighting and napkins folded in the shape of swans. The lighting in here wasn't subdued, anything but, and the place wasn't particularly full — in fact Herr Lehmann was the only customer. It'll take time to catch on, he thought, but he felt confident that it would survive. It hadn't been open long, and it didn't matter if nobody came to begin with. In the long run, he told himself, there'll be plenty of people who appreciate a kofta as good as the one they make here. And kofta was what he ordered now, as he had on the last two occasions, plus some rice and a lot of 'that salad made of parsley and stuff', as he told the man behind the counter, who hardly spoke a word of German but produced koftas which, in Herr Lehmann's opinion, brought tears to the eyes.

Besides, he thought as he sat down at a table against the rear wall and waited for his food over a glass of tea, everything's so well lit in Mediterranean countries. It cheers you up, the way their snack bars and restaurants are always so nice and bright. The Turks are fond of bright lighting, he reflected, stirring two lumps of sugar into his small, waisted glass of tea, but the more they integrate the gloomier and more Teutonic their establishments become. They'll be putting bull's-eye glass panes in their windows before they're through.

But there was no question of that here. On the contrary, everything was brilliantly illuminated, and the entire outer wall was occupied by a picture window. Herr Lehmann sipped his tea, feeling as if he were on vacation. It's time to think positively again, he told himself. Just as long as Katrin got back safely from the east, he thought, that's all that matters. Still, nothing bad could have happened to her. She didn't do anything wrong, he told himself reassuringly, and she didn't have any money they could confiscate. He tried to banish the depressing thoughts he'd entertained on the way to the *Savoy*. It's pointless being so negative, he thought. There are plenty of reasons for not taking everything so seriously. Then the Turk brought his meal on an oval metal dish and everything was fine. Even the fact that he couldn't have a beer here didn't really bother him.

He had just finished his kofta and fetched himself another tea when Katrin walked in with Kristall Rainer. They didn't see him. They stood at the counter with their backs to him, holding hands while they chose their meal. Then, to make matters worse, Kristall Rainer took his hand away and ran it over Katrin's back, lower down rather than higher up, as if he were doing so purely for Herr Lehmann's benefit – as if Herr Lehmann were particularly slow on the uptake. And Katrin not only let him do it; as far as Herr Lehmann could tell from her rear view, she seemed to enjoy it.

Herr Lehmann couldn't believe his eyes. He just sat there with his back against the wall, glass of tea in hand, and stared at them incredulously. He didn't think anything at first, but when he did think something, he thought: My God, they must be blind, surely they must have seen me when they came in, I'm not sitting behind a screen or anything, it's like daylight in here, this isn't the *Goldener Anker*, and then he realised that this wasn't really the problem. She's with Kristall Rainer, he thought. You don't hold hands with a man like Kristall Rainer, you shove a wheat beer without lemon at him – it's as simple as that. But the realisation didn't make him feel any better.

They seemed to stand there for ages discussing the menu with the Turk, who had obviously taken to them. Then each of them got a drink, a cola for Katrin and a Fanta for Rainer. Not a Fanta, thought Herr Lehmann, that's impossible; Kristall Rainer can't possibly drink a Fanta. This made him think it might all be a hallucination – a reassuring idea that didn't last. I must seize the initiative somehow, he thought eventually. I must speak to them, catch them on the wrong foot et cetera, but then he thought: No, wrong, it won't work, there's nothing I can do that wouldn't be wrong, a hundred per cent wrong. If only this lousy dump had a rear exit, but they don't even have a toilet, and if you don't have a toilet you're only permitted to have stools and pedestal tables. I ought to report them to the health inspector, he thought, and then he briefly wrestled with an urge to weep. It's been a long day, no wonder I'm feeling a bit emotional, but tears are out of the question. It would be the end if they turned round and saw me blubbing, especially Kristall Rainer, he thought as he fought back the tears, but he still had no idea what to do when they turned round, and sooner or later they would do just that. He toyed with the notion of ignoring them and looking at something else – of intently studying the Koranic suras on the walls, for instance – but that, he realised, would be even more ridiculous than blubbing, so he had no choice but to grit his teeth, hold the glass of tea to his lips with tremulous fingers, and wait until they turned round.

And turn they eventually did. Having conversed with the totally uncomprehending Turk in what Herr Lehmann considered to be an offensively ingratiating manner, they turned round simultaneously, soft-drink cans in hand, and looked at him. They could hardly do otherwise, since he was the only other customer and seated facing them with his back to the wall. He raised a hand in greeting. They froze, and their cheerful expressions faded, or so, at least, it seemed to Herr Lehmann. Katrin likewise raised a hand, the one with the can of cola in it. Looks as if she's toasting me, the silly cow, he thought. She essayed a smile — it was an utter failure — then murmured something to Kristall Rainer and came over to him on her own.

'I know what you must be thinking,' she said when she reached his table.

'I'm not thinking anything at all,' said Herr Lehmann. 'What should I be thinking?'

'Listen, Frank,' she began.

'Better sit down,' he said. 'It's making me nervous, sitting here with you standing over me.'

She sat, put her cola down, and unzipped her anorak. Kristall Rainer paid the Turk and went out.

'Where's your plain-clothes man gone?' asked Herr Lehmann. 'Lost his appetite, has he?'

'Oh, stop it,' she said. 'I told him I wanted a word with you alone.'

'Okay,' he said, 'carry on.'

'Where did you get to?'

'They searched me and took the money off me,' he said. 'Infringement of customs and exchange control regulations. Why? Were you consumed with fear? Did you ask Kristall Rainer for help? Did he happen to be in the east? Did you bump into him there?'

'Why do you want to know?'

'What a stupid question,' said Herr Lehmann. 'Why wouldn't I want to know? I'd planned an outing with you. They detained me, questioned me, confiscated the money and sent me back, and I, like an idiot, was worried about you. Then, a few hours later, you breeze in here with Kristall Rainer, pawing and cooing over one another. That raises a whole host of questions, doesn't it? I'm quite entitled to start by asking where you picked him up today. Or he you.'

'All right, if you really want to know: yes, I ran into him in East Berlin. At least he made it across the border.'

'What was he doing there? Drooling after you as usual, or did he have some undercover assignment over there? Is he a secret agent as well, or what?'

'Don't be so silly. I met him there by chance.'

'By chance! You met him in East Berlin *by chance*?'

'That's not what this is about.'

'So what *is* it about?'

'It's about commitment. You don't have any claim on me.'

'Did I say I had any claim on you? Have I ever lodged any claim?'

'No, but you behave that way.'

'Just a minute. How do I behave, exactly?'

'I told you how it is. I told you right at the start: I'm not in love with you.'

'What do you mean? You *did* say you loved me.'

'No, I said, "I love you, of course, but I'm not in love with you."'

This is just like East Berlin, thought Herr Lehmann. It's the same kind of shitty argument as I had with the frontier guards.

'What does that mean in practical terms?' he demanded. 'Where does Kristall Rainer come into the equation? Do you "only" love him too, or are you in love with him as well?'

'Oh, Frank . . .' She looked at him as if she pitied him, and he hated that more than anything else. Stupid bitch, he thought.

'Oh, Frank . . .' he mimicked. 'What does "Oh, Frank" mean? Oh, Frank, you poor sod, or what? Oh, Frank, what happens now? Oh, Frank, you don't understand these things. You waltz in here, holding hands with Kristall Rainer, you talk bullshit of the first order, you don't answer reasonable questions, and you have the gall to let off an "Oh, Frank" like a cold fart! Am I crazy, or what?'

'Don't get so worked up.'

'Why not? Be honest, why shouldn't I get worked up? I love you, damn it all, and if I can't get worked up over you coming in here billing and cooing with Kristall Rainer, I'm dead, get it? If I can't get worked up over that, then there's nothing left to get worked up about. Then nothing matters. You think it means nothing when I say a thing like that?'

'But I told you it's different for me. I told you you mustn't make any claims on me.'

'Okay, I won't – I haven't in any case – but I'm upset, and I'm entitled to be. Goddammit, at least I can be upset, I've every right.'

'All right,' she said defiantly, 'then *be* upset.'

'"I ran into him by chance . . ." Don't make me laugh!'

'Could I help it if you were stupid enough to get stopped at the border?'

'Did I say it was your fault? Did I? Did I say: It's your fault I got stopped at the border? And is that the only reason you let yourself be pawed by Kristall Rainer, the fact that I got stopped at the border? What would have happened if they hadn't sent me back? Would everything still be the way it was, or would we have had a quick threesome in East Berlin? How long has this been going on?'

'How much do you know?'

'Nothing. That's just it, I don't know anything. I suppose it's been going on for quite a while, huh? Maybe all I need to do is ask Heidi – she always knows everyone else's business. Maybe I should ask her: Have they been screwing for a long time, Katrin and Rainer? I bet Heidi knows something, she always does.'

'That's enough,' she said, glaring at him. Two vertical furrows had formed above the bridge of her nose, as they always did when she was angry. Herr Lehmann loved those two furrows, but there was no room for such an emotion now. It's all over, he thought, feeling faintly puzzled that this failed to surprise him. It was probably never on, he thought erratically. You can only switch off a light that's really on; you don't switch off a dim light, you merely dim it down to zero. He didn't exactly know what he meant by this, but he found it vaguely consoling. 'That's enough,' she repeated. 'You can't talk to me that way.'

'I can talk any way I like.'

'It's over, Frank.'

'Don't tell me it's over, that's bullshit. It isn't for you to say it's over, that's in *my* script. And I'll tell you something: it's over. And I'll tell you something else: not only am I not in love with you any longer; I don't love you any more either. To me, they're one and the same.'

'I don't believe you.'

'What don't you believe? That they're one and the same to me?'

'No, the other thing.'

Typical of her not to be able to believe it, thought Herr Lehmann. *She* can say it's over, he thought, but she can't conceive of *me* saying so.

'Well you'd better believe it,' he said. 'And now, off you go to Kristall Rainer. You make an ideal couple.'

He rose and put a twenty-mark note on the table.

'Here, settle my bill. There should be enough left over for "Fanta" Rainer.' He couldn't help laughing. 'Fanta' Rainer was good.

He was still laughing as he walked out, he couldn't stop. Fanta

Rainer . . . He laughed till the tears came and passers-by turned to look, which was unusual, because in this part of town nobody ever turned to look at anything.

18 COMMUNITY SERVICE

FOUR DAYS LATER, when Herr Lehmann was in the thick of one of his wild and woolly afternoon dreams, the telephone woke him. It was Erwin.

'Frank, you've got to come to the *Einfall* right away.'

'Honestly, Erwin, this is too much. You woke me up. Call someone else for a change.'

'This is different, you clot. Karl's here.'

'So?'

'We don't know what to do with him.'

'What's the matter with him?'

'He's crazy, really crazy. Besides, he keeps talking about you. We just don't know what to do with him.'

'Who's we?'

'Everyone. Verena, me, Jürgen, Marko, Rudi, Katrin.'

'Who's Rudi?'

'It doesn't matter, damn it. This isn't the time for small talk, Frank. It's serious.'

'I'm coming,' said Herr Lehmann, who had already pulled on his trousers one-handed and was looking for a pair of socks. 'Is he drunk?'

'No idea what he is. That too, probably. But that's not the problem.'

'Cool it, I'll be over right away.'

'Be quick, I don't like the look of things.'

Herr Lehmann got to the *Einfall* five minutes later. It was a curious scene. There were no customers present. Verena was standing behind the counter while Jürgen, Marko, Erwin and a youth he didn't know, presumably Rudi, were clustered around a table in the far corner. Karl's big, bulky figure occupied a chair in the middle of the establishment. Katrin was talking quietly to him but keeping her distance, which looked kind of odd. The tables and chairs surrounding Karl had been pushed aside, all higgledy-piggledy, to form an open space with him in the middle and Katrin on the edge.

'You see?' said Katrin. 'Here he is.'

'What's going on here?' Herr Lehmann inquired of the room at large.

Verena, still behind the counter, was trying not to weep. 'It's really awful,' she said. 'He's out of his mind.'

Herr Lehmann went over to Karl and squatted down beside him. 'Hello, old son,' he said, patting him on the shoulder. 'What gives?'

Karl slowly raised his head and looked at him. His face looked tired and shrunken, as if someone had let the air out of it, but his eyes were wide open.

'Frank,' he said. 'It's the weather. They mess around with it any way they like.'

'Who does?'

'He's been like this all the time,' Erwin called from the far corner.

'Pipe down, Erwin. What do they do to the weather?'

'In Kreuzberg,' said Karl, 'the sun shines longer.'

'Is that what this is all about?' Herr Lehmann asked cautiously.

'You've always read the wrong books, Frank,' said Karl.

'Sometime I'd like another round of minigolf.'

Herr Lehmann looked at the others, mystified, but avoided Katrin's eye. 'How come you're all here?' he asked. He didn't care for the way they were standing around, gawping at his best friend as if he were a monkey in the zoo.

'He was quite okay a few hours ago,' said Jürgen. 'I mean, he'd been making a night of it, but he was still quite chipper in the *Abfall* at five this morning. He didn't want to go home when we closed, so he came and had breakfast with us at the *Schwarzes Café*.'

'The *Schwarzes Café*? You went there for breakfast specially?'

'Sure, why not? We felt like it, that's all. He was still okay at that stage, a bit fidgety but quite quiet. He was already talking a bit weird, but what the hell? We eventually took a taxi home, but he wanted to carry on – we had a hard job getting rid of him. I mean, everyone needs a bit of shut-eye sometime.'

Erwin took up the story. 'Anyway, then he turned up at the *Markthalle*. They didn't really want to serve him – I mean, he was into whisky and stuff, and he was already out of his skull.'

'And then he came and woke me up,' said Jürgen. 'Nearly kicked the door down, he did, and talked all kinds of bullshit. We've no idea what he got up to in the interim.'

'He was up all last night, you say?'

'And the night before that, I guess,' said Marko.

'He's right round the bend,' said the youth Herr Lehmann didn't know. Herr Lehmann glared at him. He couldn't have been more than eighteen or nineteen.

'And who might you be?' he asked.

'This is Rudi,' said Erwin. 'He works here now.'

'If I want your opinion, Rudi,' said Herr Lehmann, controlling himself with an effort, 'I'll ask for it. Till then, button your lip. Not another word.'

'Now look here,' said Katrin.

'You stay out of it. He can keep his trap shut, the little runt.'

'Don't *you* start,' said Erwin. 'We've had a hard enough time of it with Karl. I mean, look at this place.'

It was only now, as he surveyed the room, that Herr Lehmann noticed all the broken glass on the floor. 'You don't seem to be Karl's flavour of the month, Erwin,' he said, and looked back at his friend. Karl, who had been listening intently to their conversation, smiled, but it wasn't a nice smile – it didn't suit his weary face. 'Erwin,' he said, breathing heavily, 'is nuts.'

'Sure, Karl, sure.' Herr Lehmann stood up. 'I'll see he gets some shut-eye,' he said, but his first priority was to get Karl out of there. He hated the way they were all looking at him. 'Come on.' He slipped his arm under Karl's and hoisted him to his feet.

'We're going home,' he said.

Karl stood there irresolutely, swaying a little. He looked round vaguely.

'Come on, off we go,' said Herr Lehmann. He put a hand on his best friend's back and gently propelled him towards the door.

The light was already fading outside, and Herr Lehmann had his work cut out. Whenever he let go of Karl, his best friend promptly veered off course. He was very erratic and forever wanting to go somewhere else. 'Let's go and have a drink at the *Potse*,' he kept saying. 'Where's my Phillips screwdriver? It's bad for the health, all that chlorine they put in the Prinzenbad . . .' Herr Lehmann did his best to counter these effusions – 'We've never been to the *Potse*, it isn't our kind of place . . . You don't need that now . . . Okay, so we won't go swimming there . . .' – but it was absolutely pointless, Karl never stuck to one subject and didn't react to his answers. Like a wind-up toy without a will of its own, he kept changing the orientation of his thoughts and words – and, consequently, of his footsteps. Each new idea set him off in a different direction. Herr Lehmann didn't like to grip his arm, it looked so policeman-like, and Karl seemed to dislike it too, but Herr Lehmann was scared stiff he would run off, possibly out into Wiener Strasse and in front of a car, so he took his hand as if he were a little child, and that helped. Karl calmed down and walked along beside him unresistingly, but without interrupting his ceaseless flow of nonsense.

'What's going on between you and Heidi?'

'Why should anything be going on between me and Heidi?'

'It doesn't matter.'

'What doesn't matter?'

'Scotch without ice is undrinkable.'

'A lot of people would disagree.'

Herr Lehmann eventually gave up. He wasn't getting through to him, and it didn't seem to matter whether he said anything or not. Maybe he'll be better when he gets home, he thought in despair, maybe all he needs is a good sleep. Two nights on the trot, he thought – anyone would go nuts.

They made their way across Görlitzer Park, which was still the building site it had been for years, and which, so it seemed to Herr Lehmann, would never be anything else. He couldn't remember how it had looked originally. They made a strange pair, he and his huge friend, as they trudged hand in hand across the soft, churned-up ground. Karl never stopped talking, except that now he just muttered to himself, and Herr Lehmann only caught a few snatches. 'Bastards . . . all the same . . . you have to do it sometime . . . it's being renovated at last, and high time too. *It's high time*,' Karl shouted suddenly, coming to a halt in the middle of the park.

'High time for what?'

'For them to pull their socks up,' said Karl. 'Or they'll never get it done.'

'Yes, Karl, but nobody's working here at the moment,' said Herr Lehmann. Maybe I can keep him on the subject awhile, he thought desperately – maybe then he'll start making sense. 'It's a funny thing,' he went on. 'They've got all this earth-moving machinery standing around the whole time, excavators and so on' – he pointed to the excavators and bulldozers parked among some big mounds of sand on their left – 'but nobody's working. They haven't done any work here for days. I mean,' he said quickly, to avoid breaking the flow, 'today is Thursday and it's four o'clock, well, maybe four-thirty, so it's probably knocking-off time, but they haven't done any work at all in the last few days, or if they have I don't know how much, because this place has looked the same for weeks.' I'm talking irrelevant crap, thought Herr Lehmann, but I've got to keep him on the subject. That's the answer, a regular conversation between us on the same subject, he thought nervously, then everything will be all right again. 'I think they're running out of money,' he went on mechanically. 'This is probably a general contractor's project, and they always have to pay in advance by instalments, which have to be approved by the district council . . .'

Karl came to a stop. Raising his head, he peered in all directions like a meerkat on the lookout for predators.

'. . . and they never have any money, of course. Yes, that must be the problem.'

'Sure, sure,' said Karl. 'All you ever want to do is get laid.'

'You're not making sense, Karl. Let's go.'

'Where to?'

'Your place. It's time you had some shut-eye.'

'It's nice at my place.'

'Yes, Karl, it's great there. It'll be fine.'

'What will?'

'Everything. You need a good sleep, that's all.'

215

Herr Lehmann towed him along by the hand. They kept to the park for as long as possible because he wanted to avoid the worst of the traffic. If Karl slips his lead, he thought, there'll be no stopping him. Then it occurred to him that he was already thinking of his best friend in canine terms, and he found the idea distasteful. I mustn't start that, he told himself.

'Sleep, sleep,' said Karl. 'Yes, okay. And clean the windows.'

'You can do that later.'

'I wanted to be a window-cleaner once upon a time.'

'Of course you did, Karl.'

'At the district hospital. Round and round.'

'That's okay, you can still be one.'

'When you've cleaned them all you start again from scratch.'

'Very practical.'

'They make cars these days.'

'Who makes cars?'

'In Charlottenburg. If they aren't careful.'

'If who isn't careful?'

'Look, a dog.'

'There isn't any dog, Karl.'

'He's cute.'

It was true, there was a dog. *The* dog. Herr Lehmann thought it far from cute, but that was unimportant. It was rooting in the mud dead ahead of them, but Herr Lehmann hadn't noticed it, he'd been too busy steering Karl round any puddles they came to. The dog looked up and wagged its tail.

'Good dog,' said Karl, squatting down. The dog trotted over and licked his hand.

'I know that dog of old,' said Herr Lehmann. 'I came across it in Lausitzer Platz, early one morning.'

'Good dog,' said Karl. He sat down in the mud. The dog leapt at him, knocking him over, and licked his face. Karl laughed, kicking and waving his arms around.

'Hey, Karl, steady on,' Herr Lehmann said cautiously. He was glad in principle that his best friend was talking normally, even if he wasn't making sense, but it couldn't be good for him to roll around in muddy puddles.

Karl took no notice. He wrestled with the dog and rolled over until he was lying on top of it. The dog yelped and whimpered under his weight.

'What's the matter with him?' Karl asked.

'You're lying on top of him – you're hurting him.'

'Oh, I see.' Karl got up and the dog ran off.

'Stupid mutt,' Karl said with a laugh. He was covered in mud from head to foot, but he didn't care.

'We ought to go back to your place, Karl. You could take a shower and grab a little sleep, maybe.'

'I don't want to go home,' said Karl, and set off in the opposite direction. Herr Lehmann hung on to him.

'Don't be daft, just look at yourself. You can't go anywhere like that.'

'All right,' said Karl, and he marched off, this time in the right direction. It was all Herr Lehmann could do to keep up, Karl took such long strides. He marched straight through all the puddles to the park's Görlitzer Strasse exit, but they'd only just left the park when he came to a stop again.

'Got some shopping to do.'

'Forget it, Karl.'

'No, I've got some shopping to do.'

'You'll have to go home first, you can't go shopping like that.'

'What?'

'You can't go shopping in that state.'

'All they want to do is get laid,' said Karl. He made a sweeping, semicircular gesture with his right arm. 'All of them.'

'There's no one there, Karl.'

'Yes they do, all of them. Heidi too. You've got a specially soft spot for Heidi.'

'Sure.'

Herr Lehmann took Karl's hand again and dragged him across Görlitzer Strasse into Cuvrystrasse. Everything'll be fine once he's home, he thought. Karl followed him obediently and said no more.

'Let's have the key,' Herr Lehmann said when they reached Karl's shop.

Karl just stood there, looking around him with an air of interest.

'The key,' said Herr Lehmann. 'Give it here.'

'Do you remember when we shared the same digs?'

'Yes, of course. Give me the key – either that or open the door yourself.'

'You were always making chocolate blancmange.'

'I've never made chocolate blancmange in my life. I don't like chocolate blancmange.'

'It was yummy.'

'Come on, Karl, give me the key.'

'Got to get something first. From the *Markthalle*.'

Karl turned to go. Herr Lehmann caught him by the sleeve.

'Please, Karl, give me the key.'

'Haven't got it.'

Herr Lehmann groped in Karl's anorak pockets and found an enormous bunch of keys.

'Which one is it, Karl?' he asked, but Karl just stood there grinning.

'Everything's fine,' he said.

Herr Lehmann sighed and tried a couple of keys. The third one worked. He pushed the door open and hauled Karl into the gloomy studio, then shut the door and switched a light on. The scene that met his eyes resembled a battlefield. All the works of art that had stood there until recently had been smashed, and their welded metal components lay strewn around.

'What happened?'

'Deconstruction,' said Karl, laughing happily. 'Deconstruction,' he repeated.

'But it's all your stuff for the gallery, Karl.'

'Deconstruction.' Karl sat down on the floor and picked up a piece of scrap metal – the sprocket wheel of a bicycle, from the look of it. 'I could make something out of this.'

Herr Lehmann was shocked. Still, he thought, pulling himself together, this isn't the moment to worry about art. I must put him to bed, that's the first priority. To reach Karl's apartment, which was situated above the shop and exactly the same size, one had to ascend a wobbly cross between a flight of stairs and a ladder leading upwards from the back of the studio. The apartment did, in fact, have another entrance, but Karl never used it and Herr Lehmann was uncertain whether a key for the other door existed.

'Let's go upstairs, Karl.'

'I could make something out of this.'

'Karl, you smashed it all. Leave it the way it is.'

'Herr Lehmann,' Karl called, looking up at him, and all at once he began to weep. Herr Lehmann felt like weeping too, but that, of course, was out of the question.

'Come on,' he said, and helped him to his feet.

'Herr Lehmann,' said Karl, 'you're a brick.'

'Sure,' said Herr Lehmann. 'Now we're going upstairs to your apartment for a bit of shut-eye.' Christ, he thought, I'm talking like a male nurse or something.

Karl allowed himself to be shepherded across the studio and

up the stairs. The stairs proved a problem. Herr Lehmann had to brace both hands against Karl's buttocks and shove, and he was terribly afraid his best friend might fall backwards on top of him. They ended up in Karl's kitchen, where the situation was even worse. The place reeked of mildew and stale fat and anything capable of putrefying. Dirty plates were stacked in the sink and on the kitchen table, the floor was littered with trash and more chunks of scrap metal, which Karl must have taken upstairs with him after his orgy of deconstruction. Karl sat down in the middle of this mess and proceeded to tear a deep-frozen pizza carton into little pieces.

'Karl, you've got to get those clothes off.'

'We ought to make a trip together sometime.'

'Does your shower work?' Herr Lehmann looked doubtfully at the shower cubicle in the corner. He himself had a similar one, a decrepit contraption with laminated hardboard walls, and you had to preheat the water. This took some time, if the boiler worked at all. Oh well, he thought, Karl can always have one when he wakes up.

'You've always taken advantage of me.'

'What do you mean?'

'I don't want to go under the shower with you.'

'You don't have to, Karl.'

'I'm going to make myself some chocolate blancmange.'

Karl jumped up, went over to a small kitchen cupboard, and rummaged around in it. Herr Lehmann heard rustling noises, then a crash that sounded as if a shelf had fallen to the floor. He hauled Karl away.

'Stop that, there's no point. You don't have any milk.'

'I must go and get some.' Karl broke free and made for the stairs.

'Stop it, Karl, there's no point. You've got to lie down.'

'If you say so.' Karl went into the room next door, which functioned as a living room complete with a sofa and bookshelves, and crossed it to the small bedroom that lay beyond. All this contained was a mattress, a TV, and a big mound of dirty washing. Karl turned a light on, lay down on the mattress fully dressed in his wet, muddy clothes, and pulled the blanket over himself. 'Okay like this?'

'Yes,' said Herr Lehmann. He turned out the light and shut the door. If he's been up for two nights, he thought, all he needs is some sleep. Then there'll be peace for hours to come.

The living room was in good condition, unlike the kitchen. Looks as if he's hardly spent any time here, thought Herr Lehmann, and then only for destructive purposes. It was already dark outside. He could hear Karl snoring through the bedroom door and breathed a sigh of relief. He lit a cigarette and decided to do a bit of clearing up in the kitchen before the rats did.

He found a roll of bin bags under the sink and had just filled one to capacity when he heard a commotion next door. Hurrying in, he saw Karl standing in front of the bookcase in the dark. He was pulling out books one by one and hurling them at the floor. Herr Lehmann turned the light on. Karl grinned at him.

'Got to be done,' he said.

'Why aren't you still asleep, Karl?'

'Asleep? I wasn't asleep.'

'But I heard you snoring.'

'Snoring, maybe, but I wasn't asleep.'

Herr Lehmann couldn't help laughing. Karl was still pretty good value, even when deranged.

'Get back to bed, Karl. You've got to get some sleep now, honestly.'

'Take your hands off me.'

'I haven't laid a finger on you.'

'I don't want them to see my stuff.'

'What stuff? And who's "they"?'

Karl thought for a moment. He was sweating profusely, and the perspiration was streaming down his face.

'You're full of shit,' he said eventually.

Herr Lehmann was getting sick of this. It's all so pointless, he thought. I can't do a thing right.

'Got to go now,' said Karl, and he set off down the stairs at a rate that staggered Herr Lehmann.

'No, don't go!' he yelled, hurrying in pursuit. 'Stay here!' Karl was almost out of sight by now, but he managed to grab him by the collar of his anorak. Karl stopped short.

'You've got to get some sleep, Karl. You're completely done in.'

Karl came back upstairs and made a beeline for the bedroom, where he started to get undressed.

'It's what you've always wanted,' he said.

'Bullshit.'

Karl only had his underpants on now. He lay down on the bed and pulled the blanket up to his chin. 'I'm asleep already,' he said, making snoring noises with his eyes open. 'Night-night, Herr Lehmann.'

Herr Lehmann shut the door and deliberated. Then he went over to Karl's desk and searched it. It took him a while to find what he was looking for: a slip of paper bearing a phone number beginning with 691, the prefix for Kreuzberg 61. He assumed that it was the number of Karl's girlfriend Christine, or at least of the *Savoy*. Karl's bogus snores continued to resound as he dialled it.

'*Savoy*. Inge.'

'Can I speak to Christine?'

'She's not here.'

'Is she at home?'

'No idea.'

'Look, I badly need her home number. It's urgent.'

'Who is this, anyway?'

'Herr Lehmann. It's about Karl.'

'Who?'

'Karl. Her boyfriend.'

'I'm new here.'

'Look, I need her number. She must have left a note of it somewhere.'

'You can't expect me to give you her private number. You could be anyone.'

'I realise that, but it's important. A matter of life or death.'

Herr Lehmann felt embarrassed by his own dramatic turn of phrase, but there was no alternative. It was the sort of crap a barmaid might believe.

'What do you mean, life or death?'

'All right, I'll tell you something: it's really important, understand? I'm not kidding. If you won't give me her number, just do this for me: call her, and if she's there please tell her Herr Lehmann phoned and wants her to call him on Karl's number, urgently. It's very important.'

'One thing at a time. Where is she to call you?'

Herr Lehmann ran through it all again, then asked her to jot down the salient points. She took umbrage at that and said he had a nerve, whereupon he repeated that it was a matter of life or death. He eventually extracted a promise that she would call Christine. After that he went into the kitchen and looked for some beer. He actually found an unopened bottle behind the trash can. It was warm, but who cared? He'd just taken a swallow when the snores ceased. He's gone to sleep, thought Herr Lehmann.

But no, his best friend suddenly appeared in the doorway. He was wearing his underpants, nothing else, and he didn't speak, just shuffled from foot to foot. He looked incredibly sad.

'Got to go and get something,' he said. 'Where are my things?'

At that moment the phone rang. Herr Lehmann hurried over to it so as to get there before him, but there was no need, Karl seemed oblivious.

'Karl Schmidt's place,' said Herr Lehmann.

'What's up?' asked Christine, the woman from the *Savoy*. 'What's all this life or death crap?'

'It's Karl,' said Herr Lehmann. 'He's—' He broke off. He could hardly tell her Karl had gone crazy in Karl's presence. 'He's ill. Very ill.'

'So you call me, huh? Is that all that occurred to you, to call me? Nobody calls me when Karl's fine, they call me when something's wrong with him. Great! Was it his idea?'

'No, of course not. He's far too ill.'

'What am I expected to do? What's the matter with him?'

'He's . . . well, not quite himself.'

'Not quite himself?' she mimicked. 'I thought it was something serious. That's his normal condition. Anyway, he's still got my keys. The bastard took the whole bunch with him, bar keys and all. I'd like them back. Is he there?'

'Yes.'

'Let me speak to him.'

'I don't think that's possible right now.'

'I don't think that's possible right now,' she mimicked again. It was really getting on Herr Lehmann's nerves. 'Come on, let me speak to him.'

'She wants a word with you,' Herr Lehmann told Karl, who was now sitting on the floor picking his toes.

'Who does?'

'Christine.'

'I need a pee.'

'I'm sorry,' Herr Lehmann said into the phone. 'I don't think it's on at the moment, he wouldn't take it in. Look, I'm being serious when I say he's not himself. Mentally, I mean.'

'What are you talking about?'

'Well, medically,' Herr Lehmann whispered. 'He really isn't his normal self.'

'How do you mean? Has he flipped his lid, or what?'

'Yes, he really has. He needs treatment, I guess.'

'Oh, hell,' she said, and he thought he heard her crying. 'Oh, hell.'

'I mean it, honestly. He's right off his trolley.'

'Leave me alone,' she sobbed. After an interval that seemed everlasting to Herr Lehmann, because he couldn't bear it when other people wept, let alone on the telephone, she seemed to have pulled herself together. He heard her blow her nose. 'If he needs treatment,' she said defiantly, 'take him to a doctor, that's what they're there for. Or a hospital – how should I know? I'm not a psychiatrist. Two years . . . We've been lovers for the past two years, did you know that? Or are you still at an age when I ought to say "We've been going together"?'

'No,' said Herr Lehmann, who found the phrase vaguely appealing. Perhaps I only 'went with' Katrin, he thought irrelevantly. 'I'm not as young as all that,' he said. 'I'm exactly the same age as Karl.'

'You could have fooled me.'

'What should I do?'

'I don't know. I can't take any more – I'm sorry, but I can't,' she said, sniffing. 'Do me a favour: look after him. I honestly think he's fonder of you than anyone else. He thinks a lot of you. You're the only person he was always talking about. You mean a lot more to him than I do. And I can't take it any more.'

'That's all right,' said Herr Lehmann, afraid she would start crying again. Besides, he was touched. He looked over at Karl, but Karl was just sitting on the floor, fiddling with his toes. He must be cold, thought Herr Lehmann, but Karl had started sweating again. Big drops of sweat were rolling down his chest, and he was breathing heavily. 'I've got to go now,' he said into the phone. 'I'll take care of it.'

'Please do that,' she said. 'Please!' she repeated.

Herr Lehmann felt uncomfortable. 'It's all right, don't worry,' he said. 'So long.' Then he hung up.

He went into the kitchen and fetched a towel. Having rubbed his best friend down, he found a T-shirt and a sweater and pulled them over his head. Karl offered no resistance. The trousers were more difficult. He located a pair of jeans among the dirty washing. They still looked reasonably presentable, but dressing Karl in them was a laborious process requiring much persuasion. This is what it must be like to have young children, Herr Lehmann thought as he buttoned Karl's flies, threaded a belt through the loops and buckled it, but he was glad his best friend had quietened down and submitted to everything so readily. Then he went to the phone and called a cab.

19 THE HOSPITAL

WHEN THEY REACHED the district hospital, Herr Lehmann took Karl straight to the ambulance entrance. He knew his way around, more or less, having been there twice before, once because of an inflamed scrotum and once when he'd cut his hand on a glass while washing up. Although both visits lay several years in the past, nothing had changed since then.

'What's the problem?' asked the man at reception, who was ensconced in a kind of glass booth with all-round visibility. He was in a jovial mood.

'We need to see a doctor,' said Herr Lehmann. Karl was standing impassively beside him. 'It's a kind of emergency.'

'What's the trouble?'

'It's my friend here.'

'What's the matter with him?'

'He's feeling ill.'

'Ill in what way?'

'Well, mentally.'

'You mean he's not quite up to snuff?' The man gestured as if screwing a light bulb into the side of his head.

'Something like that.'

'Drugs?'

'I don't know. Could be.'

'Hey-ho.' The man sighed. 'Go in, then. Through that door over there. Does he get violent?'

'No, he doesn't, actually. Not really, at least. Well, maybe. I don't know.'

'All right, go in and sit down. Someone will be with you shortly.'

Beyond the door was a passage that doubled as a waiting room. It smelt of disinfectant and stale tobacco smoke. They were the only people there. Herr Lehmann sat himself and Karl down on some plastic chairs against the wall and lit a cigarette. Suddenly, Karl jumped up.

'We can't stay here,' he said in an agitated voice, and made for the door. Herr Lehmann hung on to him.

'They won't be long, Karl.'

'I've got to feed the dog.'

'You don't have a dog, Karl.'

Karl was sweating again.

'People ought to work harder,' he said. Then he started crying. Herr Lehmann sat him down again. Not long afterwards a door opened and a woman in a white coat emerged.

'Are you the one who brought him in?' she asked Herr Lehmann.

'Yes,' he replied.

'Right, come with me.'

They went into a small room containing a couch, a washbasin, a small desk, and two stools. There was also a cupboard full of dressings and other stuff.

'Sit down.'

Herr Lehmann tried to sit Karl down on one of the stools, but Karl remained standing.

'Come on, Karl, sit down.'

'No.'

228

'Come on, sit down.'

'No.'

'Leave him be,' said the woman. '*You* sit down.'

Herr Lehmann did so. Karl stretched out on the couch and made snoring noises.

'What is your friend's name?'

'Karl Schmidt.'

'What's his trouble?'

'He talks nonsense, and he keeps sweating in such a funny way. He can't sleep, either. He hasn't been to bed for two nights, but he still can't sleep.'

'Is he responsive?'

'That depends. Not as a rule, I mean, or not really. I mean, you can talk to him, but what he says makes no sense.'

'Have you been with him all the time?'

'All the time?'

'Ever since he's been this way.'

'No.'

'How long has he been like this?'

'Well, he was like this when I saw him this afternoon. Some people told me he was still relatively normal this morning.'

'Right, another doctor will be with you shortly. All I need now are a few particulars.'

She asked Herr Lehmann a lot of questions about Karl, many of which he couldn't answer. His health insurance scheme, for instance. He didn't even know whether or not his best friend was insured, nor did he know his parents' address or the names of his two sisters.

'That is a bit of a problem,' the woman said. 'In cases like this,' she jerked her head at Karl, who was now pacing feverishly up and down the little room, 'it's important to contact the next of kin. Does he have a girlfriend?'

'Strictly speaking, no.'

'What does that mean?' she asked with a smile. 'Loosely speaking, yes?'

'No, no girlfriend.'

'Any friends in the neighbourhood apart from you?'

'No.'

'Where's he from? Berlin?'

'He's been living here for ten years. His parents live somewhere in eastern Westphalia – Herford, I think. I'll see if I can locate them.'

'If his surname is Schmidt, you'll have your work cut out.'

'I'll manage.'

'Next point: does your friend have any allergies? Any adverse reactions to antibiotics, for instance?'

'I don't know.'

'Is he a heavy drinker?'

'Depends what you mean by heavy.'

'A daily drinker?'

'I guess so.'

'Just beer? Wine? Spirits?'

'Yes.'

'The lot?'

'Sure.'

'Hm . . . What about drugs? Does he take drugs?'

'I guess so – I assume so, I mean. If he can go two nights without sleep . . .'

'Which?'

'Now you've got me.'

'Cocaine? Amphetamines? Heroin?'

'Not heroin. I don't think so – in fact I'm sure.'

'Cocaine? Amphetamines? Speed?'

'Probably.'

'LSD?'

'Does it still exist?'

The woman smiled. 'You don't keep abreast of the times, eh?'

'No, drugs aren't my scene.'

The woman got up and went over to Karl. 'Herr Schmidt?' she said. Karl was now sitting up on the couch with his head bowed. 'Look at me a moment, Herr Schmidt.' Karl looked up. His face hung slack on the bones beneath, his eyes were red with weeping but wide open. The woman peered into them closely, then held her hand over them and removed it twice in succession.

'Come on, react,' she said, then added, 'It must have been something quick-acting.'

'Yes, well . . .' said Herr Lehmann.

'All right,' she said. 'Think you could wait here with him until the other doctor comes?'

'Yes, of course. No problem.'

'I'll make sure he isn't long.'

'Good.'

She headed for the door, then turned. 'Oh, yes,' she said, 'I'll need your particulars as well.'

She sat down again and made a note of his name, date of birth, address and telephone number.

'Very well, Herr Lehmann,' she said with a smile, 'I'll go and get my colleague.'

And she went out, taking her papers with her.

The other doctor appeared shortly afterwards. He seemed rather young to Herr Lehmann. He can't be much older than I am, he thought, and somehow that pleased him. The doctor, who looked tired, gave him a limp handshake. Having brought the papers with him, he sat down and read them through. Then he looked at Herr Lehmann.

'What's the trouble?'

'It isn't me,' said Herr Lehmann, 'it's him.'

'Aha, that's logical,' said the doctor. He went over to Karl. 'What's his name?'

'Schmidt. Karl Schmidt.'

'Of course, it's down on the form, silly question. Herr Schmidt?'

Karl, who was sitting on the couch, looking at him, didn't respond.

'How are you feeling?'

Karl smiled at him. 'You're a cunning bugger,' he said.

The doctor nodded. 'Let's hope so. Anything else?'

'We ought to take another vacation together,' said Karl. He started crying again.

'Hm,' said the doctor, resuming his seat. 'All right,' he said to Herr Lehmann, 'fire away.'

Herr Lehmann told him the whole story, or as much as he knew of it: the exhibition, Karl's destruction of his sculptures, his peculiar behaviour, his bouts of sweating, and the way he'd eventually flipped his lid. The few questions the doctor asked were designed to make Herr Lehmann go back over ground he'd already covered and explain things in greater detail. He really is a cunning bugger, Herr Lehmann told himself.

'Okay, okay,' the doctor said at length, 'that's all quite informative.'

'What now?'

'Now I'll take a good look at him.'

The doctor went over to Karl. 'Yes, stay sitting there like that,' he said. 'That's just the job. You're doing fine . . .'

He felt Karl's pulse, peered into his eyes, his nose, his mouth, then checked his reactions to various things and engaged him in a brief conversation.

'Have you eaten anything today?'

No answer.

'Come on, you must have eaten *something*.'

'I've got to go.'

'Go where?'

'To get something.'

'What do you want to get?'

'Herr Lehmann smokes too much.'

'Oho!'

The doctor turned round. 'Herr Lehmann, eh? Is that what your friend calls you?'

'Usually,' said Herr Lehmann. 'But only to other people. It was meant to be a joke, but it caught on.'

'*Do* you smoke too much?'

'I've only just started.'

'Congratulations.'

'Thanks.'

Karl was growing restive. His breathing quickened and he broke out in another sweat. The doctor looked at him and felt his pulse again. 'Hm,' he said with his back to Herr Lehmann. 'What about drugs?'

'I don't know, exactly. He hasn't slept for at least two nights.'

'That fits.'

'In what way?'

'It's part of the pattern.'

'What pattern? Drugs?'

'Drugs aren't the crucial factor here. This doesn't look like a drug problem to me. The drugs are only secondary.'

'I must go,' said Karl, standing up.

'I can't stop you,' said the doctor. 'First, though, have a drop of water.'

He went over to the washbasin and filled a small plastic mug, then took Karl by the arm. 'Sit down again for a moment,' he said, leading Karl gently back to the couch, 'and drink some of this.' He handed Karl the mug. Karl took the mug and stared into it. The doctor went to the cupboard, opened it, and rummaged around inside. He was holding something in his hand when he straightened up.

'Open wide,' he said. Karl complied and the doctor popped the something into his mouth – tablets, no doubt, not that Herr Lehmann could actually see them. Then he guided the hand that held the mug to Karl's lips and made him drink. 'Have a good swallow,' he said. He waited awhile, watching Karl as he did so. Then he felt his pulse again and nodded. Karl relaxed.

'By all means lie down if you feel like it,' the doctor said, lifting Karl's legs on to the couch. 'You've been up and about long enough.' He watched Karl lying there a while longer, then sat down facing Herr Lehmann. Herr Lehmann was still looking at Karl, but his best friend seemed to be feeling fine and was lying there quietly.

'Well,' said the doctor, making an addition to his notes, 'there's nothing seriously wrong with him physically. He's a bit dehydrated, and he's probably electrolyte-deficient as well.'

'Electrolyte-deficient?'

'Yes, does that surprise you?'

'Well, he's a great one for potato crisps.' Herr Lehmann felt relieved. It's a good thing to call in the pros, he thought. It's the same with gas stoves and so on, tinker with them yourself and you'll blow the whole place sky-high.

'And not just potato crisps, I'd say. He looks as if he likes all kinds of things. How about you? Drink much beer?'

'Yes, why?'

'It shows a bit. Don't get me wrong, but beer bloats you, unlike wine. On the other hand, it doesn't burn up your liver so quickly. Oh well, each to his own.'

He made a few more notes.

'What about him?' Herr Lehmann asked impatiently.

'He should fall asleep soon. That's the first priority. We'll see what happens after that, but we certainly ought to keep him in overnight. Ah . . .' He glanced at Karl, who had started to snore. 'Anyway, you can hardly take him with you, can you?'

'No. Will he be okay once he's had a good sleep?'

'Hard to say, but I doubt it. Your friend is probably suffering from depression. A mixture of depression and nervous exhaustion. We often get it here.'

'But what causes it?'

'Well . . .' Having tipped his stool backwards until it almost overbalanced, the doctor decided to clasp one of his knees instead. 'Uncomfortable things, these,' he said. 'But to get back to your question: it's often associated with the disintegration of a person's self-image – at least, that's my own explanation. Perhaps your friend has discovered that he isn't what he always thought he was.'

'Why shouldn't he be what he thought he was?'

'Good question. I suspect he's a depressive type. Take this art exhibition. Perhaps it was a kind of moment of truth, and he got scared.'

'Perhaps' that's going a bit far, thought Herr Lehmann. 'Scared of what?' he asked.

'Of failing – of discovering that he may not be a genuine artist after all. Then everything else fell apart too. Life here is easy when you're young: a little work, cheap digs, plenty of fun and games. In the long run, though, most people need something more – something that'll validate it all. If that goes phut . . . Bang!' The doctor unclasped his knee and threw up his hands to simulate an explosion. This almost sent him toppling over backwards, and he only just managed to save himself by grabbing the desk.

'Whoops! Still, as I said, that may or may not be the problem. We'll have to see. But we often meet it here, and in his case everything fits. Insomnia is self-perpetuating. People get wound up, turn life into an endless party. They go two or three nights without sleep, do some drugs, debilitate themselves, and: bang!' The doctor threw up his hands again but was better prepared this time. He rubbed his eyes.

'Sleep isn't as important as all that, physically speaking, but lack of it will drive you crazy in the end. That's why it's hard to tell the chicken from the egg. Did your friend flip because he hadn't slept for so long, or did he go without sleep for so long because he'd flipped?'

'You tell me,' said Herr Lehmann.

'A bit of both, I'd say. That's what we've got to find out. It may be only temporary, but it may also be a fully developed manic-depressive psychosis.'

Herr Lehmann looked over at Karl, who was lying on his back like a stranded whale, snoring. He fought back the tears. I'm becoming unstable myself, he thought. If I go on like this, bang!

'What would that mean?' he asked.

'It takes time. In such cases I always recommend that patients be sent back home for therapy. The vast majority come from West Germany.'

'You mean he'll have to go back to Herford?'

'If it's bad. Sometimes it helps, but sometimes it's counter-productive. Coming home in such a situation can also be regressive. It depends on the family, too. The condition can be congenital, and who wants another nut in the family?' The doctor laughed. 'The question is, though: What'll he want to do tomorrow? Will he want to discharge himself? Should we keep him here against his will because he's a danger to himself or others?

Should we start by sedating him, then slowly open him up and take a look? It's impossible to tell at this stage.'

'And now?'

The doctor rose. He went over to the couch and secured Karl to it by means of two straps.

'Now I'm going to take him off to the ward, where they'll transfer him to a proper bed. You can visit him tomorrow, if you want.'

'Yes, of course,' said Herr Lehmann.

The doctor took the papers from the desk and deposited them on Karl's stomach, then bent over them once more. 'We have your address and phone number, right? And you'll inform his parents?'

'If I can find them.'

'Good. By the way, it's the ninth today, isn't it?'

'Yes.'

'In that case, happy birthday.'

'Thanks.'

'Could you open the door for me?'

Herr Lehmann did so. The doctor wheeled Karl past him and out into the corridor. Herr Lehmann followed, closing the door behind him. He was treated to another limp handshake.

The doctor looked down at his hand. 'I could beef it up,' he said abruptly, 'but I don't care to. People read too much into a handshake.'

'You said it, I didn't.'

'Look in tomorrow. Ward 7.'

'Okay,' said Herr Lehmann, and they went their separate ways. The doctor headed for Ward 7, Herr Lehmann went off to celebrate his birthday.

20 PARTY TIME

HERR LEHMANN DIDN'T feel like going home, where nothing awaited him but a few books and an empty bed. Maybe I ought to get another TV after all, he told himself. He guessed it was around eight o'clock. A good night for getting drunk, he thought. He had the night off, which was a rare enough occurrence, so there was no question of his going to the *Einfall*. He'd made it a rule never to patronise the bar where he happened to be working – it made you look as if you'd no other friends and nothing better to do. Besides, he had no wish to see any of the crowd who had hung around there that afternoon, gawping at his best friend in helpless amazement. He didn't want to hear their questions or provide them with explanations, let alone hear their views on what was wrong with Karl. He shuddered at the thought of the idiotic hubbub that would break out if he reappeared among his acquaintances, who all, if he was honest, had some connection with the *Einfall*. Or with Erwin, at least. It's all over, he thought, and it struck him only now how much the end of his affair with Katrin had thrown him off his stride.

I ought to have kept a closer eye on Karl, he thought as he left the hospital and walked slowly along the canal. But he'd spent nearly all of the last few days asleep. It was always the same when he was lovesick: he developed an inordinate need for sleep and left the house only to eat. I ought to have kept an eye on Karl, he told himself, instead of hankering after that silly cow. But it seemed so good at first, he thought sadly – it could have been so good with her. On the other hand, maybe that's just crap. He recalled how she'd kept trying to get him to change his life. Perhaps I didn't try hard enough, he thought. On the other hand, why should I have? Things are fine the way they are, except that I ought to have kept a closer eye on Karl. It's no fun without Karl. Take that guy Rudi, he thought – he can't be more than twenty. Where's the fun in working with someone like that? Just then he noticed the *Irish Pub*, which he'd always overlooked before, and thought it would be a good place to start getting drunk in.

He'd always hated Irish pubs, and this one, he saw at once, was as thoroughly hateful as the rest. How can they do it? he asked himself. It's all fake, he reflected as he took stock of the pub's interior. All this dark wood, all this panelling, it's all kitsch, he thought as he sat down at a table on which stood a bottle with a candle stuck in the neck. And this dim lighting, he thought, having ordered himself half a Guinness, it's like something from the 'seventies. And he recalled the Bremen bars of his youth, the *Storyville* among others, most of which were so dark you couldn't see your hand before your face, and where you could only see the person you were with in the vicinity of a candle, and the candles were few and far between.

Oh well, he thought indulgently, after getting his Guinness, which turned out to be only nought-point-four of a litre, not a half, and after taking a good pull at it, this place has got something going for it too, of course. It doesn't really matter what a place looks like, he thought, and he warmed a little to the Dubliners, one of whose tracks was issuing from a loudspeaker. He could even hum along with them a bit, and they made him feel agreeably sentimental. His elder brother was always listening to the Dubliners at the age of fifteen or thereabouts. These days Manfred wouldn't want anything to do with them, thought Herr Lehmann, or maybe he would. Maybe I should pay him a visit, I've got a little money saved up − although it's more than a little, it ought to be quite a lot by now. Or I could go to Bali, with or without Heidi. Bali might be fun with all those bird-eating spiders and tropical diseases, he thought, and ordered another Guinness. Got to move on after that, though, he admonished himself, you've got to keep moving when you get drunk on your own, so he paid as soon as the second Guinness arrived and smoked a couple of cigarettes to make it go down faster.

Once outside he found himself back in something of a cleft stick. Should he carry on drinking in this neighbourhood or switch to somewhere nearer home? The latter alternative presented a risk of running into one of Erwin's bums, as he now called them in his head, and of having to talk about Karl; the former of falling asleep with boredom while he drank. Better the latter, he told himself, and crossed the Landwehr Canal at the Kottbusser Damm. Then he made his way along Mariannenstrasse to Heinrichplatz, where there were a few bars he hadn't been into for a long time.

I've already had one at the *Irish Pub*, so I may as well move straight on to the *Red Harp*, Herr Lehmann thought as he stood in Heinrichplatz and wondered where to go next. The *Red Harp* is another lousy joint got up to look old, or maybe it really is old, he thought − who knows? The customers certainly were. Herr Lehmann saw, as soon as he walked in, that he was one of the youngest people there. That's not so good, he thought, and besides, they only had beer on draught. He ordered half a litre, and this time he got a genuine half-litre. That's rare these days, he thought, feeling the weight of it in his hand. I've got to get it down, he told himself, although he was a bottled-beer man through and through, of course, and had an automatic urge to order another after downing two-thirds of the half-litre, purely for emotional reasons. It was the daftest thing they could have done, putting half-litre bottles of Beck's on the market, it really was the daftest thing imaginable. They first turned up at the *Blockschock*, and Karl and he could hardly believe it the first time they held one in their hands. Oh, Karl, he thought, and paid.

Then he got up and went into the *Elefant* next door. It was lighter and shabbier in there, and he promptly felt better. It's better when it's lighter, he reflected, trying to remember the last time he'd thought that. It wasn't long ago, he felt sure, and had some connection with Katrin, but that, alas, was water under the bridge. He sat at the bar and downed a bottle of Maibock. Lousy muck, this, he thought as he drank. It's hard to get down, but at least it packs a bit more of a punch, which helps, and he briefly debated whether it wouldn't be possible to get so drunk they'd have to cart him off to the district hospital, in which case he might wake up next morning alongside Karl in Ward 7. That would be true solidarity, he thought.

All at once Sylvio appeared beside him. 'Hello, Frank,' said Sylvio.

'Hello, Sylvio, what are you doing here?'

'No idea. I was in the *Dick* just now, but the place is dead. Besides, I'm sick of the Kreuzberg gays. They're zombies.'

'The straight zombies aren't much better,' said Herr Lehmann, glancing over his shoulder at the bar room. It was deserted save for a few morose figures staring into their glasses. 'Still,' he said, 'it's early yet.'

'True. How's Karl?'

'How did *you* hear?'

'Everyone's talking about him. Heidi called me earlier on. She told me the whole story.'

'She would,' Herr Lehmann said angrily. 'The sooner she pisses off to Bali the better.'

'How is he?'

'Not bad. Asleep.'

'Asleep? That's an improvement, I guess. He's been hitting the bottle pretty hard lately.'

'Yes.'

'What'll he do now he can't work for Erwin any more?'

'Don't know, have to see,' said Herr Lehmann. 'Art, maybe.'

'Ah.'

They both ordered another beer and clinked bottles.

'Isn't it your birthday today?'

Herr Lehmann looked at Sylvio. He was surprised Sylvio knew his birthday. Perhaps I mentioned it sometime, he thought, but fancy him remembering . . . He felt gratified. Sylvio's the only one of the whole bunch I could endure on a night like this, he thought.

'Yes.'

'Heidi told me. Happy birthday. How old are you?'

'Thirty.'

'Thirty? This calls for a real celebration.'

'Oh,' said Herr Lehmann, 'please not.'

'Okay.'

'You know,' said Herr Lehmann, 'there's a film from the 'seventies or thereabouts. It's set in the future, with people living under a dome or underground or something, and whenever they reach a certain age they have to go in for repair, as it's called. They really get bumped off, but they have to go in for repair whether they want to or not. And they all think it's normal.'

'I know that film. I saw it on West German TV when I was still in the east. Michael York was in it.'

'That's right. Anyway, they all think it's inevitable – they think you can't become any older, because they've never seen an old person. And then two of them manage to escape somehow—'

'Yes, Michael York and some girl, I've forgotten her name.'

'Exactly, and they come across an old man and can't understand it.'

'Peter Ustinov, I think it was.'

'Right!'

'Well?'

'Well what?'

'What are you getting at?'

'I don't know. Somehow this place puts me in mind of it.'

'There's no shortage of old folk in here.'

'No, it isn't that, it's just . . . Somehow I keep feeling I ought to go in for repair myself.'

'I wouldn't think about it too much, Herr Lehmann.'

'Frank.'

'Sorry, Frank. I wouldn't dwell on it too much. Perhaps you'll get repaired automatically.'

'Time will tell.'

'*Che sarà sarà.*'

'I reckon we should go somewhere else. This place is getting me down.'

'Good idea.'

'But not to any of Erwin's dumps. I couldn't stand the sight of all those bums, not tonight.'

'That makes two of us.'

'We could always go to the *Kaffeebar.*'

Sylvio pulled a face. 'That's a dump too, Herr Lehmann.'

'Let's have another here, then,' Herr Lehmann suggested. 'But let's sit down at a table. My back's been playing up lately.'

'You work too hard.'

'What else should I do?'

'Like take a vacation. Go on, take a vacation with Karl, he needs one too.'

'Oh, yes,' said Herr Lehmann, 'he needs one badly. Maybe we should go to Herford together.'

'Tell me, is something the matter?'

'No, why?'

'You sound kind of bitter. You aren't letting this thirty shit get you down, are you?'

'No.'

'That's all right, then.'

They left the Elefant two hours later. They'd had enough of the place, and they were drunk and ready for the *Kaffeebar*. 'I feel like a touch of perversion,' as Sylvio put it.

The *Kaffeebar* was in Manteuffelstrasse. It had once been a small bar no bigger than a living room and furnished accordingly – peculiar but nice, somehow, as long as you knew the people. Now it was a huge establishment. The landlords, who had come into money and redeveloped the building, had enlarged the bar in the process. Sylvio and Herr Lehmann sat up at the counter, watching the doings of the mostly male customers, many of whom wore boots and army trousers, which reminded Herr Lehmann unpleasantly of his national service.

'Regular hetero bruisers, they are,' Sylvio said with a wry smile. 'Ugh, I think I'm going to puke.'

Herr Lehmann was past caring about anything. 'They could be worse,' he said soothingly.

'Since when have you been so tolerant?'

'Well, at least Kristall Rainer isn't here.'

'Oh, him . . . I wasn't going to ask, but is it all over between you and Katrin?'

'Yes.'

'Heidi told me that too. Depressing for you, man.'

'Yes.'

And so it went on. Around 1 a.m. someone came in, stationed himself beside them at the counter, and ordered a beer.

'Have you heard?' he asked the barman.

'What?'

'The Wall's open.'

'Come again?'

'The Wall's open.'

'Well, I'll be . . .'

'Did you hear that?' asked Herr Lehmann, pretty drunk by now.

'Hear what?' said Sylvio, who was already showing signs of nodding off.

'The Wall's open.'

'So what?'

'Didn't you hear, Sylvio? I mean, you're from the east yourself.'

'It's been getting on my tits for weeks. Whenever I turn on the TV: east, east, east. Is it my fault I'm from the east? What do you think it was like, living among those assholes? Being a gay in the east is the bitter end. What does it mean, the Wall's open? The asshole's open.'

Herr Lehmann looked round. The barman was telling other people and the news seemed to be spreading, but there was no great excitement. Everyone carried on as before.

'Well, if it's true . . .' said Herr Lehmann. 'It might be, after all.'

'Even if it is, what does it mean, the Wall's open?'

'How should I know?'

They ordered another beer. When they'd drunk half of it Sylvio suddenly woke up.

'We ought to take a look,' he said.

'Let's go to the Oberbaum Bridge,' said Herr Lehmann. 'There's a checkpoint there.'

'Okay, we'll just take a look.'

'Let's drink up first, though,' said Herr Lehmann.

They finished their beer and walked down Skalitzer Strasse to the Oberbaum Bridge. Nothing much was happening in the street. Probably just another rumour, thought Herr Lehmann.

But people were actually coming across when they reached the Oberbaum Bridge, though not many of them. Perhaps the initial rush is over, thought Herr Lehmann. If the Wall is really open, surely there'd be more than a handful of people coming across. He and Sylvio joined the Kreuzbergers who were standing there, watching. People were crossing the border on foot, quite peacefully, one after another, and going on their way. There's no real atmosphere, thought Herr Lehmann.

'They really are coming across, just like that,' Sylvio said wonderingly. 'Is it the same everywhere?' he asked a man standing beside him.

'You should see the other crossing points,' said the man, who wasn't entirely sober himself. 'These pedestrians are just small beer.'

Herr Lehmann scrutinised the people from the east, who seemed a little uncertain and were looking around them intently. 'It looks just the same here as it does on our side,' he heard a woman say.

'These pedestrians are just small beer,' the man repeated. 'I'm going back to Moritzplatz. At least there's some action there.'

'Funny thing,' said Sylvio.

'Let's go to Moritzplatz,' Herr Lehmann suggested.

'Balls, I can't walk that far.'

'I'll treat us to a taxi.'

'I don't know. What's the point?'

'Come on, Sylvio. Just for a look.'

'You'll never find a taxi.'

'Sure I will.'

They walked to the Schlesisches Tor. Herr Lehmann was in luck. A taxi not only came at once but stopped when he flagged it down.

'Are you from the east?' the cabby asked when they got in.

'Sure,' Sylvio said with a grin. 'Man, it's incredible here in the west.'

'Where do you want to go?'

'The Heinrich Heine Strasse checkpoint,' said Sylvio. 'My relations are coming across by car.'

Herr Lehmann said nothing. Sylvio was proving a sudden source of surprise. He'd never seen him like this before.

'Got any western money?' asked the cabby.

'You bet.'

'In that case . . .' The cabby drove off. 'What's it like for you, being here in the west?' he asked.

'Just incredible. I don't know how to describe it.'

'I can imagine. How come you've got some western money?'

'From my granny.'

'Oh, I see.'

They couldn't drive all the way to Moritzplatz, the streets were choked.

'Let's get out here, Herr Lehmann,' said Sylvio. 'Otherwise it'll be too expensive for us,' he told the cabby. 'We have to be careful with our western money.'

'I can imagine.'

'Give me some western money, Herr Lehmann. Here, keep the change.'

'Thanks,' said the cabby. 'Why is your friend so quiet?'

'He's a Party member. This is a sad day for him.'

'Serves him right.'

'He isn't a bad sort.'

Herr Lehmann had expected to see jubilant crowds in Moritzplatz, but it was probably too late for that. There was just an endless avalanche of cars coming from the east, entering the traffic flow, and dispersing in all directions. The noise was terrific, the air reeked of exhaust fumes.

'Christ Almighty,' said Sylvio. 'Christ Almighty.'

'Where are they all off to?'

'The Kudamm, probably.'

'Why the Kudamm?'

'Where else?'

They stood there watching for a while. Then they grew bored.

'I've had enough,' said Sylvio. 'I'm going. I'm off to Schöneberg.'

'What do you plan to do in Schöneberg?'

'See what's cooking at the *Sub*. That's where the gay action is right now, you can bet your life. Besides, I may run into a few friends from the old days.' Sylvio grinned and winked at Herr Lehmann. 'Looks like party time.'

'I guess I'll have another drink somewhere,' said Herr Lehmann.

'You do that. And don't hang your head like that, on account of being thirty et cetera. I know what I'm talking about, I'm thirty-six already.'

'I don't believe it.'

'I told Erwin I was twenty-eight,' said Sylvio. 'He'd never have taken me on if he'd known how old I am, but Erwin isn't the type to ask for your papers. Although . . . maybe he is. So long, Herr Lehmann, my gay antennae are quivering.'

'How are you going to get to Schöneberg?'

'Anyone'll give an easterner a lift tonight.'

Sylvio waved down a car in Oranienstrasse, spoke briefly to the driver, got in, and away he went.

Herr Lehmann stood there like an island in a sea of traffic, feeling empty inside. He didn't want to go home, where nothing awaited him but a few books and a bed as empty as himself. Maybe I should get another TV set after all, he thought, or take a vacation. In Bali with Heidi. Or in Poland. Or make a completely fresh start. Alternatively, I could have another drink someplace.

First off, he told himself, I'll start walking. It'll all work out somehow or other.